Stephen blocked her path. Just as when they danced, his eyes stayed fixated on her hairline and then her lips. To create space, Lexi pressed her hands against his chest and wrapped the top of the apron strings around his neck. "Turn around and I'll tie you."

"You'll tie me up?"

Laughter of relief broke the strange tension between them. "In your dreams. Now here, I'll need you to continue stirring the grits while I cook the shrimp."

Thankfully Stephen did as she asked, stopping every so often when she needed to add some cream, tomato paste, spices and lots of butter into the grits while her shrimp sautéed. They cooked together in silence but rhythmically, reminding her of how they danced together. On the dance floor he took the lead, but in her kitchen she did. He stepped out of the way when she added something new to his pot and back into the empty space. The spiced shrimp took no time to cook, and in her haste to get out of the kitchen, Lexi reached for the handle of the pan to pour everything into a serving dish behind her. She underestimated the weight of the pan and her wrists weakened. Stephen anticipated her misstep and swooshed right behind her, wrapping her in his arms and his hands over hers.

"Here, let me help," he whispered in her ear.

Dear Reader,

Welcome to Southwood, Georgia. Home to Grits and Glam Gowns, where the one-of-a-kind dresses can bring you good luck or scandal. And when the wrong dress gets in the wrong hands, sometimes you get both.

Allow me to explain that each plotted scene written was fueled with laughter and based on revenge—sort of. In the process of writing *The Bachelor and the Beauty Queen*, my family grew from a four-member house to an eight-member house. I love my boys, but the testosterone in my home is through the roof. My personal hero, my husband, felt having four boys in the house would be a piece of cake. This of course sparked the idea of placing an alpha male in a predominately glitzy pageant world.

Carolyn Hector

The
BACHELOR
AND BEAUTY
THE
Queen

Carolyn Hector

HARLEQUIN® KIMANI™ ROMANCE

Recycling programs
for this product may
not exist in your area.

ISBN-13: 978-0-373-86444-7

The Bachelor and the Beauty Queen

Copyright © 2016 by Carolyn Hall

For questions and comments about the quality of this book please contact us at CustomerService@Harlequin.com.

Printed in U.S.A.

Having your story read out loud as a teen by your brother in Julia Child's voice might scare some folks from ever sharing their work. But **Carolyn Hector** rose above her fear. She currently resides in Tallahassee, Florida, where there is never a dull moment. School functions, politics, football, Southern charm and sizzling heat help fuel her knack for putting a romantic spin on everything she comes across. Find out what she's up to on Twitter, @Carolyn32303.

Books by Carolyn Hector

Harlequin Kimani Romance

The Magic of Mistletoe
The Bachelor and the Beauty Queen

Visit the Author Profile page at
Harlequin.com for more titles.

I would like to dedicate this book first and foremost to my husband and our growing family of now five boys and one young lady. Thank you for allowing me the time to write. And much love to Monique and Pablo Baez: thanks for inspiring me all the time, as well as setting the example on how to raise a big family.

Acknowledgments

I have to acknowledge my office family,
Amy McDonald, Elizabeth McGhee and Debra Brock
(who always listened patiently whenever an idea hit),
and my Tallahassee Romance Writing Crew
who helped me put the ideas in motion.
The fabulous ladies helped raise the writer in me!

Chapter 1

"Mr. Foxx," Lexi Pendergrass began with a big, toothy smile, hoping to distract the elderly couple seated before her from the thumping music outside of her office. "I assure you this proposal of mine will not attract what you'd call *riffraff*."

Mr. Foxx, the man holding the deed to the shop next door—the deed to Lexi's dream of expanding her Grits and Glam Gowns Boutique—relaxed his pinched shoulders and gave a squeeze to the hand of his wife of over forty years. Lexi did her homework. She understood Mr. and Mrs. Foxx wanted to sell the inherited piece of prime property located between her boutique and their café.

"You are aware Mrs. Foxx and I plan to retire soon?" said Mr. Foxx, squeezing his wife's hand once again. Mrs. Foxx tilted her head up toward her husband and smiled. Lexi swore the woman batted her lashes, as well. "And though we won't be here, we do want to leave this block in good moral standing."

Commercial property in Southwood, Georgia, sold like hotcakes these days. Morality seemed to be the invisible clause in every contract. Everyone wanted to make the move to the small Southern city to enjoy the peace and security. Companies were moving into town, buying up properties and turning them into businesses with a down-home hospitality feel. Like many twentysomethings trying to find their way, Lexi had left her job and apartment in Atlanta and came back to her hometown. Instead of staying with her parents, she had tried to pay a small rent to her grandmother until the day Grandma Bea sold her Victorian home. With the money Grandma Bea made from that, she'd given Lexi the funds to start her own boutique, a dream the two of them had shared since Lexi played with dolls.

Now, with her business booming, she needed the space next door to expand. She just needed to assure the owners she would take care of the property. Armed with a 3-D model of what the block would look like once the renovations happened, she'd just given the best pitch of her life. Knowing what was at stake, Lexi was wondering why her assistant, Chantal, had decided now, of all times, to turn up the music.

"Yes, sir, I am aware." Still holding her smile, she tried to brush off the condescending tone in the man's voice. This man spoke of decency, morality and Southern hospitality when he never as much as lifted a hand to wave when they passed each other on the block. This morning she'd jumped through hoops with a model, the speech and a finger-sandwich display, set up in case they were hungry on the credenza propped against the wall opposite the mirror.

Lexi's eyes moved toward the one-way mirror positioned against the soft pink wall to the right of her desk. The mirror typically helped Lexi pick out the customers having a little trouble deciding on a dress. Today, during the biggest meeting of her life, the one-way mirror provided the image of a tall man dressed in a dark suit, with a bald head and dark beard. His lean frame belonged on the runway. She was always a sucker for a man in a suit, and he'd easily caught her attention. The tailored suit fit well against his broad shoulders and tapered waist. Glasses rested on his sleek Roman nose and chiseled cheekbones. The close-cropped black beard covered his square jawline. The flat line of his luscious lips indicated he was not a man to mess with—dangerous, even—yet tempted the curiosity within her of what those lips might feel like against her neck. The mirrored glasses covering his eyes added to the mystique of the stranger. For the first time in a long while, Lexi felt a faint quiver of desire for a man.

As far as beauty pageants went, this man scored a ten in at least half of the eight score categories. He owned poise, beauty, stage presence and overall appearance. What he'd win in swim, evening, interview and special category were yet to be determined. If he stuck around until after she finished with the Foxxes, she might try and find out. He stood at the counter holding a dark garment clenched in his fist. With no sound she heard no words but knew from the frown on his face the customer was not happy. Given the chance, she would never leave this man unsatisfied.

Clearing her throat to distract from the commotion on the floor, Lexi stood up and smoothed the palms of her hands against the wrinkles of her black pencil skirt and flattened the point where her black-and-white pin-striped shirt tucked into the waistband. She waved her French-manicured nails toward the small structure of the city block where their businesses were. "You both may have noticed my kitchenette when you entered. I would love to patronize your establishment, maybe buy your coffee every day or send the customers' families to you while they wait on fittings and things along those lines. And so…"

The whole purpose of standing was to distract the Foxxes, but Lexi's attention suffered. The stranger slipped his sunglasses off his face. His onyx eyes pierced the one-way glass. When he half smirked, Lexi gulped and clutched her neck, stumbling over her words. The slow ease of his lopsided grin sent a shiver down her spine. She'd been so focused with the store and resettling in town that she'd unknowingly set her carnal desires aside. Chantal had failed to keep the chaos outside contained.

"Are you all right, dear?" asked Mrs. Foxx. The dangling green-stemmed daisy flower at the top of her hat caught Lexi's attention.

"Yes," Lexi exhaled.

The door to her office banged open. Poor Chantal, her mocha cheeks filled with red, flattened herself against the door as the massive man stormed through. At five foot eleven, Lexi took notice of men taller than her, especially when she wore her signature four-inch heels. Quickly, she came around her desk offering an apology to the elderly couple, who were now coming to their feet at the intrusion.

With as much grace as she could muster, Lexi crossed the hardwood floor of her office and patted Chantal's arm, excusing her with a smile of assurance that this was not her fault.

"Good afternoon, sir," Lexi said steadily as she looked up into the man's angry eyes, "but if you wouldn't mind sitting outside, I will be with you in a min—"

"I will not sit and wait." The man cut her off. "I came to find out who would be so reckless as to sell a provocative gown to a sixteen-year-old." He cast a glance up and down Lexi's long frame. "Now I understand."

"I beg your pardon!" Lexi gasped and reached for the pearls around her neck. This morning she'd smoothed her honey-blond hair into the perfect chignon. She knew her high cheekbones became heated with red after being reduced to some scolded teenager.

Mr. Foxx's voice rose, "Young man, is there a problem?"

The man peered over Lexi's shoulder and offered a half smile. "Please forgive me," he said, offering a dazzling smile in Mrs. Foxx's direction.

This time Lexi did not miss the batting lashes, though she did not blame the woman for blushing. Two seconds ago, she would have melted at the same smile. Despite the angry tone, his deep, velvety voice purred in her ears.

"I needed to come back and hand deliver this piece of *garbage* this woman sold to my young niece. You ought to be put in jail for this." He clenched the black material in his fists and shook it in the air.

Over her shoulder, Mrs. Foxx gasped. Lexi twirled a pearl between her thumb and forefinger as he held up the barely there dress she'd designed and worn once during her youthful indiscretions. Of course, seeing the black dress held up in this man's meaty hands caused Lexi to finally understand her parents' concern at the time on her direction in life. Mary Pendergrass had warned her about it coming back and haunting her one day.

At the time, Lexi had paid no attention to her mother. Lexi was never quite the angel her sister, Lisbeth, was. She had designed the dress in order to get noticed by design schools and modeled it, something she did to supplement paying for college when pageants weren't covering the bills. Designers wanted the iconic dress in a vault. Lexi wanted it burned. Her assistant, Andrew Mason, had insisted on holding on to the dress as a memento, reminding her what launched her career.

"Do you deny this belongs to you?"

"Well, yes." Lexi bit the corner of her lip. The last time she'd laid eyes on it, she'd played a game of tug-of-war over it in her loft upstairs with Andrew, who wanted the dress hung on a platinum hanger and sealed in a glass case. How the dress had come to be sold was beyond her.

"Miss Pendergrass." Mr. Foxx stepped forward with his wife, who adjusted the strap of her purse on her shoulder. "We'll be leaving now."

Lexi's heart sank even before Mr. Foxx made his excuse to leave. Mrs. Foxx offered Lexi a curt smile as they quickly exited the office. Once the door closed behind them, Lexi craned her neck toward her intruder.

"Are you serious?" Lexi ground her back teeth together. Her body began to shake with bubbling anger.

"Did I ruin something for you?" the man spat out, sarcastically amused. "Imagine how I felt being called down here from an important meeting, only to discover your garment on my niece."

"I don't understand how your niece got my dress."

"Clearly you're in need of some capital." He strolled over to the 3-D model of her proposal on her desk and she followed. "And you want to get it by any means necessary, so you sold a skimpy dress. No decent woman would even think about wearing this." For emphasis, he shook the garment in the air again.

Typically, Lexi always liked to keep her cool, but this man had possibly cost her a building sale—not a dress sale, but a building sale. She narrowed her eyes at the dress before reaching out and snatching it from his hands. "Look, I have no idea how this dress got in your niece's hands."

"Of course you don't," he said folding his arms across his broad Black Label Ralph Lauren suit.

As a designer, Lexi familiarized herself with the difference between an off-the-rack ninety-nine-dollar suit and one costing two grand. This man reeked of money and entitlement. And armed with the knowledge, Lexi realized he would not give up—or leave—without an apology. She wanted him out of her office. She wanted him out of her store, hell, out of her life. "Look, Mr.—" Lexi realized he'd never even given his name before ruining her day.

"Reyes," he provided in a clipped tone, "Stephen Reyes."

Thanks to the suit and the introduction of his last name first, Lexi imagined him as some secret spy, like in the movies. Instead of a James Bond British accent, she detected a slight Caribbean accent, which wasn't the point. Lexi shook the image of him in a black tuxedo holding a vodka martini out of her head.

"Mr. Reyes," Lexi said with a slight nod. "I cannot explain how my dress ended up in your niece's possession. It has never been on the floor. I apologize."

"Are you telling me you don't know who you sell your dresses to?"

Lexi's mouth gaped open for a moment at his belittlement. She braced herself by placing her hands on the edge of her desk. "Did you hear the part where I apologized for this mix-up?"

"I heard it. I want an explanation. Do you not keep track of your customers and their purchases?"

"For the most part, yes," she said, pressing her lips together and biting the inside of her cheeks. "We don't make a habit of carding customers."

"So you carelessly sell hooker dresses?"

"Hold on one damn minute, Mr. Reyes!" Her employees glanced toward the mirror as her voice rose. "I am sorry your sixteen-year-old got ahold of this dress, but I do not understand how. Either way, you have no reason to hurl insults at my work."

Mr. Reyes closed the three-foot gap between them. His square jaw twitched as his back molars ground together. His dark eyes narrowed on her face, judging her, as his creamy, café-au-lait skin turned a slight red. "Your *work*—" he used air quotes "—nearly got a sixteen-year-old assaulted at a club."

Immediately Lexi's mind wheeled. The dress would certainly bring unwarranted attention to a naive woman. Her mouth dropped open. "Assaulted? What a woman wears has no bearing on an attack. Is she okay?" She didn't know what to say.

"No thanks to you." Mr. Reyes took a step back and sniffed the air. His eyes skimmed over the pictures and trophies of her beauty pageants on the shop walls.

"Again, I am so sorry for the mix-up."

"Sure you are," he said, as if no longer interested in her explanation. His eyes fell on the curios representing her past.

The accolades ranged from her time as a teen pageant queen and crossed over into her world of modeling and her Bachelor of Fine Arts degree from Parsons The New School for Design. His eyes focused on Lexi's party-girl images, including one of her wearing the infamous dress his niece had somehow got ahold of. The corners of his mouth turned into a frown; obviously her accolades did not help her apology. Just as her mother had predicted, people were going to judge her by her past.

Lexi cleared her throat, "Please let me know if I can do anything to help. I have two—"

Whatever Lexi wanted to say fell on deaf ears to Mr. Reyes. He snapped his gaze back at her. Not sure what had brought on his newly formed coldness, she shivered and stepped backward.

"What you do with your…whatever is your business. You need to keep underage girls out of here, so you don't influence them with floozy dresses."

"Floozy?"

The smirk spreading across his face chilled her. "If the dress fits, lady."

"I suggest you keep a better eye on your niece, instead of looking to blame other people." Her statement clearly shocked him. With him off guard, she continued. "I think you should leave, Mr. Reyes," Lexi said, tight-lipped, her heels clicking across the hardwood floors as she opened her office door. When the door swung open, Chantal and Andrew jumped back half a foot. "We're done here," she told him.

Mr. Reyes cocked his head to the side. The smile turned into a snarl as he approached. Stopping in front of her body, he leaned in close to her ear. Lexi turned her head, hoping to block out the delicious scent of this arrogant man.

"Lady, after what my niece went through, we're far from done," he whispered before straightening upright and squaring his shoulders at her assistant.

Andrew squared his lineman-sized shoulders backward. To the naked eye, Andrew appeared to be just a six-foot-tall mass of muscle with a long scar that raked down the left side of his cheek. One might assume the scar came from a knife fight, but in actuality it was from a hard lesson learned after running with scissors. Thankfully, today

Andrew puffed his chest. Most people found him intimidating before they realized he was a teddy bear.

Mr. Reyes was not most people. He cast a rueful glance over his shoulder and laughed at the lack of danger. "I'll be seeing you around, Ms. Pendergrass." Without another word or glance he walked out. Lexi stood in disbelief.

"Who in the hell does he think he is?" Chantal breathed.

"My future boo."

Giving a heavy sigh, Lexi rolled her eyes toward the natural lighting of the sky roof. "Too soon for jokes, Andrew, too soon."

The emotional roller coaster Stephen had ridden in the past twenty-four hours was beginning to take its toll on him. At least sitting down in the backseat of his Lincoln Town Car, while his driver rode through the streets of Southwood with the air blowing on full blast, allowed Stephen to get a grip on his mental state before seeing the girls. He did not believe the ferocious protectiveness he'd felt when he learned his sixteen-year-old niece was in danger.

Since the death of their parents, Stephen had indulged his two nieces' every whim. When Ken and Betty Reyes had passed away earlier that year, Stephen, along with his younger brother Nate, tried to honor the will and testament that left them with guardianship of the two girls. Together, the brothers tried to keep the living arrangements as simple as possible. They both packed up their respective homes in Atlanta and moved into Ken's house.

The living arrangements weren't ideal. Neither of the brothers wanted to move into the master bedroom, which left both of them taking two of the smaller bedrooms downstairs. Stephen didn't put up a fuss. He wanted the girls to still live in the house they grew up in and attend the same school as their friends. The uncles let Kimber and Philly spend as much time with their elderly maternal grandparents as they wanted, from which stemmed part of the problem.

Stephen had no problem packing up his business in North Atlanta to move into the girls' home. The business he created allowed him to work from any location, which currently meant out of the bedroom he occupied. Reyes Realty provided a number of services. One was helping families find their dream homes, and the other was Stephen's brainchild. As a location scout for producers in the entertainment world, whether movies, television or musical productions, Stephen traveled a lot. To make up for things he missed out on, he knew he overindulged the girls, especially Kimber, who had taken her parents' death hard and become withdrawn in the first few weeks. Finally, after spring break, Kimber had started to open up.

The night in question, Kimber had asked permission from Stephen and Nate to spend the night with a friend instead of going over to her grandmother's. Now they had learned Kimber and her friend had sneaked out of the two-story home to attend a party across the Georgia-Florida border. "Another spin around the block?" His driver, Keenan, hidden behind a pair of mirrored sunglasses, craned his neck to see through the rearview mirror into the backseat.

"I think I'm good now, Keen." Stephen inhaled deeply and blew out a smooth breath. Seconds after leaving Grits and Glam Gowns, Stephen's breath had been ragged and quick. Lessons from anger-management classes had taught him to breathe through his emotion. Something about Lexi rubbed him the wrong way, in a way he did not expect. Miss Pendergrass's tantalizing perfume clung to him. The time spent in the car cooling off should have helped Stephen gain control of himself and his recent interaction with the boutique owner. Much to his dismay, he had a soft spot for women who smelled as delicious as her—a mixture of flowers and cake. Stephen shook his head, snapping himself out of his erotic daze, and reassured Keenan of his decision.

Women like Lexi Pendergrass came a dime a dozen. He'd had her number the second he stormed into her office. Gold trophies, diamond tiaras, sashes, photographs of herself and what he assumed were her parents posed in front of a mansion-style home. She was a spoiled party girl with an expensive hobby to keep her occupied until— judging from her ringless finger—marriage.

The dress confirmed his impression. The dyed blond hair paired with her maple-sugar skin, while sexy as hell, supported his theory, as well. Stephen loosened the knot of his tie and tried to focus on the matter at hand.

As an uncle, he needed to look beyond the tempting Miss Pendergrass and remember what a bad influence a woman like her was on impressionable young girls. Kimber had nearly gotten herself attacked when she was wearing such a provocative dress. The police had no new information on her attackers, but someone needed to pay. He had decided to start with Lexi Pendergrass and her store. She needed to be put out of business.

As one of the top realtors in the nation, Stephen recognized a sales pitch when he saw one—especially when it came with a 3-D model. The boarded-up business next door to the gown shop had clued him in even more. Lexi Pendergrass planned to expand her shop? Over his dead body.

While he wasn't a parent himself, he relished his role as uncle for two very impressionable nieces. If Lexi thought she would update the wardrobe of this sleepy town, she had another think coming. It would serve her right if he outbid her on the purchase of the bakery next door. Stephen had started off his career as a location scout for a Hollywood producer and kept up with his connections. A lot of the Southern producers in Atlanta were looking for a picturesque, one-streetlight town; Southwood, Georgia, could hold the title. Norman Rockwell couldn't have painted anything better. *Hell*, he might just keep it, considering his bedroom-slash-office was becoming cramped.

The locksmiths were pulling out of the driveway by the time Stephen's driver dropped him off. He shook hands with the elder man and thanked the crew before waving them off with the invoice for the completed job in his hand. The two-story brick home with black shutters sat in a typically quiet neighborhood. The setting reminded Stephen of the street he grew up on in Florida. They were far away from the hustle and bustle of downtown but not too far for a morning job. One of these days Stephen planned on taking the girls down to the park, but with a pool, slide and jungle gym in the spacious, fenced-in backyard, he'd become lazy. Things were going to change around here.

The unmistakable catchy tunes of a PBS show echoed down the hall. Five-year-old Philly had clearly returned from weekend visitation with her grandparents. The beige carpeted steps were littered with pink doll clothes and shoes. Sticky pink handprints covered white walls right under the family portraits leading the way to the second floor. Thank God for wipe-away paint.

"I'm home," Stephen called out, shutting the door.

"Uncle Stephen!" Philly, in her favorite pink tutu and purple unicorn top, came tearing into the foyer and threw herself into Stephen's arms. "I had cotton candy."

"I can tell." Stephen shifted Philly onto his hip and walked into the family room. The child ate like a horse but weighed next to nothing. Her biggest downfall was her sweet tooth, something her grandparents overindulged. "Did you have fun?"

Philly nodded, the two ponytails high on her head, wrapped with pink ribbons, bobbing back and forth. "We went on a picnic this morning."

Sprawled out on the couch, Kimber Reyes glanced up and rolled her hazel eyes toward the spinning ceiling fan. She sighed heavily and stomped one foot on the hardwood floor, then the other. Was she supposed to be mad at him? And when did she get her phone back? Stephen was sure he'd taken the bedazzled gizmo from her. Her colorful nails swiped the pink screen of the phone in her hand and she popped a piece of bubble gum between her teeth.

"Philly, will you find the coloring book we were using last week, the one with the princesses?" Stephen leaned over and placed Philly on the ground. Knowing he'd put the book up in the desk in his room, he banked on a few extra moments of quiet with Kimber. Stephen turned off the TV and sat down on the empty cushion beside her.

An audible sigh emerged from her, clearly warning him to tread carefully. "Kimber, put the phone down."

In dramatic fashion, Kimber tossed it beside her and folded her arms across her chest. "Do we have to do this?"

"What?" Stephen chuckled. "Talk? I can't help being concerned about you, Kimber. What were you thinking?"

"I was thinking I would hang out with my friends. Some of them happen to be boys."

"Boys?" Stephen spat.

As he choked on her news, Kimber pleaded with him, batting her lashes. "C'mon, Uncle Stephen, don't act like you didn't date when you were my age. Abuela told me all about you, Daddy and Uncle Nate. She didn't imprison you in your home."

"I dated," he said with a nod, "but growing up in Villa San Juan back then was a whole lot different than growing up here where you're sneaking out at all hours of the night, dressed as you were, to meet up with…*boys*." The term barely came out of his mouth. "Besides the new bars on your window, I've also eliminated some of the other temptations."

Kimber turned her face toward his. "What did you do?"

"I went to the dress shop. Can you believe the owner claims to not recall selling this to you?"

Kimber banged the back of her head against a pillow.

"Tell me you didn't." Kimber, a miniature replica of her beautiful mother, turned bright red. "You went to Grits and Glam Gowns?"

"Where did you think I went?"

"Maybe the police station or something." Kimber gaped. "I wish you wouldn't have gone."

"I wish you'd tell me where you got the nerve to put a piece of trash on and walk out of the house."

"Okay, fine. I went to meet my boyfriend, okay?" Her bottom lip quivered.

The sound of bones cracking when he rolled his head filled the family room as Stephen squared his shoulders and cracked his neck. He glowered at his niece and clenched his fists together at the idea of some boy trying to grope her. Wasn't it last Christmas she'd asked for a Barbie dream house? "You're sixteen."

Kimber hugged herself and shrugged, not making eye contact. He doubted Ken would have allowed such shenanigans. "I'm not too young."

"Okay, Kimber." Stephen chuckled. "I don't know what's going on here or who even said you could have a boyfriend, but I say you're too young. Do you understand how much danger you were in last night? Thank God that police officer spotted you."

"I wouldn't have had to walk to meet Marvin if I had a car."

The absurdity of this request for a car did not fall on deaf ears. Stephen found the other part of what she said important. "Who in the hell is Marvin?"

"Uncle Nate met him."

Stephen's mouth twisted into a crooked smile. Marvin was not the name of some three-hundred-pound high school boy with the arms of an octopus. Marvin was the name of some pimply, brace-faced bookworm kid. "Don't even bring Uncle Nate into this." Stephen shook his head and tried to focus on the matter at hand.

Kimber blinked innocently at him. In an instant his

anger disappeared. She needed the guidance of a woman. Obviously, she'd been at a loss, and he quickly put two and two together. Kimber must have befriended Lexi Pendergrass and under that friendship had gotten some seriously bad advice.

He softened his glare and smiled gently. "Listen, I'm not good at this parenting thing. I almost had a heart attack last night."

"I'm sorry."

"I still don't get what possessed you to sneak out."

Pressing her lips together tightly, Kimber shrugged. "I don't know. The football team had an overnight game, and I needed to see Marvin and I thought…"

The thought of his niece dating a football player at an away game at a hotel and in that dress—Stephen covered his face with his hands and shuddered. "You thought wearing a dress like that would get his attention?"

"He's a senior and all the girls around here are throwing themselves at him!" Kimber squeaked.

Any minute now, there would be tears, which Stephen did not handle well. He hated when his girlfriends cried, and buying something sparkly for them did the trick. "Look," he sighed, "sneaking out to meet him is not the way. I need to meet this Marion."

"Marvin," Kimber drawled out with a whine.

"Whatever. I need to meet him first before you start giving yourselves labels."

Kimber's brows shot upward with excitement like a kid on Christmas morning. "You can meet him at the fair tomorrow!"

"Who said you could go? You're still grounded." Stephen stifled a smile.

"I have to go. Philly's in the pageant and I need to help."

He frowned now with the thought of Lexi Pendergrass and her case full of trophies. His anger shifted once again to the dress-shop owner. He still was not through with her.

Chapter 2

Cursing under her breath, Lexi cringed at the ring of the front bumper of her car banging into the meter on Sunshine Boulevard as she misjudged how much room she had for her diagonal parking space. Lexi shared the blame for her lack of parking skills with the eye-catching Sale Pending sign wedged in the boarded-up glass window of Divinity Bakery. Her heart soared and all she wanted to do was run over to Mr. and Mrs. Foxx's café and thank them. Their sign however wasn't just turned over to Closed, but an On Vacation notice hung below the sign.

All week, she and the elderly couple had passed each other like two ships in the night. Considering the way things had ended Monday morning, Lexi feared Mr. and Mrs. Foxx had reconsidered selling the store. Now finally, she was inches closer to achieving her goal, having an all-in-one boutique. "Well, damn, girl!"

After reminiscing over her past the previous night, Lexi had decided today to wear a pair of skintight denim jeggings with an old T-shirt knotted to the side.

"Safe to assume the sign is good for us?" Andrew asked, pulling her into his arms and then dipping her backward, causing Lexi to gasp. "Did they call you from the road?"

Lexi straightened herself upright and shook her head. "I only saw the pending sign when I pulled up. I hope they left a message on the machine. Did you hear anything?"

"I haven't checked yet," said Andrew.

"Uh, no, ma'am. I don't care what day of the week it is." The corners of Chantal's mouth turned upside down as she shook her head back and forth. "You haven't dressed like this because you're a businesswoman now, a consultant, the owner of a one-of-a-kind dress shop with a reputation for being the good-luck charm for every girl that comes here for a dress. Everyone knows a dress bought from your shop is guaranteed a placement, if not a title, in any pageant. If one of the sponsors or parents comes in here while you're dressed for the club, you're going to lose a lot of credibility with the mothers bringing their kids in for the pageant workshop."

With Chantal following Lexi into her office and rattling off the agenda for the day, Lexi picked out more appropriate work attire from the closet. She chose a red A-line skirt and matched it with a scoop-neck red-and-white polka-dot sleeveless blouse.

To generate an interest in pageants in town, Chantal had set up a workshop for two Saturdays a month where kids could learn the art of energetic and confident pageant walks. She spent at least thirty minutes of each workshop making the girls practice holding their wrists and hands in a cupcake-like style. Her team, made up of Chantal and Andrew, helped hone talents and emphasize their beauty.

The classes ended up overcrowded with young parents eager to find a venue that would put their kids on track for a reality show.

As a business major at Lexi's college, Chantal had recognized the full potential of Grits and Gowns by adding pageant coaching. She had approached Lexi and asked her to take Chantal on as an intern to help maximize the boutique. "Roll your eyes if you want, Lexi Pendergrass," Chantal continued, "but you know I am right. Expanding costs money. So I need you to dress appropriately for the kiddies at the fair trying to win one-on-one time with you."

Chantal quickly crossed the room and took hold of Lexi's elbow, steering her toward the dressing rooms. "I'm making sure you don't ruin your reputation—because of what some jerk said to you," Chantal scolded. Her eyes darted outside the large glass window. "We have a lot at stake here. Your pageant workshop was so successful. Let's concentrate on the next few paying classes."

"Fine." Lexi sighed at Chantal. "I'll go upstairs and change."

"On second thought—" Chantal snapped her fingers "—I made sure we have all the dresses ready for pickup for the Peach Blossom Pageant tonight."

At the beginning of every summer, the town held its annual Four Points County Fair. Lexi had once held the title of Miss Peach Blossom. Once she was in high school she went on to bigger pageants.

"The girls' dresses are already steamed and in the back for them to try on," Chantal said. "I need to go over to the hardware store and get the tape so the girls know their marks when they're walking."

"Don't worry about taping anything." Lexi snatched up her keys. "I'll run upstairs to the loft. I'm sure I have some." A few months ago she'd purchased a condo in the downtown district after spending several months living out of the loft above the boutique.

"Well, hurry up." The bell above the door jingled. A strange vibration filtered through Lexi's veins when the man stepped fully inside. The afternoon sun glowed behind him, but warning bells went off in the back of her mind as she realized the visitor's identity. The room went silent with awkwardness.

"Mr. Reyes?"

The way his black eyes pierced her, she felt naked, exposed. She reached for the collar of her T-shirt and gave the material a modest tug. Mr. Reyes's eyes focused on the two other people in the room before settling his glare on Lexi and giving her body a once-over. Once again, he earned a perfect ten on her personal score card in overall appearance and stage presence. Decked out in khakis and a white button-down Oxford, he commanded the attention of everyone in the store. Even the music stopped when he walked inside.

She didn't scare easily, not really. At least not usually. Lexi folded her arms beneath her breasts and raised an eyebrow, hating herself for giving him a perfect ten for his walk. He'd strutted into the shop with confidence. "May I help you?"

"I just was looking for Mr. and Mrs. Foxx."

"They're gone." Andrew perked up and offered. "If you would like coffee, I can make you some while we wait for them to return."

Mr. Reyes gave a tight smile. "No, but thank you for the offer. I came by to get the keys. They didn't happen to leave them with you, did they?"

"Keys?" Dread washed over Lexi. In the back of her mind, she replayed his eyes scanning over the model of her planned expansion. She mentally calculated the price of his suits, guessed the ballpark figure of his net worth. Her heart sank into the pit of her stomach. A tear threatened to form in the corner of her eye. The lack of a phone call and the Sale Pending sign next door... The blood rushed to her head and swelled against her ears.

"Yes, the property next door." Mr. Reyes gave a half smile, clearly enjoying dropping this news. He pointed toward the space standing between her boutique and the coffee shop.

"Mr. Reyes, I am busy."

"Yes, you are." His voice trailed off as his eyes cast disapprovingly over her. "Please, since we're going to be neighbors, call me Stephen."

As a former beauty queen, Lexi held her composure with a stiff smile. All this over a dress? What a petty man. Contestants received extra bonus points based upon behavior. Stephen's score now dropped to a zero.

"Neighbors?" Andrew asked for her.

"Well, we need to go over the legalities," he said casually, "but I need a place to move my business, so I put a bid on the place next door."

"This is ridiculous!" Chantal spouted what everyone thought. "You seriously outbid her because of a dress?"

Stephen's attention turned toward Chantal for a brief moment, then to Lexi. Unlike Chantal, Lexi did not cower. She squared her shoulders and jutted her chin forward.

"You gave me some sound advice," he said to her. "You told me I needed to keep a better eye on my niece, so here I am—making sure she never sets foot in this shop again."

Silence fell over Lexi, who was not sure what to say. "I did promise we weren't done."

"All this because you *think* I sold your niece a dress?"

"I don't think," he clipped.

Lexi inhaled a sharp breath. "I would like to meet this niece of yours. No one here has sold my personal dress to a child."

"So now my niece is a liar?"

"I am saying there has been a mistake."

"She's either a liar or a thief?" Stephen raised a brow.

The room grew hot. Lexi's cheeks flushed red. She had to get her bearings. Pressing her nails into the palms of her hands as she made a fist, Lexi slowly breathed in and out. "If you would be so kind as to bring your niece in here, we can get to the bottom of this mystery."

"Ha!" he scoffed. "I think you've done enough damage to my family."

Lexi opened her fists. "So this is like some sort of revenge plot?"

Stephen sniffed the air and contemplated his next words. "Actually, it's going to be a lot like that. I think, instead of never selling my niece a dress again, I may decide to have you never sell a dress again, period."

From the arrogance in his voice, Lexi imagined him to be the type of man to stroll into a restaurant without a reservation an hour before closing and order Lobster Thermidor or a rack of lamb. His entitlement irked her.

"Well. I see that no one left my keys here with you. I guess I'll be on my way to their home and pick them up." He nodded his head goodbye in Chantal and Andrew's direction.

Once the bells over the door stopped chiming, Lexi let out the breath she hadn't realized she'd been holding. "What just happened?"

Turning a bakery into an office would take most of the summer, but doing so made sense. Things in his current home office were too close for comfort. Technically he blamed himself for the loss of his keyboard. One of these days he needed to remind Philly not to take food out of the kitchen. The wonderful cotton candy her grandparents had bought deflated and brought in a trail of ants on his desk. The new building was hardly turnkey ready. Thankfully he had Nate and his toolbox to help get things in order to open up the brand-new location of Reyes Realty. He needed this space. The fact it irritated the beauty queen was icing on the cake.

The brief glimpse of upturned pink lips displaying her disappointment, however, did not satisfy him. For a brief moment, a twinge of guilt hit him. Stephen did not, by nature, set out to be cruel to women—just women who threatened his niece. Is this what parenting did to a person? Made them vengeful and spiteful? Stephen refused to believe her story about not selling the dress to Kimber. Anyone could have made the sale.

The sound of the gravel crushed beneath the tires of his brother's SUV reminded him of the crushing of Lexi's dreams. Since last seeing her, he couldn't get her face out of his mind. Sad or mad, the woman was beautiful. He wondered what a happy smile looked like on her, or better yet—a satisfied smile after being thoroughly made love to.

"Are you smiling because we're going to the fair?"

The sound of his brother's voice broke Stephen out of his daze. In the passenger's seat, he glanced over to his left at Nate behind the wheel and offered a lopsided grin. "Of course." Stephen cast a glance toward the backseat, where the girls sat wearing matching Atlanta Braves jerseys. He wanted to be able to peer over heads at the small fair and locate any of them if they got separated. "I'm ready to get on some rides and eat some food. How about you, ladies?"

"I'm ready for my crown," Philly called with a bright smile from her booster seat. Her soft brown hair, pulled back into one ponytail by his own two hands, bobbed back and forth. It had taken him six tries, but finally Stephen had gotten the ponytail to stay.

Nate groaned and banged his head against the headrest. "Did you remember to bring your caboodle?"

"Her what?"

"Her caboodle," Nate replied. "The pink case holding all of her makeup—"

"Makeup?" Stephen choked as they parked. Three of the four doors opened while he remained firmly in his seat. "What are you talking about?"

"The Miss Peach Blossom contest?" Nate said with a slow mocking tone before he stepped out from the car. "Where has your mind been all week? It's the only thing Philly's been talking about."

How did parents keep up with two children? What an ass he'd been. And again, he placed the blame on Lexi. If she hadn't sold the dress to Kimber, he would be able to focus on everyone.

"I didn't realize this contest included makeup. Kimber and I already spoke about growing up so fast, and now you want to put makeup on the baby?"

Someone opened his passenger door and Philly stood in front of him with her hands on her hips, glaring up at him. "I am not a baby!"

He reached out and, like a child, Philly eagerly climbed into his arms. "Sure you're not a baby." She smelled like one—baby lotion from the pink bottle, to be exact.

"It's just make-believe, Uncle Stephen," Kimber said, patting Philly on the back. "Soap and elbow grease."

"I don't like the idea."

Inside the walls of the county fair, a wave of screams shattered the air. Metal wheels screeched through the daylight, and the shadows of the fast-flying cars zipped through the air and circled into a loop with another wave of screams.

Nate rolled his neck around. "Can we go *inside* the gates now?"

"Yeah, everyone is staring at us." Kimber popped her pink bubble gum against her back teeth while she looked up from her turquoise cell phone.

Stephen's brows furrowed together. He was sure he'd taken away a phone earlier this week that was pink and then purple. Was he going crazy?

"Marvin is waiting by the corn-dog stand," Kimber informed them.

Stephen didn't give a flying flip where Marvin was. Instead of saying something rude, he tightened his hold on Philly and tightened his smile. "Well if he's waiting..." he said sarcastically.

"Uncle Stephen," Kimber said in a warning voice. "You promised."

"Yeah, *Uncle Stephen,*" Nate mocked with a wink, "you promised."

He couldn't make any guarantees. Maybe since he'd done one not-so-nice deed today, his time at the fair could be tolerable.

Whatever his mood had been prior to walking through the gates of the county fair, it dissipated the minute he entered. He inhaled deeply and a nostalgic smile spread across his face. It was something about the smells of the fair. Smells of animals, hay, popcorn, elephant ears and other fried inventions mixed throughout the breezy air.

The weather was unusually cool for this time of year. Philly insisted on getting a candy apple before seeing her favorite part of the fair, the animals. The barns were filled with pigs, llamas, goats and other animals that kids could feed by hand for only a quarter's worth of carrots. Stephen fed the zebra caged in the corner, while Kimber pretended not to be interested but held control over the plastic Baggie of veggies.

Stephen let the five-year-old dictate where they would go for the late afternoon. Gnats clung to the humid Southern air. Employees taunted fair patrons, challenging them to win prizes. Not able to resist his basketball skills being tested, Stephen played a few rounds and won an oversize Scooby-Doo dog. Kimber's *friend*, Marvin, met up with them. The tall, lanky boy, with his thick Coke-bottle glasses and a mouth full of metal braces, smiled. *Kimber is too good for him*, he thought defensively. But on the positive note, a guy like him would be easy to intimidate, which he had to do the few times Marvin and Kimber held hands.

Ah, to be young and in *like*. Him being "so old," as Kimber called him, he barely remembered the days when he looked forward to spending time with his high school crush. "Dang, bro," Nate said, snapping his fingers in Stephen's face. "You going soft on me?"

"What?" Stephen said, checking his phone as it buzzed. He chalked up Mr. Foxx's all-caps message to unfamiliarity with electronic mail. The keys would be delivered to the house in the morning.

"Whatever." Nate nodded. "What's got you smiling, then?"

"I made a business transaction."

"So soon?" Nate's voice and brows went up.

"We've been here for six months," Stephen reminded him. "I can't work out of my bedroom forever."

"At least this way you'll get out of the house and start meeting people, meet you a nice woman."

"Not interested in any women from this town," he said. The image of Lexi flashed through his mind, causing him to envision her hips swaying to the salsa beat on the dance floor or in his bed.

They continued their trip around the fair. Stephen reluctantly purchased the young couple a pair of unlimited passes and gave them one hour to meet back at the tent for Philly's pageant. Philly bossed her way around, holding both their hands so she could dangle and swing her legs. Stephen offered to get her another corn dog when Nate stepped in and vetoed him.

"She'll be too sick to perform tonight." Nate looked down and tweaked Philly's nose. "And you're going to be a rock star tonight, aren't you?"

Philly smiled brightly. "I'm gonna rock!"

Stephen tried to keep his upper lip from curling. "Seriously, Nate, a toddler pageant?"

"What?"

"Is this why you guys had me watching those stupid reality shows?"

"Philly enjoyed the workshops last month."

The picture of one pageant queen in particular popped into his mind. All this beauty talk forced *her* image in his mind. Southern belles were quiet and demure. She was loud, flamboyant and obnoxious to say the least. Stephen's anger worked him up all over again. Irritated, he talked himself into being glad he'd bought the property next door.

"You've got an evil grin again," Nate noted.

Stephen shook his head. "This time it is a woman."

"So you agree this beauty pageant workshop is a good way to meet women?"

Maybe that was exactly what Stephen needed, a woman. It had been six months since he last went on a date.

Oblivious to the grown-up part of the conversation, Philly tugged on Stephen's right hand. "If I do real good today, I get to compete in the next pageant where you used to live."

"Where I lived?" Stephen kneeled down to her level.

She beamed at him, batting her long lashes. "Yep," she answered proudly, "the winner today gets a big trophy and a trip."

"And if Uncle Nate is lucky," Nate chimed in, "Philly will share her prize with him."

Stephen straightened to his full height and ignored the pain in his knees. What prize did Uncle Nate think he was going to get out of this?

"A dress!" Philly jumped excitedly. "I get a new dress and I get a personal coach until the big pageant."

Off in the distance, Stephen's eyes narrowed on a long gold Cadillac behind the pageant building. He'd seen the car earlier today and had wondered who owned the old-lady car. While Stephen craned his neck, Nate pumped Philly up with encouragment. He held her by the arms and she swung her around in the air. Philly's legs accidentally kicked Stephen in the process just as he locked eyes with Lexi Pendergrass.

"I get to wear a dress from Grits and Glam Gowns!"

The words sank into Stephen's brain. As she sang the name of the dress shop, Stephen swore he'd heard wrong. "What?"

"Grits and Glam Gowns," Nate provided, "is my part of the prize. When Philly wins tonight, she'll get more lessons from the one-and-only Lexi Pendergrass. Man, Stephen, you ought to meet her."

His brother practically drooled. Stephen began to shake his head. "We've met."

"When? You've barely left the house since we came down here."

"She's the one who sold Kimber the dress," Stephen said quickly as Nate's words slowed down. Taking in the revelation, Nate closed his mouth and bit his lip. "Did Kimber tell you that?"

Philly's hand tugged his arms. "Yes, baby?"

"Uncle Stephen, look!" Her fingers pointed toward the doorway of the pageant building. Her voice gave a melodic tone to the word *look*. "There she is!"

Both of the brothers turned, Nate staring, as well. This time, he made no attempt to stop drooling. "Yep, the future Mrs. Reyes."

The back molars in Stephen's mouth ground down as their eyes met again. Philly dropped her uncle's hands and went running the few feet in front of her, arms wide-open, and barreled into *her* arms—Lexi Pendergrass.

Chapter 3

Something magical always took away Lexi's bad mood when it came to the variety of treats offered at the county fair. She knew she'd have to work a little longer with her Zumba workout disc, but it was totally worth it. Sort of. A mouth filled with a bit of exotic fair food—a fried Oreo cookie—was not the way Lexi wanted to remeet Stephen Reyes. But as she swallowed down her treat, the horrific frozen smirk on his face lessened the humiliation of being caught stuffing her face.

"A pleasure seeing you again." Lexi washed down her treat with a sip of tea through her long swirly straw before extending her hand, silently praying not to have any of the chocolate cookie on her teeth. The smug smile he'd showed off earlier in the day faltered when Mr. Nate introduced her to him as the judge of tonight's pageant. Stephen's hand wrapped around her icy one, cold from holding her drink, and sent a sizzle through to her skin.

"Yes, my brother mentioned you two already met?" Stephen dropped her hand and gave a quick nod.

Lexi's attention turned toward his brother. She'd met Mr. Nate a few weeks ago when he brought his five-year-old niece to Grits and Glam Gowns for the Saturday-morning workshop. In fact, Nate had unknowingly spawned the idea of buying the café when her kitchenette did not have the space to accommodate his fan club.

So when Nate introduced Stephen as his brother, she wasn't sure she could keep her perfected pageant smile from faltering. How was it possible the two of them were related?

Earlier, Lexi had given Stephen a ten in the evening-wear department, but if tonight was a casual look, he definitely earned another perfect score. She hated him for making a pair of denim jeans and a blue Atlanta Braves jersey look so good. Even his choice in shoes, a pair of tan Timberlands, was perfect. He oozed sex and confidence and she hated herself for noticing. *So what?* Not like she hadn't seen a handsome man before.

Stephen cleared his throat and ran his large hand over his bearded face. "We're hoping after tonight we'll spend more time together," said Nate.

The double innuendo was not lost on Lexi's ears but she did not encourage with a flirtatious smile. She did not get involved with parents of clients. *Not anymore*, a bitter voice whispered in her ear.

"Not if I can help it," Stephen injected over a cough into his balled-up fist.

Lexi cocked her head to the side. "Bless your heart, are your allergies getting to you?"

"We went to see the animals," Philly Reyes said, tugging on the pocket of Lexi's denim overalls.

She'd forgotten about the attire for the judges, the camaraderie it gave the panel, and now she bit her bottom lip. Dressing up as a farmhand wasn't Lexi's first choice, but she knew how to make it work, accessorizinng the attire with a pair of red cowboy boots. "Hi, sweetie," Lexi cooed, and squatted down to get to Philly's eye level.

"I am going to remember my cupcake hands." Philly beamed, holding her hands out to her side and pretending to cup the invisible hem of an invisible cupcake dress. The five-year-old nailed the movement. A lot of other girls from the pageant workshop kept curling their fingers under as if holding a bar. Philly held her arms out to the side and left her hands limp at the wrists, as Lexi had taught her.

Proud, Lexi gave Philly a hug. Smart of whoever decided to dress the family in matching clothes. At an event like this, things became crowded. Already she'd seen a bouncy house filled with lost kids waiting for their parents to arrive. "I can't wait to watch, Philly. Don't forget to have fun, though."

"You've met Philly," Stephen's deep voice said. He loomed over them with a smirk across his devastatingly handsome face. "Here comes our other niece, Kimber."

The niece in question practically skipped over toward her two uncles before skidding to a halt when Lexi stood up. Things began to click in Lexi's mind. Nate had come into the boutique followed by an entourage of women and their daughters. With him had been Philly and another girl. During the chaos, Kimber Reyes had appeared to be in the middle of an argument with someone on the phone. Lexi recalled the girl being close to tears and that she had allowed her to use the private bathroom in the loft—where the dress was kept. Given the teenager's wide, deer-in-the-headlights stare and the way her barbaric uncle had overreacted, Lexi planned on keeping Kimber's secret—for now.

"Kimber," Stephen said, his eyes steady on Lexi, "you remember Lexi Pendergrass."

Kimber chewed nervously on her gum and avoided eye contact with everyone. Instead she studied her canvas-covered feet. "Um, yeah, hi," she said, tugging a strand of hair behind her ear.

"Hi, Kimber." Lexi tried to keep her voice cheerful. Stephen stood behind Kimber with his arms folded across his judgmental chest. Screams from kids on death-defying rides filled in the awkward silence.

"Um, Uncle Nate, can me and Marvin get on the Ferris wheel?"

"Marvin and *I*," Stephen corrected. Lexi mentally rolled her eyes. Of course he'd correct the child. The boy named Marvin gulped.

Kimber cocked her head to the side. "You want to go on the Ferris wheel with Marvin?"

"Girl, go," Nate growled. "Be back in time for the pageant."

Kimber took off, grabbing Marvin's hand and dragging him away with her. Lexi shook her head and smiled, watching the two run off.

Her attention was captured by Stephen clearing his throat. "Well?"

"Well, what?" she asked him.

"Does seeing her bring back any memories for you?" Stephen asked. He stepped close to her, toe-to-toe. His dark eyes searched hers for an answer she did not want to give. Lexi did not waver. She folded her arms across her bibbed top and raised one brow, challenging him.

"What's going on here?" asked Nate.

Behind them, someone sounded a cowbell. Lexi cringed at the noise. "Well, there's the cue for me to get over to the judging table. I'll see you all around." Lexi smiled sweetly at Philly, waving toward her. "Don't forget—have fun this evening." Before leaving, she nodded at Nate, then purposely dropped her smile at Stephen.

A lot of cupcake dresses from Grits and Glam Gowns adorned the stage. The above-the-knee dresses with the layers of tulle were the bestsellers. The tulle material helped poof them out at the hem. The bigger the better and these dresses sold quickly.

Philly definitely stood out in her peach-colored *OOAK*, as Lexi had dubbed the garment. The one-of-a-kind dress stopped above the knees and was fluffed out with layers of tulle and stones. Andrew had worked hard and today it paid off. Nate had chosen the right color for his niece to represent the festival, as well as the state symbol. What did Stephen think?

Settling her nerves, Lexi took a seat next to the judges' table beside one of Southwood's first ladies, Mrs. Ramona Ramsey. Her daughter, Rosalind, had attended Cypress Boarding School for Girls with Lexi and was one of her best friends in the world. The Ramseys had encouraged Lexi to open up her boutique downtown.

"Stop turning around, dear," Mrs. Ramona scolded, tilting her head to the side.

"Was I?" Lexi realized when her body relaxed that she had been twisting around.

Mrs. Ramona nodded her head and patted Lexi's denim-clad thigh. "Who is the young man?"

"Who said I was staring at a man?"

"Because the stage has been filled with all types of gorgeous gowns and you have yet to coo over any of them," Mrs. Ramona noted.

Lexi grinned. "Because I created most of them," she replied with confidence. "But if you must know, there is a gentleman back there who accused me of selling something to his niece, and I did not."

"Well, if you were honest, what's the problem?"

"I don't know." Lexi shrugged. "It doesn't sit well with me he thinks so little of me."

Ramona Ramsey stopped fanning herself. "Since when do you, the Southern Hellion, care what other people think of you?"

The beauty walk for the young girls of the Peach Blossom began, and Lexi smiled and clapped for all those who attended her workshops. The Peach Blossom Pageant, held every year, was made up of girls from all four local counties. Not every parent took their child to a pageant coach, and Lexi respected and understood, but she easily picked out the girls who did not have any training. She also noticed the beauty walks of some girls whose parents clearly took them up to Atlanta for some coaching. The judges were going to have a hard time here. Things always took a turn during the talent portion.

The other judges were Mrs. Beaumont, Lexi's retired Sunday school teacher; a veterinarian from the nearby town Samaritan; and a teacher from Peachville. From peering over everyone's shoulders, Lexi guessed the judges gave tens to their hometown heroes. But after the talent completion, they were all on the same page. Every time the judges smiled and nodded at Philly Reyes singing on stage, Lexi cast a glance over her shoulder to catch Stephen Reyes clenching his powerful jaws together.

"So that's him?"

Lexi turned her attention to her best friend's mother and accepted the napkin-covered plate she handed her. Mrs. Ramona blinked aimlessly at Stephen.

"Yes."

"Well, he is hot, if you like the type." Mrs. Ramona shrugged her shoulders.

Afraid he was her type, Lexi took one last glance over her shoulder. Stephen returned the glance, his dark eyes frowning toward her. She dismissed the cold chill and turned her attention back to the stage. As the judges took a break to deliberate and grab a bite to eat, the contestants were allowed to wander off. Philly stayed on stage with a few girls from the workshop and played ring-around-the-rosy. She clearly stood out from the rest. She sported a natural smile and knew how to work the judges, even when the spotlight wasn't on her.

"I am not shallow," Lexi said. "I care more about a man's character than his appearance."

"Right," Mrs. Ramona drawled out. "How long has it been since you went on a date?"

A date? What was a date? Where a man came to her house to pick her up in his vehicle and took her to dinner and a show without expecting anything? Since the falling-out with her parents, she had no one setting her up on blind dates. Who would have thought she'd miss those not-so-random meetings her mother used to arrange?

Single men without children did not come into her shop—well, not every day, she thought, refusing to cast another glance in Stephen's direction. To get out and find a date for herself took too much effort. After working at the shop, doing alterations, making calls and critiques, or whatever her daily routine called for, she was too tired. Thankfully, her neurotic brides had already picked up their dresses for the June weddings. Dealing with them was a job all in itself.

Lexi sighed sadly and lifted the paper napkin. She smiled at the powdered-sugar-covered elephant ear and mentally tacked on another thirty minutes for her workout regime. "A while."

"I understand, but you need to make time, Lexi." Mrs. Ramsey gave a sad sigh. "Now, what are we going to do about McHottie?"

Caught off guard, Lexi inhaled a bit of the confectioners' sugar and began to cough. "Who?"

Mrs. Ramona jutted her chin in the direction of Stephen Reyes. "Him."

"He's the uncle of a potential client," Lexi said as if that explained everything.

"*Nathaniel* Reyes filled out the paperwork for Philly as her guardian, not McHottie. So there's your opening, dear."

She thought about Stephen's pending sale on the property next door to her shop. Hell-bent on avenging his niece's mishap, he clearly planned on being a daily bane of Lexi's existence. Recalling his pettiness reminded Lexi of the low score he'd earned in congeniality. No amount of hotness would bring his score up from such an act. This was a man to hate, not desire. Pondering her decision, Lexi cast one last glance over her shoulder before vowing not look at him ever again. He met her eyes with a raised brow and a smug smirk across his devilishly handsome face.

By the end of the afternoon, thirteen girls stood on the stage. The three judges never turned to Lexi for her input. The votes were unanimous and their scorecards all matched. In with a group of other girls ranging from five to thirteen, Philly stood perfectly still in front of the smaller trophies she'd already won—most photogenic, best walk and best face. The poor girl's arm had to be sore from constantly raising her hand when her name was called. No one seemed surprised when little Philly Reyes won the overall title. Lexi's services, part of the package for the winner, allowed her to stand onstage with Philly.

Team Reyes approached for a photograph. Nate stood on one side of her with Philly in his arms; due to their height, Lexi and Stephen were forced to stand together. Bulbs flashed, blinding them. Through it all, Lexi smiled and gritted her teeth.

"Well, neighbor, looks like I'll be spending more time than you thought with at least one of your nieces."

Stephen Reyes hated to lose.

He hated being proven wrong more. The tables of revenge had turned on him and karma bit him hard. He watched his family circle around Lexi Pendergrass as if she were a celebrity. Nate nearly tripped over his tongue.

Stephen did not deny Lexi's beauty by any means. She made denim overalls sexy. The entire time he stood adjacent to her, his eyes kept falling on the curve of her waist right where the snaps of the overalls and the white T-shirt she wore underneath did not quite meet. His fingers itched to test the softness of her skin.

Typically he did not date women with children. Women with kids—like Lexi and her clients—wanted a father figure for their child and he did not make for a good role model. His job kept him too busy. Nate, on the other hand, liked a woman with kids because the relationship never got any further due to the kids. Given both circumstances, Stephen needed to step aside and let Nate continue to make a fool of himself over Lexi Pendergrass. She was not the woman for him. Despite the way Philly wrapped her arms around her neck, despite the way Lexi stroked Kimber's hair, despite the way Kimber hung on her every word, there was nothing motherly about Lexi. She didn't seem to freak out or overreact when Philly's second candy apple got stuck in her hair. She just smiled and pulled it away.

"Can she come with us, Uncle Stephen?"

"What?" Stephen found himself blinking at Kimber.

Kimber's eyes blinked back innocently. "Can Miss Lexi come with us to celebrate?"

"Oh, Kimber..." Stephen tried to think of a reason why Lexi shouldn't come with them. For starters, she was dressed like a farmer's daughter. He didn't want to embarrass her by going out to eat at a five-star restaurant. "We don't want to pull Miss Lexi away from her evening plans, now do we?"

"According to my itinerary," offered the petite woman from the clothing store, "she's free."

Thankfully Lexi tried to decline. She shook her head back and forth, the pigtails she wore flipping over her shoulders. Stephen found himself focusing on the rubber bands securing the ends of her hair. He wondered if he pulled them loose, how soon her hair would untangle from the braids.

"I wouldn't want to intrude."

"Well, it's settled," Stephen said cheerfully. "She doesn't want to intrude."

Lexi paused for a split second. Her left eyebrow rose in amusement. "Well, if you guys don't mind?"

His nieces cut her off with cheering and chanting her name. Even Nate chanted along. Stephen willed his brother to shut up. "Apparently, they don't think I'd be intruding," Lexi told him.

Women didn't challenge him. "We're going to DuVernay's." He ignored Nate's raised brows. The only plans they had discussed were to go to the local Dairy Queen for ice cream. DuVernay's had come highly recommended by the concierge at his hotel. "I'm not sure if you've heard of it..."

"I am from here, Mr. Reyes," Lexi said through her gritted teeth.

"I'm sure, then, you're aware of the dress code." He gave her denim outfit a once-over.

With Philly in her arms, Lexi dramatically clutched her heart. "Oh, my bad!" She gaped, mouth open so wide, offering him a view of the white gum in the back of her mouth, "You think I can't clean up?"

As she spoke with a snarky tone, he understood she was taunting him. *Game on.*

"She owns a dress shop, Uncle Stephen," Kimber volunteered.

"Don't remind me, Kimber." Stephen gave a tight-lipped grin.

"On any occasion, I promise you, I clean up nicely," Lexi said through the thick tension. "Unfortunately, I am going to decline." She hiked her thumb over her shoulder. "I've got to take my friend home."

"I am not an invalid," said the elegant woman walking up behind her. "Lexi, dear, may I speak with you for a moment?"

She'd said "friend," but from the way the woman had leaned in and chatted with Lexi during the pageant, Stephen guessed an aunt or close relative. He cocked his head to the side, hoping for another glimpse of Lexi's skin. As Lexi spoke with the other woman, she twirled her hair around her finger with one hand while wrapping her arm around the woman's waist with the other.

Nate stepped into Stephen's view. "Whatever you did to Lexi, you better undo it tonight," he warned his brother, then turned around and called out to the two ladies, "Lexi, I insist you bring her along. We're going to—where'd you say, Stephen?"

"DuVernay's," Stephen gritted out from between his teeth.

"What do you say we head over to DuVernay's to celebrate Philly's win?" asked Nate. "We ought to all get to know each other, since we're going to be spending a lot more time together."

"DuVernay's?" the older woman said. "That's—"

Whatever she planned on saying died away when Lexi tugged the woman's arm. "Well, if you insist."

"Of course," Stephen replied.

"I think we should all head home and change into something a bit more celebratory," Nate went on, looking down at his jeans.

"Lexi." The larger guy from the shop made his way over; obviously he'd been listening. "I'll grab your dress you wore earlier. You can change in one of the rooms in the back."

Lexi gave Stephen one more tart smile before she handed Philly back to him. "I think I'll at least shower first. What do you say? Plan to meet in an hour? Your reservations are under your name? Or should I ask for Nate Reyes?"

Not wanting to lie to his family, Stephen shifted Philly in his arms and bluffed. "We'll meet you in one hour."

One hour later, the Reyes family was dressed to a T. Keenan opened the backseat door of the car for the clan to step out. A line formed outside the small restaurant located in the center of town by city hall. Well-dressed children played in the last of the daylight while their parents waited for their reservations. People waited in line, dressed in heels, gowns and shawls. Men wore suits and ties, and no one seemed to mind the evening heat. Did everyone decide to celebrate tonight? Stephen wondered if he should have left well enough alone and taken everyone to the Dairy Queen.

"You say the reservations are in your name?" Nate asked, tightening the knot of his paisley tie. They walked on the red carpet, bypassing the waiting guests, and headed inside to the hostess.

"I'm Stephen Reyes," Stephen said cockily. "I don't need to make reservations."

Behind him, he heard a chuckle from Kimber and Marvin. He preferred that over the groans he'd got from them when he'd forced them to dress up for tonight's occasion. Hell, they needed to give him a medal for allowing Marvin to come along.

Philly couldn't wait to spend time with Lexi. *You'd think the woman walked on water.* After the way things had happened between yesterday and today, Stephen admitted there was a slight wave of nervousness flittering in the pit of his stomach from the idea of being with her again. He couldn't wait to see what kind of attire she concocted tonight.

"I'm sorry, but your name is not on the list."

Stephen tilted his head to the side as he listened to a maître d' with a thin mustache and slicked-back inky black hair inform him of his nonexistent reservation. He cleared his throat. "I'm Stephen Reyes."

"I understand," the tiny man clipped, "but as you see, we're swamped. Everyone from the four counties is here tonight. Without a reservation, I can only put you on the waiting list. I will get you in within the hour."

"The hour?" Nate shook his head, "No, the kids need to get into bed."

Nate patted Stephen on the back before he had the chance to tell the little man what he could do with his hour's wait. "Guess you'll taunt Lexi some other time."

"Lexi Pendergrass?" the little man repeated.

Both men stopped in their tracks. "You know Lexi?" Nate asked.

The maître d' smiled widely as he nodded his head. "She is here already."

"She had a reservation?" Stephen heard himself asking as the man ushered the Reyeses through the ivory-covered white fence.

"No, no, no." He chuckled with a shake of his head. "Ms. Pendergrass needs no reservation."

The restaurant's interior seemed spacious, despite all the full tables. The tables scattered across the black-and-white-tiled floor were each crowded and adorned with white candles and crystal vases with two single-stemmed roses. Somewhere in the background, a live pianist played music over the various conversations and clinking of toasting glasses.

"Hi!"

Lexi appeared. She wore a champagne-colored dress made of some sort of body-hugging silk. The halter top gave him a perfect view of the swell of her breasts. Stephen cleared his throat. Hoping to stamp down the desire bubbling within, he yanked the hem of his black suit coat. The red color of her lips made them kissable and, with her long, blondish hair pulled to the side and secured with a white gardenia, his lips itched to press against her neck. Her maple-sugar skin begged for him to stroke it. The gold accents of his tie and thin stripes in his button-down Oxford couldn't have matched Lexi's attire more if he'd tried.

"I'm so glad you made it."

"We've got a special seat for the queen," cooed Lexi's assistant from before.

After introductions, everyone started to take their seats, with Philly at the helm. A waiter walked in, carrying a tray filled with champagne glasses. Lexi took two and handed one to Stephen. They lingered uncomfortably behind while everyone else got situated. Stephen took a sip, Lexi staring at him. He willed her to read his mind.

This thing between us isn't over.

She'd returned the look with a coy smile as those red lips pressed against the glass. Something about this woman irked him to no end. "Shall we?" he said, inclining his head toward the elegant table.

"Much obliged."

Everyone had taken their seats. Philly sat at the head of the table with Kimber and Marvin to her left, followed by Chantal. Across from them sat Andrew and then Nate. The only remaining seats were next to each other, as if purposely designated for Stephen and Lexi. Stephen wasn't sure why but he took the seat closest to Nate, thus leaving her to his right, all to himself.

"Lexi," Nate said, leaning forward, "thanks so much for arranging everything."

"Oh, sure." Lexi gave his brother a toothy smile and possibly a flirtatious wink. "I figured, since I have this room as a standing offer, it was probably best to let your brother's reservation go to someone else."

"You were lucky to get one," Chantal said in awe. "Du-Vernay's is in the center of the four surrounding counties. It's tradition for everyone to get all gussied up and come here after the fair."

"Really?" both Stephen and Nate chorused.

"Don't act so surprised. We're *small*-town, Mr. Reyes, not *backwoods*," Lexi said.

Chantal cleared her throat and turned the conversation on to something positive. She made a toast to Philly and to Lexi producing another Ultimate Grand Supreme.

Her words made Stephen think about what Lexi brought to the table for Philly. Obviously Philly had the right stuff because she was a beautiful child. She'd surpassed all the other children in the entire pageant tonight. Did the pageant world mean that much to her? She seemed happiest on the stage. After her parents died, Philly went into her own little world. She stopped talking as much, clung to her dolls more, and now here she sat with a crown too big for her head, the life of the party and entertaining everyone.

It was priceless. No amount of money or cool toys from Uncle Stephen brought the same smile Philly sported while seated next to Lexi. She did this.

The music from the other room filtered through to their

area. The big fella, Andrew, cooed over Philly's crown.
Nate chatted with Chantal, while Marvin and Kimber were
in their own world. Stephen pushed his chair away from
the table and stood up. He reached his hand down for Lexi
to take. For a moment, he thought she was going to stab
him with her salad fork. Her dark eyes flared at him. The
table grew quiet.

"Dance with me."

"I'm good," she declined politely.

"I didn't mean to sound as if it was a request," he said,
trying to smile, "I need to speak with you."

"No," she said, shaking her head, "I don't dance." Of
course she danced. Women with her beauty danced. They
were the center of attention on the dance floor, seducing
men with their moves. Lexi leaned in close; the sweet smell
of gardenias teased his nostrils. "As in, I can't dance. I'm
horrible."

"I don't plan on judging your skills."

He enjoyed the way her eyebrows rose in shock. What
he liked even better was that she pushed her chair away
from the table and took his hand. A spark shocked his fingers when their hands touched. Flicking them apart after
the jolt, Stephen glanced around the table to make sure no
one noticed. Everyone stared.

"Are we allowed to dance, too?" he heard Kimber ask.
Fortunately Nate vetoed the idea.

Stephen pulled Lexi away from the table and hard
against his body. Her soft skin reminded him of rose petals, her irritated glare of the thorns. Their shoes clicked
against the wooden dance floor. Her body trembled from
the stems of her stilettos. "Your legs are shaking."

"I don't like to dance."

"Yet here we are." The warmth of her body against his
made him clear his throat.

"Everyone is staring," Lexi responded in a clipped tone.
She stretched her left arm across his shoulder. He squeezed

her hand and placed his right hand against the small of her back. If his pinkie finger slipped an inch downward, he would feel her tailbone.

"Let me guess, you're not one to make a scene?"

"I'm a Southern lady. We don't cause scenes."

Oh, if only all women were that simple. The women he'd dated lived for scenes. There'd been several occasions where he'd had a drink thrown in his face for showing up to an event late due to work or simply forgetting. Women didn't like the honest truth. Women liked to play games. Lexi was playing one now. She knew he hadn't wanted her to come along. She knew that he was going to need reservations for dinner tonight, yet she let him stand there and make an ass out of himself at the fair.

"No scenes, huh." He mused over her statement. "Is that right?"

She tightened the slack in her arms. "Why did you want to dance with me, Mr. Reyes?"

For a moment he'd forgotten, lost in her dark eyes and the color of her hair. "How do you get your hair so blond?"

"I am sure you did not ask me to dance to find out about my hair-care products."

He'd dated bottled blondes. There were ways of finding out the truth. A lower part of his body wanted to find out, but his brain tried to focus. "You're right. I thought this would give us a chance to get to know each other better."

"Oh, yes, we're going to be best friends." Lexi rolled her eyes. "By the way, I know all about your type, too, Mr. Reyes. You like to throw your wealth around to intimidate people." She shook her head.

A lock of her hair fell down her back, brushing against his arm. "You still want to bring up the dress?" he said, casting a glance back at Kimber. "Let's talk about the dress."

Lexi's eyes flashed wide before falling across the table.

"Yeah, I thought not. I am willing to barter with you."

That got her attention. She looked at him sharply. "Barter how?"

"Do you believe Philly has what it takes?"

She peered around his shoulder to look at the five-year-old. A sweet smile spread across her face. "I haven't seen a natural like her in ten years."

A certain sadness twinkled in her eyes, then disappeared. Stephen was here to make a deal with Lexi, not psychoanalyze her. If she was the best, she was what Philly deserved. "So you would be willing to let go of your grudge against me to help Philly?"

"My grudge?" She stared incredulously, and if she became any stiffer she would break in half. Lexi held her face back in shock as if she'd been slapped. "Do you think I would hurt that little girl's chances to spite you? Quite the ego you have there, Mr. Reyes."

"Wouldn't you?"

The music ended and Lexi stopped moving. "I am not an arrogant ass like you."

"Did you call me an ass?" he asked humorously. Before she could step away, the music started back up and Stephen pulled Lexi back into his arms. "Uh-uh," he taunted her, "the music hasn't stopped, and you don't want to make a scene by leaving me on the dance floor."

"You're such a miserable bastard. Must you make everyone else around you the same?"

"Well, I guess we'll just have to wait and see." Stephen twirled her around and dipped her backward. "Get used to seeing more of me, Lexi Pendergrass."

Chapter 4

Sunday morning, the streets of Southwood appeared to come to a halt. Cars filled the parking lots. As they passed along the bread-box churches with steeples, Stephen searched for one long gold Cadillac, finding it parked in front of her store. His dance with the beauty queen had left him unsatisfied.

For the second morning straight, he had woken up in his pullout bed in his office-slash-bedroom, forgetting he was not a preteen boy with uncontrollable, erection-producing dreams. He needed to get over this odd obsession with Lexi. She hadn't squirmed enough in his arms Friday night, at least not until he suggested she get used to seeing more of him. Now he couldn't wait to watch her squirm when he walked through the door. As soon as Nate pulled up beside Lexi's car, Stephen's blood began to quicken.

Nate cut off the motor, and before the engine had time to cool down, the girls were out of the car and running toward Grits and Glam Gowns, pressing their faces against the window to peer inside. The leather of the driver's side seat squeaked, and Nate turned toward him, his left arm cocked on the black leather steering wheel.

"I've got this under control," said Nate. "Find something else to do."

Silence filled the front seat of the car. A church bell went off somewhere in the distance. Stephen recalled Nate's eagerness to attend the fair a second night in a row. His brother claimed he wanted to chaperone Philly while she sat in the front of the parade car. Perhaps what Nate wanted to do was catch a glimpse of Lexi. How did Stephen know? Because that was his reason for going to the fair, too. "You're into Lexi?" Stephen hated to ask, fearing the answer. They never competed for a woman.

"What I am *into* is this small town. Lexi's had a hard time here."

"And you know this how?"

Nate tore his eyes from the glare he held with his brother and stared up ahead. "I repeat," he sighed, "this is a small town."

"*We* came from a small town—" Stephen shrugged, gesturing his hand between the two of them "—on an island, secluded from the world."

"Villa San Juan is not secluded." Nate tried not to laugh, pressing his lips together and avoiding eye contact.

"Unless you had a boat or caught the ferry," said Stephen, glad the tension between them had dissipated, "you were stuck if the bridge went out."

"Look, all I'm saying is Lexi's been through a lot, and a lot of people around here won't let her forget her troubles."

"Explain to me why we want someone troubled in Philly's life." Stephen's mind grasped the nugget of information. He needed something to shake the feel of her silky skin out of his mind or the scent of her sweet body out of his head.

"If you're going to act like this, go back to Atlanta."

"I'm here."

"What about your house in Berkeley Lake?"

"Just because I didn't sell my place immediately doesn't mean I'm not committed to the girls. I told you I've already found a place to set up shop here." He inclined his head toward the shop wedged between Grits and Glam Gowns, and the café.

Nate's gaze followed, then his mouth dropped open with horror. "What did you do?"

"I made an investment in our future, a future for the girls." Stephen grinned proudly before manually unlocking the passenger's side door to step outside into the late-morning heat. Already a cloud of humidity surrounded his frame. He loosened the knot of his yellow-and-gray paisley tie. Perhaps wearing a dark suit today was not the best choice. "You cannot honestly tell me you like working out of the house."

"Is this about Philly sticking the piece of bologna in the DVD player?"

Stephen chuckled. "No, I am not upset with her for trying to hide a lunch you made. How does anyone mess up a bologna sandwich?"

"We're not talking about my cooking."

"Why are you acting so surprised? We need the office space."

Nate scrambled out of his side and stood in front of Stephen, blocking him from stepping onto the curb. "Remember when I said you need to fix whatever you did wrong? We're not destitute. We don't need to continue working for a long while. We're here to raise our nieces."

Stephen decided to leave the arguing alone. He listened to the bells over the door until they stopped chiming. The traffic downtown seemed motionless. For a minute, he swore he heard the traffic signal changing colors. In a diner across the street, a few people sat in the window, peering disapprovingly at the newcomer. A few dozen sets of eyes peered out from the drugstore across the street.

He hated small towns. The main reason he'd left Villa San Juan was to get away from everyone always being in everybody's business. As part of the Torres family through his mother, they were all subject to gossip. A major perk to living in Berkeley Lake was that he barely saw his neighbors. In Villa San Juan, you couldn't turn a corner without hitting a Torres.

Stephen reached for the set of keys, delivered to him yesterday, in the front pocket of his dark gray slacks. Despite the stares, the town truly was picturesque and moved him to the memory of when he first got excited about scouting out locations. He'd been about eighteen at the time and visiting his grandparents in Puerto Rico when he met an ambitious producer by the name of Christopher Kelly. Christopher wanted to impress his TV studio executive mother with hidden vacation spots, and Stephen, knowing all the beautiful hideaways not on the maps, was the right man for the job. After the success of his travel show for Multi Ethnic Television, also known as MET, people sought out Stephen's services. Using his shoulder, Stephen pushed against the wood frame of the door still bearing the name Divinity Bakery etched into the glass. Mounds of old newspapers nearly tripped him; dust floating through the beams of sunlight triggered a sneezing attack. The first thing he needed to do was start cleaning. The black-and-white tiled floor needed to go. Stephen preferred hardwood floors and office privacy. The only closed area so far was through the double doors leading to what he presumed was the kitchen, if he didn't count the short hallway to the left of the closed-off kitchen. Though the electricity was out, making it hard to confirm, Stephen bet the two closed doors down the dark hallway were bathrooms marked with the universal symbols.

Over the years Stephen had built a reputation people trusted and a knack of anticipating the trends in the real estate market. As a broker, he sold dreams. He sold extravagant homes to rich people who had money to spare and he sold homes to producers and directors in the film industry, who wanted authentic locations. At the high end of his real estate business, Stephen found exact replicas of movie mansions for wealthy people. Perhaps he had his mother to thank for his affinity for old movies because he had developed a keen eye for those types of homes.

Out of the three children Elizabeth Torres Reyes had raised, Stephen was the only one who managed to sit still without fidgeting through one of her beloved classic movies. Stephen never minded the rich films, which ended up helping him later in life, whether it was the dancing in *Black Orpheus*, the satire in Luis Buñuel's *Viridiana*, or the understanding of differences in the architectural structures from the American classic *Gone with the Wind*. Over the years he'd found replicas of homes like Tara, the seaside house from *Practical Magic*, the Victorian home from *Meet Me in St. Louis*, as well as colonial and Georgian houses from *Father of the Bride* and *Home Alone*.

For all his experience, Stephen lacked the ability to decorate the interiors of houses. He could find a home but couldn't put anything inside. He stood in the darkened room with his hands on his hips, knowing he needed Nate's expertise on where to construct walls. Stephen sighed and reached for his phone. There was nothing he could do right now without power.

Stephen lifted his phone in the air in an attempt to gain a bar. This morning Philly had played her favorite candy game on his device, but surely not enough to drain his battery. Light shone through the boarded-up windows of the bakery. With little effort, Stephen yanked a few of the boards and tossed them to the floor. He used his phone to snap a few pictures from each corner of the room. The icon for its battery was full and raring to go, but the internet connection said quite the opposite. He cringed at the thought of needing dial-up. In hopes of getting a better connection, Stephen stepped toward the door and held his phone toward the sun. A screen indicated a strong Wi-Fi connection came from Grits and Glam Gowns, but of course it was password protected. He debated for a moment, trying to guess the code. *Tiara? Dresses? Highly Inappropriate Dresses? Nah, too long,* he decided. Besides, after further review of what he'd seen the two times he'd been inside the store, most dresses appeared to cover every inch of a woman's leg.

The image of Lexi's long legs entangled in his sheets entered his mind, stiffening his body. Stephen shook his head. What he needed to do was clear his mind. Maybe a walk to City Hall would help. Sunshine blinded him the moment he opened the doors. With one hand, Stephen covered his eyes. The large bakery sat nestled between the coffee shop on one side and Lexi's on the other. The neighbors on his block consisted of a jewelry store, a shoe repair store and a florist before he reached a crosswalk. Every step or two, Stephen found himself taking another picture of each business, impressed with the quaint feel of downtown. He began to cross the street and lift his hand to wave at the man sweeping the top two steps of a restaurant. Black buckets of long-stemmed roses lined the wooden railing and sent out a sweet floral scent.

"Afternoon." Stephen lifted his hand.

The elderly man pressed his lips together as if deciding to acknowledge Stephen's greetings. "You jaywalked," he finally said in a gruff voice, his mouth turned down into a frown.

"Sorry, in a bit of a hurry to get to City Hall."

"You can rush all you want," said the old man. "You won't get anywhere today. Most everyone closes up on Sundays. These are things you might want to know since you're new in town."

"I stick out that much?" asked Stephen. He slid his hands in his pockets.

"You don't have to wear overalls—" the man frowned again "—but you may want to invest in some new threads."

"Thanks for the advice," he replied. He stepped forward and extended his right hand. "I'm Stephen."

"Yes, Reyes," the man said, accepting Stephen's hand with a firm shake. "I remember your brother—great man. You may call me Dave."

"Thanks for the kind words, Dave—" Stephen nodded his head "—and for letting me know what's the deal around here."

"Anytime." Dave went back to sweeping, but Stephen stood still for a moment.

"Nice flowers." Stephen nodded his head toward the buckets. "Got anything else?"

The bells over the front door jingled and out of the corner of her eyes Lexi watched everyone turn—everyone but Philly. The five-year-old remained focused. Lexi tried to regain her composure, but the image of Stephen Reyes waltzing into her store for the third time now gave her butterflies in the pit of her stomach. He wore a white button-down shirt, open at the throat, sleeves rolled up. A dark jacket hung over one forearm and he grasped a couple of flowers. White tissue paper covered the parcel cradled in his arms.

"All right, Philly." Lexi cleared her throat to recuperate. "I want you to remember there will be a couple pieces of masking tape on the stage in the form of an X. I put some down today for your markers but I want you to practice not having to look at them. Let's try a front T-formation. Pretend the judges are over there." Lexi pointed toward her right, where Nate and Kimber sat. The space Andrew and Chantal had created included a long stage stretching from one side of the room to the other and enough room outward for the girls to walk forward and work their talents.

In an attempt to point, her hand swatted against Stephen's hard chest. For some reason, Lexi mumbled an apology. He needed to apologize. He needed to be anywhere but here.

"Yes, ma'am," Philly said sweetly.

"Hi, baby girl," Stephen called out, waving his arm in the air.

"Shh, Uncle Stephen, I'm at work right now," Philly lectured. "I want to start over."

Before Lexi could protest, Philly took off behind the fuchsia curtains. Standing this close to Stephen made

Lexi's cheeks burn with heat. Well aware of his strong masculinity, she tried to focus on Philly's stride rather than how dainty she felt standing next to him. The mental score card in her head for him rated Stephen at a high nine out of ten for poise and presence. She certainly felt it.

"I wanted to give your coach these." Stephen presented the four branches of Dancing Lady orchids. Her favorite.

The corners of her mouth twitched, and she reluctantly raised his score up to a full ten. "You didn't have to." Lexi remained calm, keeping her smile to a minimum. The chocolate scent wafted upward. She closed her eyes at the memory of her Grandma Bea's backyard. The sweet smell had always enticed Lexi to linger longer at her place.

"I did."

The pep in Stephen's voice irritated her. She needed to stay angry with him. "Well, then, thank you." Her lashes betrayed her, batting against her cheeks. "You're just in time for lunch. Hungry?"

Lexi did not mistake Stephen's eyes lowering to her lips. She bit the corner of her bottom lip. The temperature in the room rose a degree or two. Why did she decide to wear the pink sweatpants and matching jacket? Maybe something had happened to the air conditioner? With the orchids in her arms, Lexi turned her attention back to the stage. "After lunch, we'll work on hair and makeup.

"Are y'all hungry?" Lexi asked the two Reyes brothers as she strolled past Stephen.

Kimber, who'd kept her eyes glued to her iPad during the entire rehearsal, glanced up and offered a half shrug of her shoulder. Lexi gave the girl a coy smile, then spoke to Nate, who stood up to close the gap between them. "We have some finger sandwiches if you're starving. Do you like cucumber or pimento cheese sandwiches?"

"Got some without the pimento?" asked Andrew, whizzing by with Philly in his arms. His heels clicked on the marble flooring of the kitchen. The bottles of jams, hot sauces and other condiments jingled as he yanked the refrigerator door open.

Rolling her eyes, Lexi shook her head. "Then you want a *cheese* sandwich, Andrew." She turned her attention back to Nate and Kimber. "I'm sorry. Someone must have forgotten to take out the platter. You know what? I have a better idea. I have some shrimp and grits upstairs ready to be eaten. Kimber, would you mind coming with me to help?"

Without making eye contact, Kimber nodded her dark head. Such great bone structure. If only she showed the slightest interest in pageantry. Lexi headed toward the back of the store to the spiral steps leading upstairs, where she kept more dresses. Expanding the store would have allowed her to separate the inventory. Now she needed to rethink things.

"You know the way?" Lexi asked, stopping to tug down the plastic covering on a sold dress.

"Yes ma'am." Kimber quietly sighed. She took two steps at a time.

The two-story building had once belonged to one of Southwood's first dressmakers. Lexi didn't break from tradition too much, hiring contractors to gut the majority of the downstairs area into a showroom floor with changing rooms and an office. The spiral steps led to an upstairs kitchenette and into the two-bedroom apartment. Lexi followed Kimber up to the second floor. Racks of more dresses, all wrapped in plastic, were lined up against the far wall, waiting to be picked up. A black-speckled marble bar with two high-back wooden bar stools separated the kitchen and dining area from the living room. Behind the bar on the black stove, a red pot simmered with what Lexi had planned on having for dinner with her assistants.

"I just need to add the shrimp," Lexi told Kimber. "Do you cook?"

"No, ma'am," Kimber answered, her head low and eyes

on the floor, probably wishing the shaggy red throw carpet would swallow her alive.

Lexi shook her head and her smile softened with the understanding of regretting doing something stupid. Kimber sat with her elbows on the countertop and watched Lexi measure the amount of water she needed to feed everyone downstairs and set the pot to boil. "Do me a favor. Turn on the fan. It's the switch by the bathroom door."

Without needing any direction, Kimber headed over to the white wall with the panel and flipped the switch. Lexi reached into the cabinet and took down her bag of grits. She smiled over her shoulder at Kimber. "Don't tell my mama you saw me using quick grits. She'll disown me."

Kimber smiled weakly.

"When cooking shrimp, I don't want to risk getting any smell on those dresses." Lexi inclined her head toward the back wall. "The dresses up here are very important to me," said Lexi. She watched Kimber slide onto one of the bar stools, head still hung down.

Kimber burst into tears. "I'm sorry I took the dress, Miss Lexi!" When she glanced up, her tear-filled eyes pleaded with Lexi.

"Oh, honey, how did you even get it?"

"During Philly's last workshop," Kimber started to explain. "I'm sorry. It was wrong of me to take advantage of you, Miss Lexi. You allowed me to use your private bathroom when I was on the phone, crying, with my boyfriend, and well, I got nosy and went through your racks of dresses. There were so many I didn't think you'd even notice."

I didn't, Lexi thought to herself.

"I was so desperate to make sure my boyfriend noticed me."

Yet again, Lexi's mother's words rang in her ears, the ever-nagging *I told you so* when it came to Lexi's decision to create and wear dresses. As she came around the kitchen bar, Lexi remembered wanting to grow up and impress a boy—it didn't make the situation right, but she understood. She wrapped her arm around the girl and gave her a hug. Hugging her saddened Lexi. With no prospects for a romantic partner, the only love and advice she'd give out would be to her niece, Jolene, and other young girls like Kimber.

"You do realize you're too young for something like this?" Lexi stroked her shoulders. "I was too young for it, and you don't want to make the wrong impression."

"Please don't tell my uncles I stole your dress!" Kimber blurted out in panic.

"I've already taken the heat, sweetie," said Lexi, thinking about how much it had cost her. "No point in two of us being in trouble."

On Friday night, while she had been in his arms dancing, Stephen claimed he planned on keeping an eye on things. She was already going to be punished. Why ruin Kimber's summer? Besides, what did Stephen plan on doing with a bakery? Did he bake? She pressed her lips together and thought of her mental score card. He might earn a few points if he did.

"For the record, I was older than sixteen when I wore the dress, over twenty-one. Whoever you were trying to impress can't be worth the trouble," Lexi continued. "He's not the kind of boy you want to be around."

"No, ma'am." Kimber shook her curly head. "Uh, Marvin's not like one of those boys."

Odd that she said Marvin. The relationship between the two struck Lexi as simply friendship. "Marvin, or whomever you're really trying to impress. Remember, it is always easy to be the bad girl," she told Kimber with a wagging finger. "The average teenager strives for the bad-girl routine, but you strike me as above average."

Hesitantly Kimber nodded her head. "Yes, ma'am."

"Promise me you'll carry yourself above the rest. Okay?"

Abruptly Kimber threw her arms around Lexi's neck. "You're the best, Miss Lexi!"

"Wow, I typically get that kind of response when I give a gift."

Startled by the intrusion, Lexi and Kimber jumped and turned around. Stephen filled the space with his massive frame as he leaned against the staircase with his hands in the pockets of his pants, head cocked to the side. Stephen's score card owned the number ten on presentation, she thought as she remembered to breathe.

"Girl talk is priceless," Lexi quipped.

The corners of Stephen's mouth twitched as if he wanted to smile, but the smile lost to a frown. "I did not mean to interrupt, but Andrew suggested I might be of some service."

Andrew needs to be fired or given a raise.

"We came up here to finish up our meal," Lexi explained, walking back around to the kitchen. She turned her back to get her bowl of deveined shrimp and butter and set it on the counter in front of Kimber. Still in the living room, Stephen ran his large hand over the cushy chair shaped like a red pump, diva-style shoe with a zebra-print heel. His eyebrow rose with amusement after spying the zebra throw rug under the fashion magazine–littered glass coffee table.

"May I help?" he asked, walking over to the bar next to his niece.

"I'm here to help," Kimber clarified.

Lexi cast a glance over her shoulder in time to catch the surprised look on Stephen's face and Kimber's boastful grin before she turned around to reach for her frying pan. She enjoyed the girl coming to her defense. Maybe Stephen could relax now.

"Looks to me like you're sitting down while Miss Lexi is doing all the work."

"Oh, no," Lexi corrected. "We've been talking and waiting for the water to boil. But this is a two-butt kitchen—"

"A what?" Stephen chuckled.

"A two-butt kitchen, meaning I can't bend over to peek in the oven if you're washing dishes."

"I see." Stephen licked his lips. His head cocked to the side, and something else began boiling in the kitchen besides the water.

Lexi gulped and shook her head. "Drinks. I have a pitcher of tea on the balcony. Kimber, would you mind?"

"Not at all, Miss Lexi." Kimber scrambled off the stool as her phone rang. "You're not going to believe where I am," she squealed into the line.

The kitchen seemed to grow smaller when Stephen came around the bar and invaded her space. "What I can't believe is I've taken Kimber's phone every day since last week. How does she keep coming up with a different-colored one each time?"

"You got me." She sighed. "Here, let me get you an apron." Lexi tiptoed toward the pantry and grabbed one off the hook. She turned and Stephen was right behind her. "Sorry," she mumbled. "I told you this is a two-butt kitchen."

Stephen blocked her path. Just as when they'd danced, his eyes stayed fixated on her hair and then her lips. To create space, Lexi pressed her hands against his chest and wrapped the apron strings around his neck. "Turn around and I'll tie you."

"You'll tie me up?"

Laughter of relief broke the strange tension between them. "In your dreams. Now here, I'll need you to continue stirring the grits while I cook the shrimp."

Thankfully Stephen did as she asked, stopping every so often when she needed to add some cream, tomato paste, spices and lots of butter into the grits while her shrimp sautéed. They cooked together in silence, but she was reminded how they'd danced together. On the dance floor he took the lead, but in her kitchen she did. He stepped out of the way when she added something new to his pot and back into the empty space.

The spiced shrimp took no time to cook and in her haste to get out of the kitchen, Lexi reached for the handle of the pan to pour everything into a serving dish behind her. She'd underestimated the weight of the pan and her wrists weakened. Stephen anticipated her misstep and swooshed right behind her, wrapping her in his arms and his hands over hers.

"Here, let me help," he whispered in her ear.

Lexi gulped and watched the shrimp fall into its bath of butter. She sprinkled parsley flakes over the edge of the pan, prolonging her time in Stephen's arms. How long had it been since a man held her? A little voice in her head reminded her that this was not being held. Stephen was helping her. The beating of her heart drowned out common sense. It took all her strength not to reach up and behind her to stroke the back of his head and neck. His lips were so close to her ears; if she turned, they might kiss. Beneath the fabric of his shirt she felt the hard muscles of his chest and abs. A bit lower and she felt the unmistakable swell of a hard erection beginning to grow. So she wasn't alone in this attraction?

The sliding glass door opening from the patio interrupted Lexi's wanton thoughts. Stephen took the empty pan and set it in the sink. "Miss Lexi," Kimber called out, "this is not a pitcher. This is a bucket." She hauled the container of brewed tea into the dinette area and turned around. "Cute apron, Uncle Stephen."

Stephen glanced down and Lexi covered her mouth to keep from laughing. "Keep Calm and Sparkle On. Nice."

"Sorry, I just reached for the first one." Lexi extended her arm. "I'll give you another."

Stephen grasped the counter behind him for support. "I'm good."

Her eyes traveled to the lower half of the apron and decided he was right. The little voice in the back of her mind spoke out again, this time reminding her of what a long summer this was going to be.

Chapter 5

"Why did you bother with the condo if you're going to sleep here?"

At the sound of the cheerful, deep voice, Lexi glanced up from the dish in front of her and gave Andrew a wink before layering the last vanilla wafer on top of the instant banana-pudding mixture. She'd gotten up this morning, took the risk of flat-ironing her long tresses in this summer heat and dressed casually in a pair of denim jeans and a white Grits and Glam Gowns shirt. "I got caught up making a dress last night."

"Perhaps a wedding dress inspired by my boo?"

Lexi responded with an eye roll. In truth, the inspiration had come from seeing Kimber standing against the balcony door with the vibrant colors of the afternoon sun behind her. After everyone left last night, Lexi grabbed the spools of red, orange and yellow, and began blindly putting together a dress. She hadn't been so excited to start on a dress in years. Andrew propped himself up at the bar stool and watched. "Why are you baking?"

"Is it considered baking when you never turned on the oven?"

"What would Mary Pendergrass say?" Andrew clutched his throat.

"Considering she's not speaking to me," Lexi joked, "not a thing."

With a heavy sigh, Andrew rested his chin in his hands and propped his elbows on the counter. "If my Southern Baptist preacher daddy can get over me giving up my chance to play in the NFL to design dresses, then your folks can get over this whatever thing."

"This, whatever—" she sighed and held her fingers up

in air quotes "—has been going on for years ever since I opted to attend a state college."

"Aw," Andrew cooed. "You poor baby. Tell me again how you were cut off from Mommy and Daddy's money, thus forcing you to model to make your own money?"

Lexi dusted crumbs off her hands, then wiped her brow with the back of her right hand as if she'd worked so hard in the kitchen. "If you're writing a book, it didn't happen quite like that."

"Boo hoo." Andrew rolled his eyes. "Poor little scandalous Southwood socialite."

"Are you here so early to bust my chops?" Lexi smirked, placing her hand on her hip.

"No, I actually came to print out more flyers on the pageant in Savannah this weekend."

"What?" A pageant took weeks to prepare for.

Andrew reached into his back pocket and extracted a folded-up piece of paper. "The Glitzy Southern Pageant is out of our district, but I thought the new crop of girls would be excited to watch."

Lexi shook her head, going over to her pantry for a red box of clear wrap for her dish. She closed the door with her hip, all the while trying to recall who would run the pageant area in the southeast region of Georgia. "Who is the emcee?"

"Waverly Leverve."

The name brightened up Lexi's smile. "No kidding. I used to train her."

"I know," said Andrew, "which is why I thought you might try to gather some troops up to bring down, you know, generate business, wear our logo and pass out business cards with our services. It is Memorial Day weekend."

"We can try."

"Try what?" asked a feminine voice at the opening of the staircase.

"Good morning, Chantal," Lexi and Andrew choroused.

Strolling in with a brow raised, Chantal looked between them. "What's the occasion?" she asked, peering over the counter.

"I owe a favor."

"You never said who this is for," Andrew pointed out. "My boo?"

"His name is Stephen," Lexi said quickly.

"Meow." Andrew swiped his hand at her like a cat. "Claiming him already?"

The last time Lexi had claimed someone, unbeknownst to her, he was already married. The humiliating act at least allowed Lexi to refocus on her career. So the only thing she owed Ernest Laing was a thank-you. The heir to the Laing Diamonds had filled her head with lies and her heart with betrayal.

"Those were some pretty flowers he bought you," said Chantal, dragging Lexi out of her stupor.

"They're Dancing Lady orchids," Lexi informed them, "and he was being nice."

"Interesting." Andrew hummed.

"You're reading too much into this." Lexi wiped her hands on the back of her jeans. "Like I said, he was being nice."

Andrew reached across the bar of the kitchen and tapped the covered dish. "So you're returning the favor by being nice?"

"Of course," Lexi said perkily. She refused to let him have one up on her. If Stephen wanted to pretend to be kind, after what he did with the lot next door, he had another think coming. What was the saying? Kill them with kindness? "I thought I'd drop this off before I headed into the shop."

"I thought the lights weren't on in his place," said Chantal.

"Oh?"

"Yeah," said Andrew. "When I asked Philly if she was

coming in for practice today, she told me no 'cause her uncle Nate had an appointment out of town."

The two assistants bumped their shoulders together when Nate's name was spoken, and Lexi rolled her eyes and inwardly admitted the handsomeness of the Reyes men. She did wonder how Stephen would handle the pageant world if he was not prepared to bring Philly in for any practice. If he didn't freak out over the way some of the pageant moms treated their kids, he might over the way they'd devour him.

A lightbulb went off in Lexi's head. She wondered how he'd handle the pageant in Savannah. In a way, she feared for his sanity. And did Andrew say Nate went out of town today? Curiosity filled Lexi's veins.

"Perhaps I'll swing by their house this afternoon and drop this off."

Andrew's eyes widened. His elbow nudged Chantal in the ribs. "They live out where your friend Rosalind used to be."

"You know this how?"

"Kimber told us," said Chantal.

"Well, I'll just shoot over there and drop this off."

Today, Lexi felt nostalgic. She left her boutique and went east, which would take her by her childhood home—if she still had the right to call it that.

David and Mary Pendergrass enjoyed being pillars of the community without actually living there. A tree-lined canopy road led the way toward the neighborhood of plantation-style homes. Already aware of her speed, slowing down for deer, Lexi brought her Cadillac to a crawl as she passed high gates covered by the low-hanging limbs of peach trees. Ripe peaches dangled off, ready for picking. Lexi resisted and sat in the car.

From this distance, three large columns blocked her view into the oversize dark gray framed windows of the living room and the formal dining room. The balcony doors were open and the long white chiffon curtains billowed in the wind. The picturesque house had stolen her heart but also her childhood. This was her parents' home. She hadn't stepped foot inside since she came home from college. They'd made their displeasure known when she decided to go to a state school by cutting off her funds. They scowled when she dropped out of pageants to model. So when the scandal with Ernest had broken out, her parents looked right through her when she bumped into them in town. Now with Grits and Glam Gowns making headlines, she hoped they might find it in their hearts to be proud of her.

Thirty minutes later Lexi pulled her gold Cadillac into the driveway of the Reyes home. A small pink bike with training wheels lay on its side in front of the white garage. The girls lived in a split-level brick home with black shutters on all the white-framed windows. Black security bars covered the top-floor windows. The manicured bushes under the bay window bloomed with fragrant white gardenias.

The bottoms of Lexi's jeweled flip-flops flapped against the pebble-lined walkway to the front door. Frosted panels on either side of the door gave an obscured view of the chaos inside the home. Pink clothes were sprinkled along the beige-colored carpet on the stairs. Roller skates at the bottom of the steps were an accident waiting to happen. A high-pitched ding sounded off in the house as she rang the bell.

Lexi balanced the covered dish on her hip and leaned forward. Nate's SUV was nowhere in sight. For the life of her she could not recall what Stephen drove, but he probably parked in the garage. Ringing the bell again, Lexi turned around to observe the rest of the neighborhood. She tucked a stray blond hair behind her ear, conscious of how much anyone might know of her past.

Once again, Lexi rang the doorbell, her long manicured

fingernail accidentally pressing the button twice. In a matter of seconds, heavy-sounding footsteps rushed to the door and in one swift swoop the door yanked open. Startled, Lexi took a step backward. As she balanced herself to keep from slipping off the step, she gasped at the sight of a shirtless Stephen Reyes. His solid torso, muscular chest and sculpted bare arms filled the door frame. A set of washboard abs dipped into a V shape, pointing toward the waistband of a pair of black-and-gray swim trunks. Her eyes fixated on the white ties holding the trunks up.

No doubt of the perfect score in her mental score card.

Unable to move, hell, unable to breathe, Lexi stood frozen for a few seconds before Stephen cleared his throat to speak first. "Lexi, what a pleasant surprise."

"Hi, um—" she lifted her gaze "—is everything okay?"

"Why do you ask?"

As he spoke, Lexi concentrated on his face—more importantly the bright blue eye shadow caked on his lids. Fuchsia-pink blush stained his high cheekbones. For a moment she thought two caterpillars were crawling under his eyes until she realized someone had attempted to place faux lashes on him. Clear glitter blotted his top and bottom lip and twinkled in the afternoon sun. The only thing missing was a black bobbed wig, and he'd be as hideous as Cary Grant in *I Was a Male War Bride*.

"Are you checking up on me?" Stephen asked when she took too long to speak. He crossed his arms over his chest. "You wound me, Miss Pendergrass."

"Are the girls okay?"

His brows furrowed together and his right eye twitched. "Why would you ask? Of course they're okay. They weren't feeling well—that's why they missed school," he spat out, rolling his eyes. "Please don't tell me Nate sent you."

"Nate? Uh, no?" She tried to find the logical reason why she'd driven over here, but the sight of his hard muscles literally made her lose her mind.

"I'm perfectly capable of taking care of my two nieces."

The absurdity of his attitude rendered her helpless with laughter. Stephen raised a brow. Lexi cleared her throat and pressed her lips together to keep from giggling. "Were you asleep?"

"What?" He choked out a nervous laugh, brushing his hand across the back of his bald head. "Why would you ask?"

"Because your lipstick is a bit smeared, here." With her free hand Lexi tapped her bottom lip.

Stephen's hand mocked hers and swiped with his fingertips and inspected the residue. Cursing, he pushed away from the door, leaving it open. His voice carried throughout the house as he called for Kimber and Philly. Not sure whether to come in or stay at the front door, Lexi nodded her head and glanced around. She took her chance and stepped into the foyer and closed the door behind her.

Unlike the Pendergrass household, the inside of the Reyes home reeked of love. Mary and David Pendergrass had never allowed toys outside of the toy room. They barely tolerated having her in the house. As soon as she hit the proper age, she was shipped off to boarding school. In contrast, wood-framed family photos lined the walls of the Reyes home. She spied a wedding photograph of Ken and Betty Reyes. Both of Ken's brothers flanked him, along with a couple of familiar faces of women from around town as bridesmaids. A cherrywood credenza by the door held a space for keys, stacks of mail and lots of colorful hair bows. At the Pendergrass house, the photos on the wall were Sotheby's certified, insured and usually purchased at an auction. Makeup and hair were done in the parlor upstairs by an artist.

"Miss Lexi!" Philly appeared at the top of the steps and took the banister down. Her lavender tutued behind came full speed ahead. The white-and-lavender-striped T-shirt she wore now bore a single dust streak down the front.

"Hi, Philly!" Lexi exclaimed, reaching down with one arm to give the five-year-old a hug. Her damp hair smelled of faint chlorine. "What are you up to?"

"I was practicing sparkly makeup with my dolls. Want to see?"

The makeup on Philly's eyelids matched Stephen's. "I'd love to, sweetie, but first I believe this needs to go into the refrigerator." She displayed the covered dish. "Will you show me?"

"Sure!" Philly beamed, stretching her sticky hand upward to grab Lexi's and drag her into a spacious kitchen.

A heavy scent of Lysol mixed with chlorine hit her senses first. The royal blue island was covered with dirty dishes. Lexi's fingers itched to start cleaning. Instead of cleaning, Lexi placed the banana pudding on one of the empty shelves inside the Sub-Zero fridge. The bare shelves cried for attention. A cardboard box of pizza filled the bottom shelf, along with a few white Chinese-food containers on the door. How did the dishes get so dirty if there was no food in the house?

"Can I have some?" asked Philly, crawling between Lexi's arms and the door.

"Have you had lunch?" Lexi countered. She checked the time; it was after two.

Philly's hazel eyes blinked at the blue-speckled pot on the stove. Lexi leaned over and spied at the contents. Burned black flakes floated in soapy water. "Uncle Nate left last night after he and Uncle Stephen got into a fight."

"A fight?" Lexi asked.

"Yes." Philly nodded and pointed toward a mason jar on the center of the island bar with the words *swear jar* in black ink over masking tape. "The cursing kind."

"Is everything okay?" Lexi didn't sense things were so bad. It wasn't as if Stephen sported a black eye or anything.

Philly nodded her head eagerly up and down. "Uncle Stephen got mad 'cause Uncle Nate burned dinner and so

Uncle Nate left Uncle Stephen in charge. And then Uncle Stephen burned breakfast."

The speed the girl spoke at was amazing. Lexi tried to take in as much as she could before Philly took a breath. She concentrated so hard she never heard Stephen's steps come up behind her.

"Blackened," Stephen's deep voice announced from the arched doorway. In the time it had taken for her to put the food away and get the scoop on what happened, Stephen had cleaned off his face and thrown on a fitted black T-shirt to cover up. A little piece of her deflated. What a shame. "I told you the food was *blackened*."

"We had *blackened* eggs," Philly told Lexi.

Amused, Lexi patted Philly on the head. "Oh, you poor thing, are you hungry?"

"She's fine," Stephen spoke up. "Did we miss a session with you today?"

"No, uh…" Lexi licked her lips. "Nate canceled."

"We missed school today," Philly informed her. "We didn't wake up in time."

Lexi's eyes glanced back in Stephen's direction, catching him as he shook his head quickly and stood tight-lipped. "You guys weren't feeling well?"

"He said I sounded *congested*." Philly annunciated every syllable of the word. As a pageant coach, Lexi had seen all kinds of maternal antics when they thought the judges weren't watching. Philly's hazel eyes looked over Lexi's shoulders and read whatever Stephen coached her to say.

Lexi glared.

"Philly, go get your sister so we can go out for lunch," Stephen ordered his niece.

Philly scrambled out of the kitchen. Her little foot-steps echoed through the hall. They were alone. The closest they'd been to alone before was dancing together the other night. The uncomfortable silence falling between her and Stephen made her all too aware she needed to leave.

"I guess I'll be leaving." She stepped around the island to escape the small space, but Stephen met her at the corner. Even though he was barefoot, he towered over her.

"You're not so tall without your heels," he said, his eyes looming over the top of her head.

"You're the first man to say such a thing." Lexi gulped.

"Why do you wear such high heels?"

Lexi flashed a pageant smile. "The higher the heel, the closer to heaven."

With that, Stephen chuckled. His pleasant laugh and smile softened the hard lines on his face. "Religious much?"

"I've been known to holler out the Lord's name before." Heat scorched her face at her blatant flirting.

Stephen's eyebrows rose. He cleared his throat and stared at her mouth for a full minute, contemplating something. What? She didn't know. For a split moment she thought he might kiss her. Did she want him to? *Hell yeah.*

"Why did you come today?" Stephen finally asked.

The rich deepness of his voice made her brain freeze. Air dried her throat. Lexi gulped, hoping to find her words. "My dessert is for you," she fumbled, then shook her head as the words left her lips, "I brought you some dessert you…" *God, please make this stop.* "You guys. You and the girls." *Geez shut up*, she told herself. Sweat began to bead at the nape of her neck. She'd straightened her hair for this?

"Dessert?" Stephen's left brow rose with curiosity. His lips curled into a lopsided grin.

"A little banana pudding." Lexi squared her shoulders with confidence. "I wanted to be neighborly."

"Neighborly to the man who stole your store?"

A sharp pang stabbed at her heart, but Lexi squinted her eyes and pressed a wide, second-place finisher smile across her face. "I am going to assume you offered the Foxxes something more favorable than what I came up with."

"I did."

"Then I don't consider what you did stealing, simply business."

Stephen's dark eyes roamed over her hair and her face, settling on her lips. She inhaled deeply, in hopes of disguising the set of chills threatening to expose her leashed desire.

"Such poise you have," Stephen hummed, still staring. "Did you learn that in your pageantry days?"

Lexi folded her arms across her chest to create some distance between them. "As a matter of fact, I did. I didn't always win."

"Hard to believe."

"It's true," Lexi said, and took a side step away from him. A sliver of bright light from outside flashed down the hallway when the door opened and quickly closed. "You don't go far in life by being a sore loser. So why not be happy for the winner? Say, how long were you asleep?"

"Questioning my parenting skills?" Stephen leaned his hip against the island.

Lexi debated whether or not to share with him what she thought she'd witnessed but decided against it when Philly and Kimber bounced down a set of spiral stairs in the corner of the kitchen. Maybe she was crazy. Maybe she didn't see Kimber sneak inside.

"Miss Lexi!" Kimber exclaimed, running to her side. "I was going to stop by and see you today."

"You're still grounded," Stephen interjected.

Kimber opened her mouth, then closed it. Lexi cocked her head to the side, noticing the faint mauve lipstick on her mouth. She wore a pair of strappy gold sandals, denim shorts frayed at the edges and a long-sleeved shirt—quite the opposite of the rest of her family members in the kitchen.

"Well, y'all," Lexi broke the tension, "I'd love to stay and chat, but I've got to get going."

"Do you have to?" Philly whined and came over and wrapped her arms once again around her waist.

Laughing, Lexi nodded her head and patted the top of Philly's head. "We'll hang out tomorrow."

"We can hang out now," suggested Kimber, "Uncle Stephen burned breakfast, so he promised to pick up lunch for us. You can stay, right?"

Unlike last time she'd been invited, Lexi did not have Stephen's glaring eye on her. Instead he nodded and smiled in amusement. "I'll take a rain check, guys," she finally said.

"Whenever you like." Stephen nodded again. "I'm not going anywhere. Here, I'll walk you out."

Lexi said goodbye to the girls and waved over her shoulder. Stephen brushed quickly by to open the door for her. *Was he eager to get rid of her?* The back of her hand brushed against the back of his as they walked down the front steps. She shoved her hands into her pocket and swore she heard him chuckle.

"If you're looking to take the kids out to eat," Lexi began, ignoring the way her shoulder brushed against his, "there's a place called Shenanigans. Kids eat free on Mondays."

"Is there something about me that strikes you as needing to find a meal deal?"

"A man who can purchase a building out of revenge does not strike me as a coupon clipper," she teased as she half grinned.

Stephen graciously accepted the playful banter with a quick nod of his head. "Cute." They reached the driveway and her car. If she didn't know any better, she'd swear they both dragged their feet.

"That's a pretty big Cadillac." Stephen cleared his throat.

"And gold, too." Lexi grinned up at him and when he flashed a grin and a wink, she looked away. Next to the small child's bike, a purple ten-speed leaned against the garage door. She swore it wasn't there when she pulled up. Quickly she told herself this was none of her concern. Stephen said he had everything under control. "You forgot to mention the color."

"I was getting to it." He winked. They reached the driver's side door. He leaned against the handle, blocking her entrance. "So what's the deal?"

"With the pudding?"

"I meant the car, but thank you for the dessert." Stephen reached out and took her keys from her hand. She knew the neighborhood and knew she did not have to lock the car, but she allowed this act of chivalry. Her mental score card went up on him.

"You're welcome," she said, then remembered the flyer Andrew had printed out earlier. "I almost forgot to give you this."

Stephen stepped forward and took the paper. His fingers caressed hers, sending a shock wave of excitement. "Thanks."

"And as for the car, well you know, it's long, lean, fast and blond." Lexi winked. Stephen opened the door for her, his mouth in a crooked smile. "What more could a girl want?"

She could want me, Stephen thought as Lexi backed her gold car into the quiet street of the neighborhood. He stood, afraid to move until he recovered from the physical desire, and waited until the red taillights disappeared. He tried to play the mind-over-matter trick, which failed, especially when he was in his swim trunks. What was it about Lexi Pendergrass that got under his skin? She was beautiful, but so were lots of women.

Lots of other women did not take an interest in his nieces, though. Sure, she'd played an intricate part in the girls' life, but he admired the way Kimber and Philly these scenes in his new town. They hung up with Stephen promising to find a place. As he swiped the red off button, the pit of his stomach flopped with anticipation of seeing Lexi again.

When was the last time he'd looked forward to seeing someone like this? High school? Having rushed into starting a career, Stephen never made time to form relationships with women. Over the years there'd been a few who kept him cozy at night, but all understood he was in no position to give in to a relationship.

They entered the noisy establishment and Stephen's senses were assaulted immediately. Pepperoni and popcorn scents wafted through the air. Bells and whistles pinged off the walls, slightly drowned out by a singing dog on a stage in the back of the room and children's laughter. Flashing lights streaming pretty much all the colors of the rainbow blinded Stephen for a moment.

He blinked several times and when his vision became clearer, it landed directly on Lexi Pendergrass's hourglass backside squeezed into a pair of tight jeans. She wore a red T-shirt tied in the back and a pair of red high heels. He'd yet to see her with her hair down. Usually she kept it up and off her neck, but tonight, even with her long tresses flowing down past her shoulders, he recognized her frame.

Even though the girls had walked into Shenanigans without him, they weren't permitted to join the crowds until he walked in and got his hand stamped, as well. With the time it took Stephen to get in and with the girls still waiting, they still hadn't recognized Lexi right off, which gave Stephen more time to watch her wiggle in front of a flashing game. A light spun around and as it neared where Lexi stood, she pressed a button. After the third time, she began jumping up and down like Sylvester Stallone after running up the museum steps in *Rocky*.

"Jackpot!" she yelled.

"There's Miss Lexi," Philly cried.

adored her. He barely got Kimber to give him eye contact, and yet his oldest niece threw her arms around Lexi.

Stephen waited a few minutes before heading inside. On any given day and with any given woman, Stephen prided himself on the ability to always have control over his body. These random pop-up erections after being around Lexi were going to be the death of him. Yesterday he had had the cover of the apron to hide his adolescent behavior. Today he needed to regain his composure before going inside to see the girls. Stephen willed his body not to respond to Lexi. He tried to recall the article written about her, word for word. The only thing popping up in his mind was the video of her honey-hued body in the frayed black dress barely covering her particulars. The article was aptly entitled "How Not Enough Is…Not Enough?"

As Stephen suspected, his internet search on her last night came up with negative article after negative article from her days after leaving the beauty-queen scene.

Now with his senses coming back to him, Stephen was ready to head back indoors and get the girls set to go out this evening. Sooner or later, either he or Nate needed to learn how to cook. The phone in his pocket began to ring. As if sensing Stephen was thinking of him, Nate's face began to appear on the screen. He swiped the green button to accept the call.

"What's up?"

"How'd the girls get off to school today?" Nate's chipper voice came through the line.

Stephen rolled his eyes toward the bright blue sky. The worst thing about being down here was the lack of breeze. Perhaps another dip in the pool would help pull double duty in cooling him down. "Why are you calling me?"

"I was on the road when I got a text the alarm went off. I'm just now able to pull over."

"Are you going to call me every time the alarm goes off?"

"Hey, you're the one who installed the damn thing," said Nate. "Feel free to have it uninstalled."

"I may," said Stephen, turning around to head back inside. "With me here, I can keep a close eye on the shenanigans."

"Speaking of Shenanigans, that's a restaurant I've been taking the girls."

"I know all about it." Stephen cut his brother off. "I got things under control."

"Then you know you don't have to make a reservation at this place."

"Funny." Stephen frowned into the phone before pressing the button to hang up on his brother. Was today Gang Up on Stephen Day?

Chapter 6

Why wasn't he surprised to spot Lexi's gold vehicle front and center in the parking lot of Shenanigans? Keenan dropped Stephen and the girls off at the front and said he'd be back in a couple of hours. With his hand on the brass handle of the door, Stephen exhaled with a mixture of dread and excitement. He and the girls had spent the past few months at the house, outside of social gatherings. Now it was time to get everyone acclimated to the town, and judging by the way Philly and Kimber took off down to the entrance and the man ready to stamp their hands, they were ready.

But it would have to wait. His cell phone began ringing from the front pocket of his blue jeans. The familiar number came from Orlando, Florida. Stephen held back by the door and answered the call from his old friend Christopher Kelly, the CEO of MET Networks.

"Chris, what's up?"

"Hey, man, I was checking in on you. Wanted to see how you and the girls were doing." Christopher came from a big family of politicians and television executives, yet he managed to be down to earth.

"We're managing," said Stephen. "I'm actually out with the girls this evening."

"Good to know. Are you working again?"

Stephen thought of his new office area. A lot of work needed to be done before moving in, but he still planned on working from his bedroom until then. "Yeah, things are progressing. What's up?"

Christopher briefed Stephen on an ideal shooting location. A TV script called for a small-town feel. Southwood came to mind, but Stephen didn't want to set up

Kimber pulled from Stephen's side and began trotting toward Lexi but stopped when someone called her name. Stephen grumbled when he spotted Marvin off by a hunting game with a bunch of other guys.

"Can we go see Miss Lexi before we get our table?" asked Philly. "Maybe we can sit with her."

"We don't invite ourselves..." His words fell on deaf ears as Philly ran toward her pageant coach, who was bent over collecting a long stream of tickets. Lexi stretched her arms out to embrace Philly with a big hug. Her eyes scanned the red booths of the dining area before finding him still at the entrance. The smile she gave him caused his breath to catch in his throat.

"Hi," she mouthed, and waved him over. Philly dragged Lexi by the hand to meet him halfway.

"Hi." Stephen returned a smile and hoped it did not come off as goofy as he thought. "What brings you here?"

"The Cyclone." Lexi held up a stream of gray tickets. Philly held on to the end, twirling and wrapping herself in them.

Stephen flattened his lips to inspect the machine. "The Cyclone, you say?"

"I'm addicted." Lexi tugged at her end of the tickets. "Hey, Philly, before you leave tonight, add these to your pot."

"Really?" His niece's face brightened, making her lop-sided ponytails even more adorable.

"Of course. Where are you guys sitting?"

"We just got here," said Philly, "Uncle Stephen did my hair."

Lexi's smile faltered, looking up at him. "Did he, now?"

"Kimber wanted to do it, but he said he can. It took him five times just to get the part in my hair straight. Then it took us forever because Uncle Stephen told Mr. Keenan to take the long way here. Uncle Stephen, can we sit with Miss Lexi now?"

It took Stephen a full ten seconds to digest everything Philly had blurted out before he shook his head. "What did I say about inviting yourself?"

"Feel free to sit at my booth," said Lexi. "I just put in an order for eight personal pizzas. Some of your classmates are over there." She inclined her head for them to follow.

They arrived at Lexi's table and she handed Philly a cup of brass coins. "Have fun, and don't forget about our deal."

"I won't, Miss Lexi!"

"Wait," Stephen called out, wanting to take the opportunity to lecture Philly about being aware, but she'd already disappeared with a group of girls wearing Grits and Glam Pageant shirts. Clearly, from the way they all giggled together, they were friends.

"She's fine," Lexi assured him. "Have a seat. Her other friends from the pageant workshop are here. When the waiter comes back with my drink, I'll let him know Philly's here."

After the death of her parents, Philly had become withdrawn and content with coming straight home after school. Seeing her happy now struck a chord with Stephen.

A lock of blond hair fell over Lexi's shoulder. She swept it away, revealing the deep V of her red T-shirt, and more importantly, the swell of her breasts. "He'll get her an individual pizza."

"And you ordered eight?"

The waiter came over with a pitcher of beer and a clear carbonated drink, along with a dozen red Solo cups. Lexi put in an order for both girls. "Beer?"

Stephen settled into the cushion and nodded. "They serve alcohol in a children's establishment?"

"If they didn't, I'd doubt they'd have this many people." Lexi turned over a red cup and poured from the pitcher. A few teenagers walked by and waved.

"Did you work here or something?" he asked. "I feel like I'm sitting at the popular kids' table."

"I sponsor a Skee-Ball Little League team for some of the girls from the after-school program at the public school."

Every time she spoke he became more impressed with her.

Lexi extended his cup toward him. "Here you go, barely any foam."

A static pop ignited between their fingertips with the cup handoff. Since Lexi didn't react, Stephen guessed it was just him. He thanked her and took a long sip. "You don't strike me as a beer kind of girl."

"Trust me, Stephen. I look forward to surprising you."

Stephen took another drink to keep from saying something inappropriate. They were in a public establishment filled with children. She was also Philly's coach. Kimber had gotten the scandalous dress from her. He needed to concentrate on these barriers, not imagine what a hellcat she'd be in bed, calling out the Lord's name.

"You like pushing my buttons." He decided to keep the friction between them.

The red cup rolled between her hands. For the second time Stephen noticed her fingers were void of any jewelry. The women he dated dripped in gold, platinum, diamonds or silver, and they would never drink domestic beer out of a plastic cup. Not as if he dated Lexi, though.

"Like I said, I like shocking you." She hid her smile behind a sip from her cup. "Let me guess, you're used to high-maintenance women? You like to wine and dine them, and then when they want more, you leave them."

Her last statement did not come off as a question but more of a statement. "Like you," he said, "I am going to enjoy shocking you."

"Let me guess about your last real girlfriend. I bet tall, thin and beautiful."

"Does liking beautiful women make me a bad man?"

The smile she'd started stopped and she rolled her dark

eyes. "Not at all. But liking a woman who takes whatever crap you have to say is."

"What makes you think I would give a beautiful woman crap?" He leaned forward, resting his elbows on the table.

"You give me crap."

"Are you saying the flowers I gave you yesterday were crap?" He enjoyed the red tint to her high cheekbones. She wrinkled her perky little nose.

"The flowers were slick. Nice choice, and I believe I said thank-you."

"By way of banana pudding?"

"I was being neighborly." She cocked a brow across the table at him and leaned forward, as well. Her lashes fanned against her high cheekbones as she took a sip of her drink. "I half expected you to be in your new establishment already."

"Nate changed his plans on me this afternoon over the phone." Stephen explained about how he and Nate had almost tussled over something as trivial as burning dinner. If Nate had listened to him, the attempt to bake a whole chicken wouldn't have gone awry. They hadn't gotten in each other's face like that since they were teenagers. Ken, being the oldest, always stopped them before their mother got involved. This being Nate's weekend away for "work," Stephen felt guilty for not fixing the problem before Nate left.

"So you stayed home with the girls," Lexi said, tilting her head to the side, studying him for the truth, "because they were sick?"

"Hey, with the spread of measles, I didn't want to risk the other kids in their school." Stephen glanced around and spotted Kimber hugging the mascot.

"So honorable, aren't you?"

Stephen turned his attention back to Lexi. Amusement swirled in her eyes. "Fine, don't tell Nate I overslept."

"You realize the administrative office accepts late excuses."

"And admit I overslept?"

Lexi gave a slow nod. "Well, at least you were able to spend some quality time with the girls. I caught a glimpse of the pool. It's gorgeous."

He agreed with her. Hanging out by the pool, napping, a little internet digging on Lexi had really helped him relax—until she showed up. "Thanks, I can't take the credit for it, but it is nice. Feel free to come over and swim sometime."

"Thank you for the offer. Did you give the next pageant any thought, or do you need to run it by Nate first?"

Stephen felt the corners of his mouth frown. "I don't have to clear things with Nate."

"I'm sorry." Lexi's perfect lips formed into an O. "Given he is the guardian listed on Philly's paperwork, I assumed he took care of the day-to-day activities." Lexi spoke a mile a minute, reminding him of Philly.

Half smiling, Stephen shook his head. "We're not an old-fashioned couple."

"I never said a word." Lexi sat back and hummed.

"Sure you didn't," he said with sarcasm. "Tell me about this pageant."

Eyes sparkling, Lexi sat up straight. "The Glitzy Southern Pageant? This one has a mix of all ages, but specifically Philly's age group will be the largest. A lot of pageant girls get their first start there."

"I'm not sure if I like the idea of all the money these pageants shell out to buy a trophy."

"Did you play sports growing up?"

"Of course," he said. "MVP in baseball every year."

"And did your parents have to pay for a uniform and a team fee? Did they have trophies at the end of your season for everyone?"

Stephen held his beer in his hand. "Of course, but we didn't have to wear makeup and look like grown men."

Lexi rolled her eyes. "Not all pageants are full glitz. Philly can win with natural beauty."

"And you still see potential in her?"

"As I told you the other night, I absolutely believe in her, as did the judging panel."

Leaning forward, Stephen rested his forearms on the table between them. "She didn't win just because you wanted to get revenge?"

"I'm a lot of things, Mr. Reyes, but petty is not one of them."

The standoffish tone in her voice didn't sit well with him. He didn't want the distance between them anymore. "Back to 'Mr. Reyes'?"

Lexi crossed her arms over her chest. "You assuming I'd pick Philly out of revenge reminds me we don't know each other at all. I had no say, but it didn't matter, she won hands down."

"All right." Stephen waved his hand in the air in surrender. "I don't want to fight with you, not when we're being so neighborly with each other. How about you show me about the game you were playing?"

"The Cyclone?" Lexi dropped her arms and craned her neck around to check out the machine. "It's not at a hundred yet. Once that number reaches a hundred, you increase your chance to get more tickets when you win."

The flashing lights over the dome read eighty. Stephen stood up and held his hand for her to take. "Show me, for practice."

Reluctantly, Lexi slipped her hand in his. Her fingers curled around the palm of his hand and set off a wave of electricity. Their eyes locked for a moment before Lexi pulled her hand away to grab a plastic cup of coins. Stephen followed her over, enjoying the view of her swaying hips as she sashayed to the game.

"All right, this game is about the right rhythm," she said, offering him the spot in front of the button. "It helps if you sing a song in your head and get a beat. Each time the light hits between the beat, press the button."

The intercom played the Charlie Daniels Band. Stephen shrugged and gave it a try, although with Lexi near him, he wasn't sure how to concentrate. She slipped a coin into the machine and he waited and pressed the button, missing the opportunity. Several tries and coins later, Lexi, subconsciously he was sure, wedged herself between his body and the button. She kept her hand over his. Each time they missed, she bent over and deposited another coin. Stephen understood how addicting the game became—or at least how addicting standing with Lexi was. By the end of the song, they won the round. Lexi jumped up and down and threw her arms around his shoulders.

"Oh, my God." She jumped back. "I'm so sorry." Her hands flew to her blushing face, covering her red lips.

Steam pooled from beneath his collar. His heart raced. Stephen shook his head and mentally shrugged off the sudden urge to go outside and smoke a cigarette. "I think our pizza is here." He nodded in the direction of three waiters bringing several pizzas over to where they sat.

Lexi caught a young girl whizzing by and told her to tell the others the food had arrived. In the mix of the younger kids, Kimber helped pour sodas from the three different pitchers and handed everyone napkins. He'd never seen her so helpful before. Did hanging out with Lexi do this?

"I must thank you for letting us crash your party," Stephen said with admiration.

"You don't have to thank me for Southern hospitality." Lexi blushed. "But speaking of offering, I can show you how to drive so you don't look so pretentious with a driver."

"You think I'm pretentious?" He couldn't recall the last time anyone dared speak to him in this way.

"Not many residents have a chauffeur."

"I don't have a driver. I have Keenan. He's been working for me for a while now, since I up and moved away from my business. Would it please you if I fired him completely?"

A grin spread across her face, which she tried to hide

by taking another sip of her beer. The corners of her eyes crinkled over the rim of her cup. Stephen licked his lips and shook his head. She was going to be the death of him one way or another.

"You're an admirable man." Lexi nodded. "But I can still show you around town."

Stephen knew exactly how to get around town. He chose not to take the quickest road—the same one that had claimed his brother and sister-in-law—but she did not need to know that. He pushed the image of the yellow tape blocking off the wreck out of his mind for something more pleasant.

The waiter arrived with an adult-sized pizza and two paper plates and served a slice to the two of them.

"You're from here, but you didn't attend school here?" Stephen asked when they were alone again.

"I am." She nodded, blotting the oil off her pizza before eating. "But my folks shipped me off to Cypress Alley Boarding School for Girls in southern Louisiana."

"Why there?"

"Because it's in the bayou, where boys can't get to you," she said lightly.

"Sounds like a wonderful place," Stephen mused, watching Kimber pour a drink for Marvin. "No boys, you say?" A sharp pain attacked his shin. "What'd you kick me for?"

"Don't you dare think about sending Kimber away."

"Okay, okay." Stephen chucked.

After playing a few more rounds of the Cyclone, Skee-Ball and whack-a-mole—Stephen drew the line at DanceDanceRevolution—Shenanigans started to close. As promised, Lexi gave her tickets to Philly and went with her and the other children to pick out their prizes. Parents arrived one by one to get their kids. Lexi walked over to the door to make sure each child got home with the correct parent. One kid was left behind. Lexi stayed and Stephen sent the girls home with Keenan while he waited an extra thirty minutes for the tardy adult to arrive. Once the mother picked up her daughter, Stephen walked Lexi to her car. He took her keys from her hands to open the door.

"Tonight was fun," said Lexi. "I hope you enjoyed it."

"I did." Stephen nodded. "I think next time I may end up beating you at the Cyclone."

"Sure," Lexi replied with a dramatic eye roll, "as soon as you try DanceDanceRevolution."

"And you said you don't like to dance," Stephen teased.

"I dance best when the steps are on a screen for me to follow."

"That's what I'm here for," he said, leaning forward. On autopilot, Stephen's right hand reached for her left and tugged her close to him. "You just need to watch me and follow my lead."

Under the pink sky, she blushed and cleared her throat. "So, um, I can drop you off if you like," Lexi offered. She rested her hip against the side of the car. The early summer's heat cooled off with a breeze through the streets. Birds began settling in the dogwood trees lining the sidewalks.

Not ready to share his lack of desire to take the short route home, Stephen shook his head and smiled. He allowed his hand to drop to his side when she untangled hers from his fingers. What had possessed him to try and hold her hand? Feeling awkward, Stephen scratched the back of his head. "Keenan should be here any minute. You go ahead."

"I don't want to leave you out here by yourself."

"Afraid something will happen to me in the mean streets of Southwood?" Lexi chuckled and waved her arms about. The sun had already begun its descent over the city buildings. Stores were closing for the evening. Cars made their ways toward the suburbs. One car, in particular, a white American vehicle, approached, catching Lexi's attention.

Stephen watched Lexi's eyes and her faltering smile. The woman behind the wheel, a caramel-hued older woman

with perfect gray hair, drove at a snail's pace with her eyes
forward and lips pinched.

"Friend of yours?" asked Stephen, touching Lexi's
elbow. A clench seized his heart when she faced him with
tear-filled eyes.

"Thanks for waiting with me, Stephen." Lexi smiled.
Keenan had the utmost timing and pulled up the moment
she'd turned to face him. Lexi reached for her door handle,
and not wanting to stand in her way, Stephen stepped aside.

Somehow a wave of disappointment washed over him
with the realization there'd be no kiss good-night. Is that
what he expected? Wanted? The Cadillac's engine roared
to life and she let down the driver's side window.

"Wait? What just happened? Who was the woman in
the car?" he asked.

Lexi squared her shoulders and smiled. Her tone became
almost robotic, practiced, even. "Well, Stephen," she began
with a toothy grin, "if you must know, that was my mother."

The bells over the door of Grits and Glam Gowns jingled
when Lexi entered her boutique the following morning,
business as usual. She could hear someone hammering next
door in Stephen's new store. Her four-inch heels clicked
against the floor and her hips swayed in her knee-length
brown pencil skirt. Already she slipped out of the matching
jacket, leaving on her sleeveless brown-and-cream polka-
dot blouse.

"You're in early," Chantal said, looking up from the
books at the register.

"Couldn't sleep," Lexi said, breezing into her office,
Chantal and her book on her tail.

"I don't like the sound in your voice."

"I'm okay." Lexi half smiled. "I saw my mom last night."

Chantal's eyes lit up. "You did?"

"Yes, I was leaning against the car, talking to Stephen
at the time."

Chantal's eyes narrowed and lips curved downward in a scowl. "Why?"

"He showed up at Shenanigans." Lexi shook her head and softened her smile, "Don't look like that. I suggested he bring the girls."

"And how did it come for Mary to catch you and Stephen canoodling?"

"We weren't canoodling." Lexi frowned, trying to wipe the memory out of her mind. She couldn't canoodle with anyone. The last thing she needed was her mother to see Lexi get sidetracked—again.

"So why did Stephen send over some more of those orchids you like? The dancing ones?" Excitement coursed through Lexi's veins. She looked around eagerly, but everything in the store was the same. "They're in your office," Chantal said drily.

"What's on the schedule today?"

A vase filled with long yellow orchids sat in the center of Lexi's desk. She walked around to her chair and glanced at the note, a thank-you card for a lovely evening. Lexi pushed it back into the envelope and listened to Chantal rattle off the list of appointments she needed to get through today, including several debutante dress fittings for the end of the month. At noon, she had a consultation with a future bride and her parents, and then later when school released, she'd have a pageant workshop, which ended with an hour of private lessons with Philly. A smile touched her lips at the thought of seeing Stephen again. Did he still feel the need to be present for every session?

Chantal left Lexi to greet the deliveryman they'd both spied from the mirror in her office, leaving Lexi to the set of designs she wanted to show the future bride. Some were her own designs and some were from other designers. She'd be a fool to think Grits and Glam Gowns would survive without buying from other sellers. After about an hour of thumbing through dresses, she met with the Keaton family upstairs in the loft.

Emily Keaton grew up in Southwood and had attended Southwood High School with her now-fiancé, Sam Marshall. Lexi was familiar with the Marshalls, thanks to their affiliation with the country club her parents belonged to when she was a kid. Lexi and her two best friends, Rosalind and Shannon, used to spend their summers floating on the blue water of the Olympic-style pool. Sam and some of his friends had teased them for being stuck-up, which amused Lexi, considering he belonged to the same club. Emily seemed like a nice enough girl, determined even to shop locally, despite her mother's pout. Mrs. Keaton didn't care for Lexi, possibly because of her modeling history or because she was offended Emily had opted not to wear the hand-me-down family dress.

On her way downstairs the clamor of hammers grew louder than when she'd met with the Keatons. Curiosity got the best of her. Had Stephen already hired a crew? Odd, how her heart did not ache as much as she expected. She headed down the steps from the loft and spied Andrew helping a girl decide between a peach and a pink dress. Lexi slunk toward the front door, and as the bells exposed her position, she heard Andrew call out to her. Intent on finding out what Stephen was up to, she slipped outside.

The afternoon sun briefly blinded Lexi. She covered her eyes with her hand and walked a few paces. Had she been able to expand into the bakery, she had planned on keeping the door where it was, with a walkway through her kitchenette toward the boutique and a pageant room separate from the area for the patrons buying dresses. Lexi swallowed down her animosity and found her beauty-pageant smile as she pushed the door open. The vision waiting for her made her mouth drop.

It wasn't the torn-out bakery case or the ripped-up black-and-white floors or the disappearance of the tables and chairs. What dried her mouth was the sight of Stephen standing in front of a scaffold, sawing away at a piece of wood. A pencil dangled from his lips. He wore a pair of dark denim jeans, which sagged just enough to show off the waistband of his boxer briefs. She wasn't sure how long she stood in the doorway without him noticing, but she enjoyed the view while she could. Biceps rippled with each powerful stroke of the saw. Her fingers itched to run along each rung of his abdominal muscles, including the V shape disappearing into his pants.

"Like what you see?"

Lexi almost jumped out of her skin at the deep voice pressing against her earlobe. Stephen glanced up to wave with his free hand. Nate Reyes stepped out from behind Lexi. The sun caught his deep green eyes, and she swore they twinkled against the lighting.

"What?" Lexi stammered.

"The bakery doesn't look anything like it did before." Nate beamed. "Does it?"

"Oh," she said over her beating heart. "Right, I would have never guessed this place was a bakery. When did all of this get done?"

Nate placed his hand in the middle of her back and guided her farther inside. "I had some free time yesterday," he said, giving his brother a look. "We're ahead of schedule."

"My brother is a bit of a carpenter," explained Stephen. He set his saw against the wall beside him and reached for his balled-up light blue crewneck T-shirt. "Were we making too much noise?"

Lexi blinked back her disappointment at his covered body. Nate brushed by Lexi. It was then she noticed he wore a pair of light blue jeans, and like his brother a moment ago, was shirtless. Nate Reyes was not the least bit modest and made no attempt to hide the massive tribal tattoo covering both shoulders. But when Stephen stepped in front of her, a set of butterflies fluttered in the pit of her belly.

"I came to say thank you for the flowers."

Stephen stepped close, so close she shivered. He reached out with his hands and inspected her palms. "What? No banana pudding?"

"Funny." Lexi pulled her hands away.

"What's this about banana pudding?" asked Nate.

"Don't worry about it," Stephen called over his shoulder. He wrapped his arm protectively around Lexi's lower back. "Nate, we're going to lunch."

The afternoon heat did not help the intense flame boiling inside Lexi. Once out on the street, she watched him glance around, contemplating which direction to go. She knew from the year she'd been at Grits and Glam Gowns that the deli across the street was filled with friends of her parents, which meant they'd report on her behavior to anyone in their circle. Lexi stepped out of Stephen's hold and began walking from her building toward the park.

"You're in luck," she said, glancing to her left, where Stephen fell into step with her. "Today is Food Truck Tuesday. There's a variety of places to grab something to eat."

"Sounds good to me. I wanted to talk more about this weekend."

Heart fluttering, Lexi stopped in her heels. "Seriously?"

"I need to find out for myself if this is something I want Philly involved in," said Stephen, slowing down for Lexi to catch up with him.

"Did you talk this over with Nate? Should we go and get him?"

Stephen half turned his face toward her. "Nate does not have the final say in what happens with this beauty pageant. We'll drive down Friday afternoon."

"We?" Lexi gulped. She and Stephen? Alone? Her palms began to sweat. She didn't realize she'd stopped walking again until Stephen turned around and grabbed her hand.

"We," he repeated. "I, rather we, will need you to guide us, and this will give me a chance to get to know you better."

Hand on her hip, Lexi cocked her head to the side and studied him. "What is there to know?"

"Oh, darling," Stephen said, his heart-stopping, devilish grin sending a shiver down her spine, "I want to learn what's beyond the beauty queen."

Chapter 7

The intention he'd had when leaving the new shop with Lexi was to take her someplace nice and quiet. Despite the occasional fly and gnat, he wouldn't change a thing, though.

During their lunch in the park, Stephen ate and watched Lexi. They shared a meal seated across from each other on a green metal picnic table. The paper wrappers their lunch came in became background noise between them as they dined on food from Southern Spin, a food truck doing exactly what the title promised. Lexi swore by the soul-food egg rolls and macaroni-grilled-cheese sandwich, so he took her up on her suggestion and added an order of pork nachos.

"You must work out a lot," Stephen said after Lexi polished off the second half of her collard green–filled egg roll.

"Are you saying something about my eating habits?"

Stephen coasted past the answer by chuckling. Better to laugh than to point out the half pizza she'd polished off last night or the three bowls of shrimp and grits the day before. Yet the woman still managed to have the most alluring hourglass figure he'd ever seen.

Lexi let him off the hook with a playful eye roll along with an explanation. "Besides work, I don't have anything else to do." She shrugged her shoulders.

"You don't date?"

She rested her elbows on the holes of the table and dropped her shoulders. Despite her posture, she still reminded him of a beauty queen. "Southwood is one of those small towns, you know?"

"I do." He nodded his head, then wiped his mouth with a napkin. "I grew up in Villa San Juan."

"Florida?" Lexi perked upright.

"I usually have to clarify not the one in Puerto Rico," Stephen chuckled. "You've heard of it?"

"You don't have to explain anything to me." Eagerly nodding, Lexi wiped the corners of her mouth with her napkin. "My friends and I passed up spring break at the usual Panama City Beach and headed over to Villa San Juan Beach. So you're from there? Why did I assume you were from Atlanta?"

"My business is there." With his mind preoccupied with Lexi lounging around on his hometown beach, Stephen absentmindedly reached across the table with his thumb and wiped away a faint smear of her red lipstick. Her eyelashes fluttered against her high cheekbones at the touch. "It *was* in Atlanta," he corrected himself and pulled his hand away.

"You sound sad."

Stephen cleared his throat. His eyes gazed across the park at the dozens of food trucks. The lines of customers were dwindling. Everyone apparently was going on about their day. "What makes me sad is I spent a lot of time in Atlanta instead of here." He turned his eyes to face Lexi. Her eyes stayed focused on his words.

"Because you dislike small towns?"

"I don't dislike small towns, exactly," he tried to explain. "I'm not a fan of everyone in my business and blind fix-ups like I'd get back at home in Villa San Juan."

A long S-shaped curl slid up and down on the front of her polka-dot blouse as she nodded. "I understand. Everyone around town knows your secrets."

It was on the tip of his tongue to ask her about her secrets. Why didn't her mother stop last night and speak to her? Why did Lexi freeze up and tear up?

"Where did you live in Atlanta?"

"Berkeley Lake."

The corners of Lexi's lipstick-free lips turned down. "Why does that not surprise me?"

He shrugged his shoulders. "Don't knock my hood."

"Berkeley Lake is far from a hood." Lexi laughed. He liked her laugh, enjoyed the way the corners of her eyes crinkled. "The last time I checked, your *hood*—" she used air quotes "—was listed as the most affluent neighborhood in the state of Georgia."

"Aw, don't make me sound *bougie*."

"Well—" Lexi shrugged "—if the mansion fits."

Stephen hollered out a laugh, something he hadn't done in a while. An elderly couple walking by stopped and turned. The woman glanced at Stephen's dining partner and shook her head disapprovingly before reaching for a phone from her pocketbook. If he didn't know any better, he'd swear she took a picture of the two of them. Lexi, still laughing, glanced over her shoulder and spotted the woman and offered a friendly wave. Stephen noticed the way the woman dropped her phone back in her purse and scurried off.

"What is the deal with you and your mother?"

The space between them quickly became quiet. The construction team across the playground stopped drilling. Even the birds stopped chirping. A proverbial needle on the record scratched their conversation to a halt.

Lexi took a long sip of her tea before deciding on an answer. When she did, her tone was low but diplomatic. "You said you wanted to talk about the pageant this weekend."

Stephen shrugged his shoulders. "Are we not allowed to discuss both?"

"What does it matter to you?" Lexi folded her arms across her chest.

"I thought we were getting to know each other," said Stephen, "being neighborly, as you said. What happened to that idea?"

A few minutes blew by, enough time to allow Lexi to process how to answer him. He interjected right before she

"Hey, are you guys done already?" asked Nate with a ght smile "I was about to come over and get you. I al- dy put in the order for the pizza." The girls' protesting ans echoing around the bare walls gave Nate reason to se. "Did you have fun?"

Yes," the girls chorused.

Nate's green eyes glanced between both girls and then . "I'm not sure how you got the two of them to agree have fun at the same time, but thank you."

No need to thank me." Lexi waved off the compliment.

Yes, don't thank her," Stephen said with light humor g off his handsome smile. "Or you'll be one-upping rever."

te rubbed his large hand over his square jaw. "I don't e problem there."

phen pushed his brother's back, jutting him forward. do."

mber and Philly giggled. Lexi recalled enjoying ing her mom and aunt argue over silly things. Ste- brotherly push appeared to be a bit harsher. Perhaps how boys played with each other. What did Lexi She only had a sister, and with their age difference, d nothing to argue about. But why would Stephen ate, especially over her? He didn't even like her— she was wearing him down.

e was no denying the attraction between them at nt, though. Lexi planned on allowing Stephen the nity to dispel his initial impression of her. She lanned on finding him so attractive in the mean- w was a woman supposed to resist a man like him? e a dimple appeared beneath his beard every time ed. And what a sexy laugh it was.

place looks good, guys," Lexi said, glancing Vas the heat on inside?

isn't too weird for you?" asked Nate.

ords Lexi thought she wanted to say were lost.

opened her mouth to explain, "And don't give me one of those rehearsed answers."

"What?" Lexi choked out. "I resent that."

"All right, I'm going to let you off the hook on your mother for now. Maybe this weekend we can talk some more about what's going on?"

"Why my mother?" Lexi shook her head from side to side. "How is your relationship with your mother?" she asked, folding her arms across her breasts.

"A bit strained right now," Stephen confessed. "Only because she blames me and Nate for not teaching the girls how to speak Spanish."

A few seconds ticked away before Lexi dropped her arms, her lips pinched into a threatening smile. "What?"

"Imagine how ashamed she was of *us* when we brought them back home over spring break."

"Your brother didn't speak in Spanish to them?"

Stephen chose his words carefully, not wanting to shed a negative light on the girls' maternal grandparents. "I think my brother had good intentions by not wanting to exclude Enzo and Jeanette."

"I remember Mr. and Mrs. Gravel," said Lexi. "She sang at a wedding I did not too long ago. This explains Philly's talent."

Stephen leaned forward, ignoring the awkward way the cold metal of the picnic table holes rubbed against his elbows. "Weddings and pageant gowns. Why both?"

"Don't forget prom gowns." As if asked this question before, Lexi nodded her pretty head and smiled, not her typical pageant smile, but a genuine one, one that reached her eyes. "I love dresses, always have. My Grandma Bea introduced me to a famous GRITS."

"What?"

"Girls Raised in the South." Lexi sighed, slightly annoyed with his interruption. "Ann Lowe."

"Who?" Stephen felt his lips press together when the name did not ring a bell.

"She was only one of the first noted African-American designers." Lexi gasped out of irritation. "She designed for a lot of actresses. Olivia de Havilland's dress when she won an Oscar for…"

To Each His Own," Stephen finished for her. When her brows rose, he explained, "I used to spend Saturdays watching old movies with my mother."

"So you want to sit here and act like you didn't enjoy the movies?"

"Nah." Stephen sat back. "I can't pretend that this didn't help me with my career."

"Do you still watch them?"

He nodded. "Every once in a while, I can commandeer the television in the living room and get one of the girls to watch with me."

"Saturday nights, this park converts into a sort of drive-in," said Lexi, waving her hand like a wand toward the open area between the swing set. A group of non-school-age children played in the sandlot while their mothers sat on the benches surrounding the square. "You may enjoy it."

"Are you asking me out on a date?" Stephen teased.

"I don't date parents." Did she want to tack on an *any-more* to the end of her statement?

"I still come even if I've seen the movie a dozen times," Lexi went on. "I love the glamorous way everyone dressed back then. I can't remember a time in my life when I didn't want to create dresses. My mama would drag me across the state to find the perfect pageant gown because there wasn't a shop in Southwood to cater to her needs, which is partly why I came home."

"Makes sense."

"What's your favorite part of watching films?" Lexi asked.

"For me, I love the scenery. I can see a broken-down home and see its potential to be something I'[...] classic movie."

"Uh-oh." Lexi sat up straight again.

"What?"

"It just sounds like we have a lot more in [...] you'd like."

With a deep exhale, Stephen sat back, [...] her news was not such a bad thing.

The sun had settled over Sunshine B[...] time Lexi returned to Grits and Glam G[...] diagonal parking spaces were filled wit[...] for the evening's workshop. A twinge of [...] staying away from the shop for so long[...] ing Stephen away from his afternoon du[...] time flew by as they got to know each ot[...] what would have happened if she had [...] on the beaches of Villa San Juan or e[...] Peach Tree Boulevard.

"Miss Lexi!"

A crowd of girls between the ages [...] surrounded Lexi the moment she set f[...] Philly in the center, leading the cha[...] Lexi practiced walks, stances and ma[...] the judges—the judges being Andre[...] ber. That last appointment came aft[...] on the teenager's body language—[...] and heavy sighs at being forced to [...] sister. To stabilize the mood, Lexi [...] help. The hour passed quickly, ther[...] girls next door. For the second tir[...] butterflies flittered in the pit of L[...] of Stephen's bare chest. He and [...] by side, setting up partitions in [...] ing area. In less than forty-eight [...] bakery into something resembli[...]

Weird, because she stood here in this new office area and lusted after a man who just a few days ago had vowed to ruin her. "Weird how?"

"I don't know." Nate shrugged. "I was under the impression you wanted to expand."

"This isn't the only place in town," Lexi said with a practiced smile. "I may have lost out on this space but I at least gained some interesting neighbors." She rubbed the cap of Philly's curly head. Stephen moved closer to her, elbowing his brother out of the way.

"Let me walk you to your car."

"We'll walk over and pick up the pizza," said Nate after a pause of awkwardness. The girls groaned again. "Let me clean this stuff up first."

The shortness in Stephen's tone sent a pang to the center of Lexi's chest. So he still held animosity toward her when it came to his nieces. She had every right to plant her heels into the pulled-up floor and stand her ground, but when his hands brushed against her lower back, something in the back of her knees went weak.

Like last night, a warm breeze blew between them. Stephen walked her to her car, but then leaned against the driver's side door. Unsure of where to stand or what to say, Lexi rested her hip by the hood and faced him. "Clearly you have something to say."

"I do." Stephen cleared his throat. "I wanted to say that I may have been wrong."

Against her better judgment, her heart fluttered against her chest. What did she care? Lexi did not date parents or fall for them. So what if his proverbial bedroom eyes stared down into her soul when they spoke? "Really?"

"Yes. I was wrong about not wanting to allow Philly into pageants. I've never seen her happier."

The fluttering stopped and crashed into her belly. Lexi plastered a smile. "I am fortunate to work with her. She is a great kid and can go far in the pageant."

Stephen slipped his hands into the front of his jeans. "So this weekend?"

"Yes. Did I convince you this afternoon?"

"You convinced me on a lot of things."

The door to the new office opened. Philly pointed out that they were still outside and Nate nudged her along down the street. They were probably headed toward the great little Italian place. Even with the variety of places Southwood had to offer, the girls still dragged their feet along the sidewalk. "Do you guys ever cook at home?"

"You saw what happened when we tried."

"You burned it," Lexi recalled.

"Blackened," Stephen corrected. "Why do you ask?"

Lexi cast a glance over her shoulders toward the corner. "I thought I noticed a bit of reluctance from the girls when your brother mentioned picking up some food. How long have you been in town?"

"Almost six months."

"Isn't it time you two stopped acting like a couple of bachelors raising two girls?"

Through his sexy beard, his lips parted for a moment to pout, then turned into a crooked smile. "Are you offering your services?"

"Sorry, I don't play house." Lexi inhaled deeply, proud of herself for not falling for his charm. She took a step backward, away from him.

"You don't date parents, either."

Lexi's brows rose. "You were listening."

"I've heard everything you've said, Miss Pendergrass." Stephen stepped closer. "I am trying to decide if I want to pay attention to that part."

"What? Why?"

"Why?" Stephen asked. "Are you going to deny this attraction between us?"

Lexi squared her shoulders and tilted her chin and answered honestly. "Yes."

Amused, Stephen chuckled and rubbed his beard. "Why?"

"Did you hear me when I said I don't date—"

Whatever she wanted to say was lost when Stephen descended upon her. His large hands snaked around her waist and drew her close and hard against his body. Her mouth opened in a feeble attempt to stop him, and she pressed the palms of her hands against his sculpted chest. Deep down inside, she knew she wanted this. She needed to feel his lips on hers, his tongue against hers. Stephen dragged his hands from her waist up the sides of her face, cupping her cheeks before delivering an earth-shattering kiss. Lexi's knees went weak. A bolt of desire from the taste of his mouth pulsated through her veins. He pulled away briefly, long enough for Lexi to savor the minty sweetness of his mouth. One hand dropped from her cheek and caressed the outside of her arm, curving to the inner delicate skin of the other side. His fingers splayed against her and trailed upward. Her mind beckoned his hands to touch her all over. Lexi leaned closer into his body. Partly obliging, Stephen cupped one breast. Beneath his thumb, her nipple hardened. An unintentional gasp escaped her lips. Stephen came in for another kiss, capturing her mouth. Deepening the kiss, his hands dragged from her body to her hair, tugging at the roots. When he pulled away for real, Lexi wrapped her arms around his neck to keep from falling.

"You need to remember one thing. I'm not any parent."

The last thing Lexi remembered was Stephen's strong arms pulling her frame against his, seducing her mind, body and soul with his kiss. She didn't recall the drive home. Maybe a vague memory of the Reyeses walking around the corner and Stephen stepping aside.

The sound of her keys hitting the glass dish on the credenza by the door brought Lexi out of her daze. An echo hollered down the hallway. Just a few months after moving in, she still lived out of boxes. She'd yet to hang any photographs on the walls. Since her refrigerator at the boutique was filled with food, she ate there. She couldn't go back to the shop to pick up something to eat now. She wasn't sure she'd be able to pull into her parking space and not reminisce over Stephen's kiss. What on Earth possessed him?

I'm not any parent.

Stephen's parting words sent a shiver down her spine. True enough, he wasn't a parent, but Stephen was still Philly's guardian. What would be the point of a relationship? Weren't the girls' lives complicated enough as it was? In her heart, she already knew Kimber and Philly had developed a fast and close bond with her—Philly because of the extra coaching and Kimber due to the secrecy of the dress. Stephen had promised he'd drop the dress matter their first night at DuVernay's. So far, he'd stayed true to his promise. But a part of her cringed with fear he'd bring it up. She vowed to hold on to Kimber's secret as long as possible.

What would happen if they dated? What if they decided to end things? Stephen Reyes did not strike Lexi as the type of man to stay in a small town. Sure, he talked the talk by moving down here, even going through the motions of setting up shop with his new office space. But what about a year from now? What happened when he got bored with a small town like Southwood?

No matter how she tried to rationalize any form of relationship, it ended badly. Sticking to her guns, Lexi called in a take-out order from the local Asian restaurant and slipped into a comfy pair of cotton pajama shorts and a tank top. She'd just piled all her hair on her head and taken off her makeup when her house line rang. The shrill startled her at first. The delivery boy always called on her cell phone if there was a problem.

Lexi took the cordless phone off the hook in the kitchen and glanced at the caller ID. Her brows furrowed. "Hello?"

"May I speak to Lexi?"

"Speaking." Lexi held the phone out for a better view of the number. The line was registered to Ken Reyes. "Stephen?"

"Did I catch you at a bad time?"

Lexi glanced down at the cartoon tiaras on her shorts and sighed. "No, not at all, just contemplating whether or not to go out tonight."

"Oh," Stephen responded in a hard-to-read voice. Was that disappointment? But he continued, "I just made sure the girls were in their rooms and came downstairs."

"Okay," she replied slowly.

"Turn your television to channel seven."

Aimlessly, Lexi padded across the hardwood floors with her bare feet over to her L-shaped cream leather couch. The cushions sighed as she sat and curled her feet underneath her legs as the television came to life. "What's up?"

"We were talking about old movies today and I noticed there's a Cary Grant marathon tonight. *I Was a Male War Bride* is about to come on. Have you seen it?"

Yes, the other morning when you opened your front door, Lexi thought to herself. "I have, but it's still a classic. Thanks for letting me know."

"You're welcome. So where were you going to go tonight?" Stephen sounded as if he were stretching, relaxing into the phone call. Lexi wondered if he was holding a cordless phone or tethered to the wall.

"Out?" she answered with more of a question. "I'm sorry, but how did you even get this number?"

"Oh, can you believe I found a book containing everyone's phone number in town?"

"A phone book?" Lexi asked with a cracked smile.

"Is that what that was? Neat, right?"

Lexi wished they were on Skype for a moment for Stephen to watch her roll her eyes. On second thought, she told herself, he might freak out at the sight of her with no makeup on her face. She never thought she wore too much, but she did not leave her house without mascara. "Stop talking about my small town."

"I'm not making fun of it." Stephen laughed. "I'm enjoying the small-town life. Aren't you? Isn't that why you returned?"

"Well, yes." Lexi gulped. His deep baritone cast some sort of spell over her, causing her to want to confess everything. "Like I said, I saw a market for a special line of dresses in the Four Points area."

"No beauty-queen answers, please. You sound rehearsed."

Irritation swelled with the deep inhale she took at his audacity. Lucky for Stephen, the doorbell rang in the nick of time. "Hang on a second." Lexi set her phone on the coffee table and went back to the hallway, grabbing her wallet from her purse to pay the delivery kid. When she returned to Stephen on the phone, her heart skipped a beat. Since when did she sit around on the phone with a boy? *He's no boy,* a little voice reminded her.

"Sorry about the interruption," Lexi said, taking her foam container out of the brown paper bag.

"It's okay. Did you order Chinese?"

Lexi's eyes glanced slowly to her left and then to her right. The long chiffon curtains were drawn and she was sure no one across the street would be able to see inside. "How did you know?"

"The bag." He let out a chuckle. "I recognized the rustling of the thick paper bag Lu's uses."

The stapled opening of the container pooled with steam from the hot vegetables and rice. "That's pretty pathetic."

"I guess it is." Stephen's chuckle turned into an infectious laugh. "I really need to do better with the girls."

"Did you at least have a salad with your pizza tonight?"

As Lexi ate, Stephen shared his routine with the girls and how he prided himself on giving them culture by trying as many different restaurants with a delivery service.

Lexi cringed at the idea of eating takeout all the time. Stephen grabbed himself some more pizza, and together they dined and watched the movie.

"I can't imagine doing that every single night." Lexi sighed, scooping the last of her garlic sauce up with her sticky rice. "When my parents cut me off…"

"They what?" Stephen interjected.

Embarrassed to admit her parents' flaws, Lexi shook her head back and forth. "You know how it is. When a young adult reaches the point in their lives, they cut them off. Kick them out of the nest, you know?"

"Parents do that?"

"Most," said Lexi.

"Tell that to some of my cousins." Stephen chuckled again. "I think a few of them are going to live off the Torres name for the rest of their lives."

"Wait." It was Lexi who sat up straight. "The Torres family, as in the Torres family of Villa San Juan? Torres Rum? Torres Towers?"

Stephen downplayed his historic family name and town. "My mother is a Torres. My father, Esteban Reyes, refused to allow my brothers and me to be raised without appreciating the value of a dollar."

"So you have been spending money on take-out food?" Lexi teased.

"Well, you saw what happened when my brother cooks," Stephen said into the line.

"I thought you burned the food."

"Blackened," he retorted. "The food was blackened and the girls did not like it."

"I see." Lexi's smile spread across her face. She focused on a picture on her mantel over her mock fireplace. In the silver-framed photograph, Lexi stood between her two best friends from boarding school and their husbands. At the time, she hadn't minded being the so-to-speak odd man out. Life without man trouble suited her just fine. "If you say so," Lexi hummed, "but so you know, on the weekends we have market days. The farmers from around the Four Points area come in and sell their produce. And don't forget we have two competing grocery stores willing to take each other's coupons. Both stores offer free cooking classes."

"Are you trying to sell me on staying in Southwood?"

Lexi sighed. "I'm trying to help a friend out. As delicious as the food is in Southwood, you're spending way too much on takeout. When my parents cut me off, I learned how to shop wisely."

"Ramen noodles?"

"Sale items," she countered. "I was trying to save money for college."

"Wait, don't your parents own Pendergrass Banks?"

A heated blush spread across Lexi's cheeks. "Don't be misled by the name. *They* have money, not me."

"I understand."

"If you did, you wouldn't be taking the kids out to eat every day." She toyed with him.

"Just because my family comes from money doesn't mean I didn't make my own," Stephen clarified. "The girls haven't seen me or my brother work in several months. We're comfortable with our bank accounts, but we don't want Kimber or Philly to think everything in life will come easy. Why else do you think I need an office space?"

The question had Lexi stuttering for an answer. "Um."

"Sorry," he quickly said. "I didn't mean—"

"It's okay." Lexi cut him off before she felt more humiliated. Here she was giving him lectures about coupon clipping, and of course he could afford to eat out all the time. "Let's not talk about it."

By the end of the movie, Stephen and Lexi had done more talking and laughing than paying attention to the film. It was after midnight when it ended, and neither was tired. They spent another two hours talking their way through another classic.

"I took up your evening," Stephen stated. She waited for an apology. It never came. After getting to understand Stephen better, she realized he did not apologize. He had yet to say sorry for accusing her of selling the dress, but he did offer to drop the matter—which Lexi greatly appreciated, seeing how she felt horrible for keeping Kimber's secret from him. Was she lying? After getting to know Stephen better, she highly doubted he'd do anything too extreme, besides placing iron bars over her bedroom windows. Who knew? Perhaps after Philly finished with pageantry this summer, she and Stephen might actually become friends.

Chapter 8

Early Saturday morning, a black stretch Hummer pulled through the garage of Lexi's condo building, just as a wave of second guessing began to wash in. Was attending a pageant the right thing to do now, or should they stay in town and practice? After Philly's private lesson Thursday night, Nate had offered to take all the other girls down in style. He had arranged everything and the eager mothers all seemed pleased with his idea.

Though Philly was Lexi's private coach, she also worked with a lot of other little girls whose mothers had all seen the fliers at the counter and wanted to enter their children. Lexi had no say over who should or shouldn't enter pageants. She provided the girls with awesome dresses and the skills of working the stage. The girls, Lexi had no problem with. Some of the parents needed to remember how to conduct themselves. Emotions ran high when people's kids were judged based on their beauty and style of dress.

Lexi wasn't too pleased this morning when Stephen called her on the phone to tell her he was on his way. She hadn't seen Stephen since the night he kissed her. They hadn't spoken since their movie marathon over the phone. With trying to go over all the rules on behavior for the young parents with daughters entering the Glitzy Southern Pageant, Lexi hadn't had time to stop over at Stephen's office space. The boards were still up in the windows and she never spotted Nate's SUV. If Stephen came into town with his driver, he did not stop by Grits and Glam to say hello. Lexi chalked up the distance over the past few days as being due to the business of their schedule. But a part of her wondered whether or not the overshare on the phone was too much for him. Something about getting to know

Stephen unnerved her. His kiss lingered. If ever there was a category for kissing, he won, hands down.

After the mortifying way her last relationship ended, Lexi never thought she'd find another man as attractive as she did Stephen. But she needed to stamp any desire down. At least this weekend she'd be busy explaining the process of the pageantry world to the newbies. God, she needed help this weekend, she thought as the doors to the Hummer opened.

A man dressed in a black jogging outfit and white T-shirt stepped out of the driver's side and she wondered if he was the infamous Mr. Keenan that Philly spoke of. He came around to the passenger's side and opened the back door to the Hummer. She'd partied in cars like this a long time ago but her drivers were always dressed in suits.

"You live here?" Stephen asked, stepping out of the Hummer with his signature neatly trimmed beard. A flash of desire raced through her veins.

"Yes, what did you think?"

The sky roof opened and Kimber poked her head out. "He thought you lived at your store."

"Seems like I do some days." Lexi half laughed.

Stephen and the driver came around to help her with her overnight bag. She caught a whiff of Stephen's cologne and she prayed knees didn't buckle. His neatly trimmed beard brushed against her cheek when he surprised her with a hello kiss, stilling her heart for a beat or two. Today he wore a pair of chinos and a white oxford shirt opened at the throat—completely delicious.

"Uncle Stephen lives at his office sometimes, too," Kimber provided. "That's why we can't live with him at his house in Atlanta."

Lexi cocked her head to the side to look up at Stephen. A spark ignited when his long fingers guided her by the elbow toward the waiting open door. "You still have a house there?"

"The market's tight." Stephen's jaws tightened.

"Well, perhaps you'll be able to check on your house at the end of the summer for the Southern Style Glitz Pageant."

Stephen's brows rose. "What are we going to today?"

"The Glitzy Southern Pageant."

"What's the difference?"

Philly stepped out and threw her arms around Lexi's waist, nearly knocking her off her four-inch hot-pink heels. Thankfully, Stephen gripped her shoulders and held her upright. The air crackled between them. How was she going to make this three-hour trip?

"I'm going to *win* the pageant!" Philly exclaimed.

"That's right." Lexi pulled away from Stephen's embrace to hug Philly. "Now let's get going so we can see how it's done."

The spacious inside of the limousine sat eighteen people, so with only four of them they all had plenty of room. Kimber dropped hints here and there about how Marvin would have been able to come along. Her complaints went on in vain as the stretch Hummer picked up the other children entering the pageant. A caravan of mothers drove behind them. Lexi swore everyone but the driver held up a wineglass in salute at the Hummer.

Folding her hands in her lap, Lexi cleared her throat. "This was sweet of you to offer to pick up all the kids."

"Sweet of Nate," Stephen clarified with a hint of a grimace. "He arranged everything."

"He's really not coming?"

"No, can you believe the bastard said he needed to head up to Atlanta this weekend?"

Lexi turned in her seat to feign a gasp. "No?"

"Yeah, I didn't believe him, either."

After containing her gasp, Lexi needed to figure out how to suppress the giggle mounting from the pit of her belly.

"Judging from the dimples popping out of your cheeks," Stephen said, "you believe I've been *Punk'd*."

"What do you know about Ashton Kutcher?"

"I'm raising a teenager, so if the television in the living room isn't on Sprout, it's on reruns from some music channel."

Lexi wrinkled her nose. "You are so hip."

"We will be on the road another two hours before we arrive at the Brutti Manor," Stephen said, his voice and smile taunting her. "Are you ready to tell me about your mother?"

"Brutti Manor?" she repeated. Legend had it two people remotely attracted to each other fell in love after staying at one of that family's residences. Lexi had always wanted to meet Gabrielle. But not at the expense of falling under the hotel's charm.

Lexi dreamed of having her evening gowns sold in Gabrielle Owens Brutti's store, Desideri. Back in the day when she needed money, Lexi would have killed for the opportunity to walk in a Desideri fashion show. Not only were the designs like those Lexi strived to achieve, the models were well paid and the money would have covered Lexi's tuition for at least four semesters.

A coy smile spread across Stephen's handsome face. "I've already made reservations at Owen's."

"Sounds delicious," she hummed.

"You've heard of them?" he said of the Brutti family's restaurant.

"Of course. I've actually been craving some of their *guanciale* carbonara." She noted his raised brows. "You don't like hog jowls?"

"Not particularly. My paternal grandparents made them when we visited Puerto Rico." He nodded. "I am surprised a woman like yourself eats them."

"A woman like me?" She took her turn raising her brow.

Stephen offered a smile of apology. "Never mind."

"Whatever." Lexi relaxed into her seat. "For starters, I am pure GRITS."

"Girl Raised in the South." He pointed with his long finger toward his temple, clearly proud of himself. "I remembered."

"Yes, and this means I like my grits buttered, my tea sweet and my pork chops smothered, and on occasion, I will eat chitlins over rice, depending on who makes them, and the same goes for potato salad. You know you can't eat just anybody's."

"What's the other thing?" The dazzling smile sent a chill down her spine. Stephen Reyes would win best smile in a contest, hands down. She needed a distraction, but the girls were too busy watching the sisters on the car movie screen deal with a snowstorm.

"Hmm?"

"You said, 'for starters.' What else were you going to say?"

Lexi's red lips formed into an O as she tried to muster her courage. "Did you say we're *staying* at the Brutti Manor?"

"Is that okay? Would you like to stay someplace else? The Brutti is the best."

"The Manor is also pretty pricey."

"You're worried about my finances?"

Lexi gave a tight-lipped grin. "Let's try to remember you tried to purchase the Cyclone game when I beat you Monday."

His mouth opened and a deep laugh expelled itself. "You cheated."

"I can't help if I know how to make the right move at the right time." The double entendre came out accidentally. Stephen shot her a lopsided grin and a penetrating stare, catching what she'd said. Lexi's hand went to the neckline of her T-shirt in case he really did possess X-ray vision. She needed space away from him. "Anyway," she huffed, "after your big purchase last week, I am sure I have nothing to worry about your finances, Mr. Reyes."

"So we're back to proper names?" Stephen cleared his throat and hesitated, seemingly understanding what had triggered the awkward moment. "Lexi," he said calmly. His baritone voice gave her chills. With the voice of a DJ and the body of a model, the man commanded the small space between them. "We're going to be spending a lot of time together this summer. But I'm one of the best Realtors you'll ever meet."

"Don't insult me," Lexi hissed under her breath. "I told you, you outbid me fair and square, and I've set my designs on something else."

"Trying to get away from me so quick, huh? Well, at least I've got this weekend to change your mind."

As the children began to start up the chorus of the "Wheels on the Bus," Lexi glanced out the window and said a silent prayer.

Nice quiet drive to Savannah? Stephen masked his chuckle with a covered cough. A few people in the chairs in front of him turned to glare for him having the audacity to make noise while their—he assumed—child painfully played the piano on the stage. Holding his phone in the air, Stephen tried to motion he was laughing at his message rather than their child on the stage. The woman in front of him snorted and rolled her eyes before turning her attention forward. He swiped his finger across the screen to end the text from his younger brother without bothering to respond. He planned on spending the car ride home figuring out ways to get back at Nate.

In the meantime, he planned on taking every opportunity to get to know Lexi better. Nate backing out at the last minute couldn't have come at a better time. Stephen could no longer deny the truth. The mystery around the woman intrigued him. He liked her tenacity at her job and the care she took with Philly and Kimber, and he needed to make sure she was the right kind of influence on them.

"You don't want to piss them off," Lexi whispered, leaning in to him.

"Too late," he whispered back. "Why not?"

Lexi nodded her head in the direction of the woman with the two-foot beehive hairdo. The leopard-print jogging outfit she wore stretched to the limit. "She is a bully, and a cyberbully, to boot."

"A what?" he laughed. The woman turned around, snarling through her mauve lipstick–stained lips and front right tooth. "You're making this up."

"She likes to talk about other people's kids on the internet. She arrives at competitions with an entourage and also sets up a conference room for her daughter to sign autographs."

A slip of a finger on the piano sent a pain deep into Stephen's ears. "I suggest her mother spend more time on her child's piano lessons."

The number thankfully ended and the entire row in front of them stood up and cheered—hooting and hollering, and Stephen swore someone used an air horn usually used at an Atlanta Falcons football game. Once the child stepped toward the edge of the stage and waved at the judges, she exited, and luckily, so did the family in front of them.

Lexi gripped Stephen's bicep. He resisted the urge to flex. "She winked! Did you see that?"

"No?"

"Philly, never wink at the judges, okay?"

Philly nodded and accepted the advice. "I don't know how anyway." To prove her point she tried to wink one eye, but inadvertently blinked both. After Ken died, Stephen wasn't sure Philly would ever smile again. Now here she sat, beaming from ear to ear. He enjoyed watching her come out of her shell.

The rest of the afternoon dragged on. If he had a dollar for every "Work it" or "Sparkle, baby" screamed out loud, he'd be a much richer man. Girls in ages ranging from five to seventeen practiced their beauty walks, talents and smiles for their mothers. The judges sat at a long table draped with a black tablecloth. When they'd arrived at the Glitzy pageant, Lexi had introduced her former pupil, Waverly, to them. The seventeen-year-old, now a pageant judge, was impressive in the way she emceed the toddler portion of the event. He imagined what Philly would do at that age. Would she still be interested in pageants? Would Lexi still be in their lives?

A much-needed intermission allowed everyone the opportunity to stretch their legs, nap or grab a bite to eat. Lexi took Philly and Kimber along with the other girls from her group up front to meet Waverly. Other contestants and their mothers stopped Lexi and asked for her autograph. Intrigued, Stephen sat up farther in his seat and wondered if he should have kept reading about her pageant life. Lexi rivaled the beauty of the current Miss America.

What was Lexi's pageant life like? The whole time she made her way to the podium, she kept her smile toothy and wide. The slow turn of her wrist as she waved to a group of women calling her name reeked of homecoming and prom queen. Stephen planned on getting the rest of the story from her tonight over dinner.

The drive down here had barely whetted his appetite, mentally and physically. As any man would, Stephen admired the way Lexi leaned over to pass out the bright pink T-shirts for everyone attending. To make things fair, she had the name of all the girls entering this pageant on the back, but the bold white glittering letters across the front read Team Waverly, and her shop's logo was on the back. Lexi handed Stephen a black shirt much like the one she wore. She claimed she'd made it for Nate, but Stephen took it with pleasure. Stephen stretched his long legs out in front of him and folded his arms across his waist while he took in Lexi's beauty. He looked forward to spending the evening with her.

That afternoon, Stephen treated the four girls and his nieces to the boat ride on the Dolphin Tour while their mothers sat back at the local seafood bar and relaxed for a few hours. Afterward, Stephen sipped on Torres Rum, his family's brand, while he paced the living room of the top floor of the four-bedroom suite. Lexi had tried to insist on getting her own room, but Stephen pointed out the ease in keeping everyone together if they stayed in one suite. He gave her the master suite, while he had his own right next door. The girls each had their own room.

One minute this afternoon, she was joking around with him and explaining the ridiculous rules of pageantry, and the next minute she was accepting autographs like a celebrity—a down-to-earth celebrity. She really won him over on the boat ride. Like the children, she sat engaged with his every word as he retold a Puerto Rican folktale. With each throaty laugh she gave, she'd tilt her head backward. She didn't care when the wind whipped her hair into her face and didn't stop once to check her reflection. Stephen couldn't figure out how she was part sweetheart and part sex kitten at the same time.

"Where are the girls?"

Speaking of sex kitten. Stephen gulped when he turned with his drink in his hand. The coolness of the ice against his glass reminded him of how sweaty and slippery his palms got when he looked at her. She stood in the doorway of her room in a fitted black dress that only amplified her curves. Her hair hung to one side, practically covering her left eye while the rest hung down her back, long and straight. Her lips were a kissable red and he itched to try them out. Stephen's eyes fell to the hem of the dress, which stopped above her knees. Her long stems poured into a pair of black shoes with heels so high she might be his height. He envisioned Lexi draped across a piano, singing a sultry song—or better yet, on his king-size bed.

Setting the drink on the coffee table in front of the couch, he sniffed and chuckled. "Funny thing."

"Why do I feel like I'm not going to laugh?"

"The kids are taking a cooking class." Stephen shoved his hands in his pockets and tried to think of something to say. "You're beautiful."

A pink blush spread across her cheeks. "So are you— well, I mean in the man version."

Silence fell between them. The long, black hands of the clock over the fireplace ticked down the seconds. Stephen wanted nothing more than to carry her into the bedroom, and considering the way she returned his stare, she'd allow him. This would be their first time being alone without the threat of interruption from kids. While a quick roll in the sack would satisfy his sexual desire, he wanted things to be different with Lexi. Now that he was living in Southwood full-time, and because of her interactions with Philly, he didn't want things to be awkward between them. He wanted to learn more about her this evening.

"Shall we go to dinner?" If he did not sit down, she would question if he was a man or an adolescent. Something about being around Lexi forced his body to respond. He needed to recite the starting lineup for the Atlanta Braves. These involuntary erections were going to be the death of him.

"You still want to go to dinner? If the kids aren't here, I figured you might not want to go out…" Her words trailed off.

"I didn't realize you wanted to get me all alone so soon," he teased. "We haven't even completed our first date."

"This isn't a date." The smile on her face disappeared but a twinkle in her eye remained.

"Yes, I know," Stephen teased. "You don't date parents. I assume your hearing is okay?"

"Mine?" Lexi cocked her head up at him.

"Because I've told you several times now," he said as he leaned over and took a chance, pressing his lips against her cheek right below her earlobe. "I'm not a parent."

"Let's go eat," she said drily.

ness in her voice returned and despite the way she smiled across the table at him, Stephen knew something wasn't right. Who was this man? What happened? He wanted to see her to smile again, and the more she talked about it, the sadder she seemed.

The fork she set down against the dessert plate clattered into the silence. "So tell me, did you always want to do real estate?"

"I sort of fell into it," he answered. Lexi propped her elbow on the table, cupping her chin in her hand to learn more. "Okay, so when I went to my grandparents' house in San Juan, the mainland," he clarified. A lot of people were not aware of the other San Juan, a small Florida island city founded by his great-great-great grandfather, Victor Torres. "While I was there, I met a guy who wanted to scout out locations to film and he was in the wrong place, so I showed him some hidden sights in San Juan and all around. He hired me on as a driver at first, and then I became his location scout and my name got around in Hollywood."

"Because you knew how to get around?"

"Because I have an eye for seeing the beauty in everything." Stephen's eyes roamed over Lexi's face, slender neck and shoulders. She sat back and folded her arms over her breasts, causing Stephen to shake his head with a chuckle. How was he supposed to be on his best behavior with her seated across from him, looking as delicious as the dessert she devoured? "Which is how I became a broker. I'd buy homes from sellers, flip them and hang on until someone wanted to buy it or use it for a location."

Lexi relaxed and her arms dropped to her side. "So you're a regular tycoon, aren't you?"

"Let's just say if we played Monopoly, I'd win," he teased.

"Whatever," Lexi poked out her tongue. "If you want to see some nice homes, remind me to show you around town."

Chapter 9

Owen's lived up to its reputation as one of the finest restaurants in the whole state of Georgia. Stephen liked the hardwood floors leading to the white-clothed tables with solid black accessories. A hanging white drape privatized the booths, drowning out the conversations nearby.

Full from a plate of the best risotto, pan-seared chicken breasts and fresh Italian greens, Stephen sat back and watched Lexi. She'd ordered the carbonara and a salad. He enjoyed watching her eat, envying the fork in her mouth. He reveled in the fact that she didn't turn down the bite he'd offered her of his food.

"Tell me about being a pageant coach. How long have you been doing it?" Stephen asked over the plate of sour-cream pound-cake tiramisu.

Lexi slid her silver fork out of her mouth. "Officially, I haven't been a pageant coach in over ten years."

"Where does Waverly fit in with your timeline? I recall her saying she was from New Orleans."

"I offer my advice to Waverly. She is family, in the sense she attends boarding school with my niece."

"I see. So, if you haven't coached in a while, why the sudden comeback?"

"Chantal, my assistant, approached me about adding a pageantry workshop for Saturday afternoons. She teaches a dance class at the center and some of the young mothers spoke up about being interested in it for their girls."

"For the girls or for them?" he asked, thinking of some of the mothers this morning.

"With every pageant, there some mothers who want to encourage their daughters, and then there are those who want to live vicariously. They're the easiest ones to spot."

Stephen felt as if a pair of jackass ears were growing from his head right about now. Lexi put out a good product. People listened to her. People followed her and they took her advice. She was driven, like him. "Chantal is wise."

"She is." Lexi nodded. "She is finishing her degree, working for me and teaching dance. She does it all."

"Including volunteering your services as pageant coach?"

"In a way, it pays for itself. All the mothers buy my dresses."

He did not want this evening to end. "Do you mind if I ask why you stopped being a pageant coach?"

The set of her eyebrows softened, as her smile faded slightly. "Let's say the time came for me to move on. I was sewing and designing dresses, but not selling them and when the opportunity came time to move on, I stopped."

"You're great with kids," he stated. "Didn't you enjoy it?"

"I did. It wasn't the kids, but more the situation."

Stephen sat back in his chair. "We have all the time. Please elaborate."

The material of her top shifted, giving a slight hint of the blush on her ample cleavage. "I'm not proud of all the things I've done."

Uh-oh. An alarm sounded off in the back of his mind.

"I told you I had to pay for school because my parents did not approve of my choice. Well, college tuition isn't cheap. I used my knowledge from my teen years as a beauty queen to get me the Miss Florida A&M University crown, which opened the opportunity for me to continue on to Miss Florida, as well as the opportunity to make more money by appearing in a few local fashion shows. Can you guess which one I chose?"

"Does it have anything to do with the infamous dress?"

"So you've seen the video?" The blush deepened and traveled to her cheeks.

Stephen nodded his head with a grimace.

"My folks stopped talking to me after that. But I was young and I had a plan. The dress was a visual essay to get into Parsons School for Design."

"Why didn't you apply there in the first place?" Stephen asked.

"Eh, I wanted to hang with my friends Rosalind and Shannon a little bit longer, but that college life wasn't for me. I partied too much.

"My Grandma Bea reminded me about how much I enjoyed sewing as a girl and encouraged me to explore the field. I went to my folks and begged them to help fund the new adventure and according to them I was an embarrassment. Folks in town threatened to leave my family's bank because clearly if my parents couldn't control me, how could my dad control their money?"

"You're not serious."

"Very." Lexi tilted her head to the side. "I think they were afraid their money would be used to bail me out of jail."

"What?"

"So I killed two birds with one stone. I created an unforgettable dress," she explained.

The image of Lexi in the dress reminded Stephen he was a man. He shifted in his seat and cleared his throat. "And pageantry?"

"Well…" Lexi sighed heavily, "Do you know how many starving artists there are in New York City?"

"No?"

"Neither did I. So when a connection opened up for me to privately coach, I took it, which of course opened up enough dialogue between me and my mother."

"Which was a good thing, right?"

A smile tugged at the corners of her red lips. "Not really since it was her way of telling me how disappointed she in me to, in her eyes, shack up with some man." The

"There you go, selling me on Southwood." Stephen reached for the glass of wine beside him and took a long sip. "I'm here to stay, but if you want to show me beautiful things, I don't have to look far." His dinner companion instantly turned red and cleared her throat. "For a former beauty-pageant girl, you certainly don't take compliments well," Stephen pointed out.

Lexi pushed the hair behind her right ear. "I can easily take them when I'm in the right, ah, location."

Would she take a compliment better in his bedroom? He didn't ask but instead nodded. "I think I can understand."

"Is real estate a family business? I believe Nate mentioned he did the same."

"At eighteen I realized it was the easiest way to make fast money legally." Stephen recalled his first sale at nineteen. He'd commissioned 7 percent and thought he was rich. "A shrink might cite my lack of parental support because my father often did not come home."

"I'm so sorry!"

"Don't be. My father chased a ghost all his life, trying to keep up with the family fortune on my mother's side of the family. By not letting his father-in-law help with finances, he let his pride work him to death."

"And so have you been able to prove him wrong? Are you as rich as you need to be and still have time for your family?"

No one had ever posed the question to him. He made all the money in the world he wanted, yet, when push came to shove, he would be damned if he couldn't be there for Ken's family. He thought of his brother's modest home in Southwood. It easily could have fit into Stephen's place. Yet Ken still had enough to provide for his wife and kids. "I guess I'm more like my father than I thought."

The way Lexi pressed her lips together bothered him. The corners of her mouth turned downward with displeasure. "You don't sound happy."

"I guess when I say the words out loud, I'm not."

"So what are you going to do to change? Ever been close to wanting to get married and settle down?"

"I married Alexia Guzman in the third grade. Does that count?"

A shriek of infectious laughter told him it didn't count. He found himself laughing, also. A waiter came over and poured cups of coffee for the two of them. Lexi put several spoonfuls of sugar in her white cup and stirred the black brew with some cream until the mixture was the same color as her skin. When they were alone again, Stephen turned the question around and hopefully masked his sigh of relief when she said no.

"Oh, don't get me wrong. Men have proposed."

Of course.

"Because no one seemed to *get* me," Lexi went on. "Look how long it took me to settle on one career in life. I had a lot to do and a lot to accomplish before I settled down. I want to come into a marriage already being worth something."

"Sounds like mother issues," he noted with a nod.

"Perhaps. My folks married because it was a match made in heaven, financial heaven. My maternal grandparents had lots of money and my paternal grandparents had a place for them to put it."

"Pendergrass Banks?"

"Yes."

Stephen leaned forward, intrigued with the idea of her parents. "How did your grandfather start things off?"

A coy smile spread across her lovely face. "Robbing banks."

"You're joking?" Of course she was, her pearly whites flashing as she nodded her head.

"Yes, I'm kidding. My great-great-grandfather started a bank a long time ago in Samaritan—the longer you stay in Southwood you'll come to learn about the Four Points—but anyway, he opened up his first bank there and branched out. He was blindsided coming to Southwood and saw its prejudices, but he kept trying to make a name for himself, hence trying to walk a straight and narrow line, and avoiding rumors and drama. It worked for a few generations, I guess you can say, until I came along. I think the drama I've caused put my folks' arrangement to the test."

His parents had married out of love, but the love ran thin after three kids.

"They're still married, right?"

"They're married, but I never thought they were happy." Lexi's lashes lowered to the flickering flame between them. "I can't prove it, but I don't think they even sleep in the same bed—since I was born."

The sadness came back to her voice. Stephen cleared his throat. "What do you think the secret is to a good marriage?"

"You got me." Lexi sighed into her coffee cup and blew before taking a sip. "My two best friends are married and have been for years. They keep it going, I guess, by being brutally honest with each other."

Under the lighting, her face lit up as she talked about her friends. "Brutally?"

"Yes, but I'd rather keep a scorecard for most guys. They have to rank high in the nineties in order to keep my interest."

A smile tugged at the corner of Stephen's mouth. "Do I have one?"

"Bless your heart, I started a card on you the minute you walked through the doors of Grits and Glam Gowns."

Stephen closed his eyes and groaned. "I can only imagine what my scorecard looks like."

"Don't worry. Your marks are at least over fifty." The corners of her eyes squinted as she bit the inside of her lips.

Stephen feigned a heart attack and clutched his chest.

"I come from a long line of annoying cousins. I can dish brutal honesty and take it."

"All right, then, try being brutally honest with me."

Stephen leaned forward, as well. "I want nothing more than to clear off this table and thoroughly kiss you again."

Once upon a time, Lexi would have taken the dare, but right now she had too much at stake. Resisting Stephen's seduction tested her willpower but at least he did not let her rejection spoil the moment. A flash of lightning struck the center of her diaphragm at his lazy yet dangerous smile.

After paying for dinner, Stephen came around to Lexi's side of the table to help her out of her chair. His hands caressed her shoulders, then fell to his side, where the natural thing to do was cup her hand in his. Instead of heading upstairs, he suggested they take a stroll and walk off some of their dinner. She did not mind one bit. Thank God for Spanx, or she'd be bursting at the seams right now.

Their footsteps fell in sync with one another. His strong, long legs had to slow down so she could keep up with him along River Street. Careful not to take a misstep on the cobblestones, Lexi leaned in close to Stephen for security. The evening's cool breeze off the Savannah River played the perfect wingman; Stephen stretched his arm around her shoulder and they cozied up together.

"These streets remind me of Villa San Juan," she mentioned.

"They do," he agreed. "You should come with me this summer when I bring the kids. I will show you the real city, rather than the tourists' side."

The idea of spending more time with him left her dizzy. The last relationship she was in involved a spoon and Ben & Jerry's—the ice cream. She missed dressing up and going out with someone. Turned out his life seemed pretty much parallel to hers; he didn't date much because of work and even spent some nights in his office.

"When was the last time you visited?"

Stephen shared with her the story of how his brother and sister-in-law perished in a car accident, and the debate as to where the kids needed to live. Her heart ached at the sadness in his voice.

"Nate and I didn't want the kids to grow up entitled like our cousins. Besides, they don't speak a lick of Spanish and we did not want them judged."

"Do you?"

"*¡Claro!*"

"Well—" she grinned "—my Spanish isn't up to par. My French is better."

They stopped walking and leaned against the black rail above the river. The lamppost behind them illuminated his handsome face. The breeze blew her hair in front of her eyes, and when Stephen reached over to brush the strands back she inhaled deeply, struggling with the idea of kissing him. She needed to focus. Maybe his eyes? No, she'd get lost in the dark orbs. She settled on his mouth, surrounded by his beard, then solely on his lips. *No*, she told herself. She couldn't get involved with a parent—or a guardian— not when she needed to rebuild her reputation.

"French is a beautiful language, especially when being spoken by a beautiful woman," he said quietly. "Tell me, what is going on with your hair?"

Absentmindedly her fingers reached the ends of her tresses. "Is it flying all over the place?"

"The color?" He grinned.

"Oh." She rolled her eyes toward the sky. Clouds breezed over the bed of stars. "Long story short, I have a great-great-great-grandfather or so who was a Viking from Denmark. Every generation or so, one of us pops up with this coloring."

"Wow."

"Yes, imagine my father's shock when I was born. Because my mother's coloring is darker, she never thought she'd be the one to have a blond child. Remember, my family didn't do controversy. Can you picture their surprise when I came out?"

Stephen's fingers stroked her hair over her left ear; his thumb caressed her cheek. Lexi searched his eyes, praying for him to say something because if he didn't, she might reach up and kiss him. A fire truck screamed out somewhere in the distance. A party in a nearby club thumped a rhythmic beat into the air. Cars swooshing by, hitting the same pothole and clunking in the air. Through all the noise she wondered if he heard her heart beating. A twitch of wanton desire fought with the pulse of sanity at the curve of her neck. Her right eyebrow rose.

"Bésame."

No need for a translator. Lexi craned her neck upward and Stephen cupped both sides of her face to draw her in for his kiss. He pulled her against him with his left hand, bringing her soft body roughly against his rigid one. His right hand snaked around her neck, coaxing her head into the right angle to match his lips. In the past, her height had made kissing awkward, but together she and Stephen were the perfect match, in size and in kissing.

As expected, she found his lips to be soft, tasty and juicy. Their lips brushed against each other for the initial introduction. Their mouths opened slightly and his tongue slipped in for a sample. Her moan vibrated against his mouth. She opened her lips wider, inviting him in for a deeper kiss. Her hands inched up his chest, toying with his tie and bringing him down to her.

A set of drunken sailors driving by whooped and hollered. A church bell rang in the distance and a passing tanker replied with a tug of its whistle. This kiss showed her the future. The church bells invoked the image of them standing in the afternoon with a set of pink flowers between them, kissing, sealing vows. At the call of the tanker, she imagined them kissing at a port with thousands of people cheering hello and goodbye. The scene frightened her. Marriage and the whole shebang did not fit in her plans. Fear told her to stop kissing him, but she couldn't. His lips, his tongue and his heart all probed forward, searching. Things were never going to be the same.

Lexi broke the kiss. She had to. "What are we doing?" She breathed heavily, resting her forehead against his chest. His rapid heartbeat thumped against her ears.

His soft yet large hands cupped the sides of her cheeks and turned her face up to his. "I think we're kissing," he said in a husky voice with a smile.

"Why?"

"The moment called for a kiss," he said simply.

"Yes, but—" she timidly bit her bottom lip "—I'm coaching Philly this summer."

"*I* did not hire you to coach Philly. She won your services. This—" he brought his lips to her forehead "—this has nothing to do with Philly. This has something to do with the chemistry between us since I walked into your office. Am I wrong?"

"No." The attraction between them knocked the breath out of her. She hadn't been kissed like that since—well, never, and she began to think it might not happen again. "Where do we go from here?"

A part of her feared his answer. What if he wanted a one-night stand? Maybe that was what they needed to break the sexual tension between them, but flings were not her thing. She wanted more. "I say we leave here and go back to my bed."

The cool wind from the water interrupted the heated blush on her cheeks. Lexi turned her face into his hand, kissing his palm. "Not happening."

"I know—" he chuckled "—but it was worth a shot. How about this? You coach Philly on Mondays, Wednesdays and Fridays, and the other days I have you?"

The words *have you* made her hot in her nether regions.

She imagined herself naked on a white-clothed table while he feasted upon her. "Stephen, I—"

He silenced her with another thought-provoking kiss. "We'll go slowly," he said, pulling their lips apart. "You coached Philly today, then tomorrow you and I will go on our first date."

"Wasn't tonight a date?"

"More of an appetizer." Stephen straightened his frame, at the same time turning back toward the hotel. He pulled Lexi's hand into his as they walked together.

If tonight was just an appetizer, she couldn't wait for the main course!

The girls still hadn't arrived back at the hotel by the time he and Lexi returned to the suite. Stephen mentally thanked the mothers for deciding to bring them downstairs to the conference room, which the hotel used for a movie night for children. Chuckling, Stephen loosened his tie and slipped his phone back into his pocket. The motor of the refrigerator kicked on in the kitchen, exposing Lexi's location.

"Are you tired yet?" he asked, entering the small area. Stephen guessed this was what she would consider a two-butt kitchen. He stood in the arched doorway to show some restraint.

With the door still open but the light off above them, Lexi straightened from her search. The light from inside haloed the left side of her frame—enough light to show off her wanton smile. "No."

Stephen reminded himself of his promise. He would take things slow with Lexi, and he meant it. Jumping into the sack right now was not a wise move. "I think *Carmen Jones* is playing tonight. We ought to call up for some popcorn and watch."

Lexi's face lit up. "Room service for popcorn, Stephen?"

"What?"

She crossed the small kitchen in two steps and stood in

front of him. Her heels were gone, toes bare, but her height made it so easy to lean in for a kiss. Lexi, in anticipation, inhaled and yanked open the pantry door. Stephen bit the inside of his jaw and shook his head at the missed opportunity to taste her again.

"I believe I saw a blue box of popcorn up here."

The height Stephen appreciated on Lexi came at a disadvantage for her. Her long legs strained in vain to reach the top shelf. He took a second opportunity to step in and reach for the box. Lexi backed herself against the opened door. Both pairs of hands were in the air. Stephen pushed the box near with the tip of his fingers and clasped her left hand in his. He enjoyed the rapid rise and fall of her breast.

"What are you doing?" she asked.

"I'm about to kiss you again." Stephen gave all the warning she needed. He leaned in and brushed his lips against hers. Her free arm wrapped around his broad shoulders, crushing her body against his.

Any thought of the movie was lost, along with Stephen's plan to take things slow. He drank from her sweet lips and intoxicated himself with her taste. Every inch of his body hardened. Lexi tightened her hand in his. Her fingertips splayed against the nape of his head, circling the spot that fueled his desire. *Take it slow*, he reminded himself. *Stay in control.* Stephen reached up and pulled her hand into his, dragging it down to their sides. The back of his hand brushed against the curve of her thigh to the apex, to the source of her heat. A groan bubbled in the back of his throat. He yanked her arm up and above her head, transferring her other hand into his.

One hand held both of hers. He traced the length of her body with his other one, starting with her neck. His thumb brushed against her bottom lip. Lexi broke their kiss and licked the tip of his thumb. Danger flashed in her dark eyes before she closed them again and continued sucking on his bottom lip. The exploration continued. Stephen's hand brushed her shoulders, his fingertips tracing her collarbone down to the swell of her breasts. Lexi inhaled as if giving him permission. Four fingers played with the material of her dress just beneath her breasts and yanked downward. One breast was exposed, and Stephen broke the kiss this time and dipped his head to introduce his mouth to her pink nipple. A sharp gasp escaped Lexi's throat.

His tongue became familiar with both of Lexi's nipples while his hands pulled up the hem of her dress. He sent up a silent prayer of thanks she'd taken off all her undergarments. His fingertips glided around the smooth skin of her belly and hips. Against him, Lexi quivered. He was seconds away from exploring the short curls between her legs when the front door of the suite slammed shut.

Lexi shoved Stephen away and crammed herself into the pantry. His senses swirled and began to make sense of the women bickering in the hallway. Myranda, one of the mothers, stood with an apologetic look on her face. "I'm sorry. Philly wasn't feeling well."

"Because she ate three helpings of ice cream," Kimber growled, annoyance pinching her face. "Not to mention she threw gummy bears and sprinkles on top of them."

"Uncle Stephen," Philly moaned, "my tummy hurts."

"Where's Lexi?" asked Kimber at the same time Philly turned a unique shade of green.

Myranda backed out of the door. "Well, I'll let you guys have at it. Philly, feel better. Kimber, thank you for helping out with everyone."

Shocked Kimber had been of service, Stephen raised his brows. "What? You helped?"

"Whatever," said Kimber, pushing by her uncle and glancing around the room. "Did Lexi go to sleep? I need her."

Join the club, Stephen thought. "She's, ah——" How did he explain Lexi was in the pantry in the kitchen with the hem of her dress wrapped around her waist?

"I found some popcorn," Lexi hollered, appearing in the doorway of the kitchen. Her long blond disheveled hair piled into a bun at the top of her head. The kiss-stained lips smiled, then parted at the sight of Philly.

Stephen turned in time to preview everything Philly ate this evening. He groaned inwardly. This certainly was a way to take things slow.

Chapter 10

"Ladies and gentlemen, I welcome you back to the thirty-fifth annual Glitzy Southern Pageant," Waverly announced into the microphone. "On behalf of the Georgia Board of Pageantry, I want to remind everyone of our bylaws, which state no toleration for physical altercations. Let's set an example for our children and let the show continue!"

Stephen settled into his seat and watched the mothers, photographers and videographers crowd together in the aisles behind a set of judges who were roped off in the first ten rows. A set of security officers sat on the sides as a safety measure. Girls between thirteen and seventeen zoomed around the lobby and into the theater with rollers in their hair, tons of makeup and racy outfits Reading his mind, Lexi, seated immediately to his right, leaned over toward him to whisper behind the program. She smelled like chocolate. He hoped she liked the Dancing Lady orchids. He made sure this morning to have her room filled with them by the time she stepped out of her shower. The fact he entered her bedroom, knowing she was naked in the bathroom, should have earned him an award. Last night had been hard. *He'd* been hard.

"I don't offer the extra padding in my outfit of choice costumes," she whispered. "I think a lot of these pageants are racy enough."

Now he had to question whether or not to let Philly participate further.

Stephen peered over to his left; Philly sat on Kimber's lap, thoroughly enjoying the cheerleaders and dancers. Her large, expressive eyes were wide and she smiled so broadly her cheeks might ache by the end of the day. Kimber seemed to be enjoying herself, as well. Stephen understood why Nate found this a haven to meet women. Despite Lexi sitting next to him, seven different women had hit on him.

Lexi nodded. "You're allowed to bring as many guests as you want to an event, but everyone needs to be listed. The promoters will run a scan on everyone for safety reasons." Lexi pointed a bare finger towards the red-lit exit signs.

On the sly, Stephen brushed his shoulders against hers. The dark denim jeans clung to her legs and the T-shirt she wore was knotted at the waist. She kept her blond hair in a loose ponytail at the top of her head.

"How long is the show today?"

Disco lights made circles and flashed against the red curtains onstage. Lexi's eyes widened and a smile spread across her face. "A few hours today. We got over the longest part with the younger girls yesterday. They're a tad bit slower and unsure of where to go."

In total, he was looking at a ten-hour day. He groaned inwardly. At least he'd be near Lexi.

A woman's shrill voice echoed through their row.

"Lexington Pendergrass?"

Beside him, Lexi stiffened. Her fingers gripped the armrest. Her knuckles turned stark white. Sure she had paled at the sight of the woman, Stephen took her hand in his.

People began to stare while the woman pointed toward herself. "It's me! Rose Laing!"

Kimber's and Philly's heads bobbed back and forth between the woman and Lexi. Stephen thought he heard a groan coming from Lexi as she came to her feet, still holding on to his hand. Kimber turned her legs to the left for Lexi to exit.

In a matter of seconds, Lexi transformed into the kind of woman Stephen came across at the golf club. A high-pitched phony laugh coming from Lexi sounded more like a *"Kill me now."*

"Well, Rose Laing!" Lexi drawled, leaning over to air-kiss both of the woman's cheeks. They held their hands in midair as if they were about to play patty-cake, but never quite hugged or touched. "I don't believe this! What brings you to Savannah? Is Vera with you? She must be sixteen now."

Amused, Stephen sat mesmerized by Lexi's ponytail bouncing over her shoulders as she craned her neck through the crowds for this person named Vera. Recalling Lexi had worked with Waverly when she was a toddler, it only seemed natural this was another former client. He deduced this must be the family she'd worked for ten years ago.

"She's competing today," Rose said. A row of diamonds hung from her neck, her rings also sparkling, but nothing beat the icy stare she gave Lexi.

"I didn't see her name on the roster."

"We did not want to intimidate the other girls," said the woman.

Though Rose appeared friendly, Stephen did not miss the catty tone—he didn't need to have sisters to understand these women did not like each other. They chattered idly. The Reyes clan all had their heads turned in their direction, as well, not missing a beat.

"Chatter in the dressing room is you've abandoned your idea of a pageant dress shop." The woman babbled on, oblivious to Lexi's success. "Did that idea fail, as well? Are you daring to make a return to pageant coaching? I figured you would have been married by now with five kids." Then she peered at the aisle and made an assumption. "Well, almost. No ring on your finger?" Caught off guard, Lexi stood, hands tucked into the back pockets of her jeans. "Oh, Lexi," she gushed, "get it together, girl! The only men you're going to find here are probably gay."

At that point, the woman nodded her head in Stephen's direction. He glanced around, assuming she must be insinuating about someone else.

"I'm doing fine, Rose. Hopefully we'll bump into each other again."

Why in the hell didn't Lexi hand this smug woman one of her business cards? It was on the tip of his tongue to ask her when she took her seat, but instead of sitting, Lexi made a beeline for the door. The woman's jaw dropped open and she seriously shook her head, thoroughly confused as to why Lexi took off. Stephen aimed to find out exactly why, as well.

It took a few turns around the corridors, but Stephen eventually found Lexi outside on a lounge chair, soaking in the afternoon sun Her tresses seemed even paler against her caramel skin. He wanted nothing more than to scoop her up in his arms and take her back to the hotel room.

"Hey," he said, softly approaching. "Everything okay?"

The bright sun did not contribute to the red tint of her high cheekbones. The woman had embarrassed her. "Yes, everything is fine," she visibly lied. "I needed to catch a breath of fresh air."

"Who was the lady?"

"Rose Laing, wife of my former boss." Lexi gave an exaggerated sigh as she came to her feet to face him, but held her head down.

"Do you want to talk about it?"

Lexi's head sharply shook back and forth. Her eyes widened. "No."

Disappointed, Stephen took her hand. Why should she trust him with her secrets? He pulled her in and held her in his arms, wondering what it would take. "You can trust me."

"Maybe some other time, I promise." Lexi gave him a weak smile. "This is not the place."

"All right, I'm holding you to your word. Let's go back inside and act like she hasn't pushed your buttons."

"If my mother was speaking to me, she would say the exact same thing." The smile she gave did not reach her eyes. They stood close together, holding hands. Anyone passing by would easily assume they were lovers.

"Your mother sounds like a wise woman."

Finally Lexi laughed. "Debatable."

"Well, perhaps at times." Stephen stroked the soft skin of Lexi's arm. "Want to tell me about things over dinner tonight?"

As she bit her bottom lip, Stephen feared she was having second thoughts about their arrangements. "We won't get in until late."

"So we'll take a late dinner, drinks maybe." Did he sound as if he was begging? He might have been. Stephen disliked her hoity-toity former employer even more now. "Dessert? The hotel makes a pretty good double-Dutch-chocolate brownie." No woman could resist chocolate. The corners of her mouth turned upward. "One brownie."

A wave of mothers ran by with their little girls in tow. Stephen pulled Lexi against him to save her from the stampede. "What the hell?"

"Crowning time. We better hurry."

Thanks to her bit of a fit from running into Rose Laing, Lexi missed Vera being crowned most photogenic. "What?" Stephen leaned in. "Our girl should have won. Myranda, I don't know what they were thinking. Your daughter had the best salsa dance I've seen from a six-year-old. I can't believe she's not getting a princess crown. She was the best."

"She pulled for a higher title," explained Lexi. Kenya, Myranda's daughter, did an excellent job. Chantal should be proud of the hard work she'd put in with the girl. "If your name is called now in this round, you're done in the competition."

"Yeah," Philly chimed in, "Andrew said we never want our name called until the end."

"She's right." Lexi beamed, glad to see Philly was picking up on a lot. "We keep our fingers crossed, but I would score her pretty high, as well. She might be the only one who did not need her mother or coach dancing in the aisle behind the judges."

"I'll learn my routine, Miss Lexi," said Philly, "I promise."

"Don't worry, sweetie." Lexi bumped her forehead gently against Philly's. "I'm not going to let you on stage unless I'm sure you're ready."

"You best believe you won't be dressed like a lot of these girls," Stephen said.

Lexi turned and gave him a wink, unprepared for the sexy grin he gave her. Thanks to her past dateless nights, she had had plenty of time to sketch and come up with a one-of-a-kind dress for Philly, filled with tons of Swarovski diamonds. "Well, you do not have to worry about that. I'm friends with a fabulous dress-shop owner.

"Waverly, you were beautiful!" Lexi said cheerfully after the final judging, wrapping her arms around her neck.

Waverly's Miss Magnolia crown wobbled. She lifted the tiara and set it on top of Philly's head. "Are you ready to win one of these crowns?"

Philly anxiously nodded her head. "Yes, ma'am!"

Waverly playfully cringed, her eyes begging Lexi for help. "Ma'am?"

"Think of this as a sign of respect," Lexi whispered.

With a deep inhale, Waverly turned to the rest of the family. "Did the rest of you enjoy yourselves?"

Lexi noticed the way Kimber's eyes widened at Waverly, all made up with her crown and dress. "What did you think, kiddo?"

With as much nonchalance as possible, Kimber shrugged her shoulders. "Yeah, it was cool, I guess."

Philly tugged Waverly's dress. "Will you be at mine?"

"You know I will!" Waverly beamed. "I can't wait to go back to Atlanta."

"My uncle lives in Atlanta," Philly decided to announce.

No one else noticed that, as Stephen stood beside Lexi, his long fingers drew circles on her lower back. Lexi tried to keep her mind straight, but his movement reminded her of the way he'd drawn circles at the nape of her neck while they kissed right outside her bedroom door.

"I do, too." Stephen's deep voice sent a chill of desire down her spine.

"I can't wait to go," Lexi told Waverly, and then, moving away from Stephen's embrace, she said to Philly, who was tapping her shoulders, "Are you ready to get back home and start practicing?"

Philly nodded eagerly.

"You *are* coaching again?"

A familiar sound of Rose's voice broke the camaraderie. The hairs on Lexi's neck rose. Stephen's hand clamped down on her shoulders and pulled her close. All three members of the Laing family strolled up behind Waverly. Vera's young face pinched. Her skin was a flawless mocha, eyes regal and dark. She wore the world's tightest pair of jeans. Lexi's eyes darted toward the man standing behind her. Close to Stephen's height, Ernest was dark skinned with a piercing glare. Dressed in a matching shirt like Rose's, he wore a pair of faded blue jeans and black boots.

Not here, not now, her mind begged, her body quivering in fear and shame. While living in the Laing household with just Ernest and Vera, Lexi had fallen into a comfortable routine with the duo. She'd fallen for Ernest's lies, hook, line and sinker. Rose had left her family but the ink on their divorce papers was not dry. Without thinking, Lexi's face broke out into a smile. If Stephen's hand weren't still clamped on her shoulder, she would have met them halfway to hug the young girl.

"Vera!" It had been ten years since the last time Vera laid eyes on Lexi. Back then, she'd sat on the top step of her parent's home, witnessing the drama. The pink lipstick plastered on Vera's lips emphasized the way they curled as soon as she laid eyes on Lexi, who recoiled into Stephen's side. "Vera, did you forget about me already?"

Eyes encased in thick, false lashes glared at Lexi as Vera shook her head. "I'm not the one who forgets things." Her icy voice set Lexi shivering. "You recall how you walked out of my life and forgot all about me?"

"Hey—" Kimber broke the silence, clearing her throat "—beautiful gown today."

Impressed with Kimber's maturity, Lexi grinned proudly. Vera turned her nose up at Kimber. "You're the one she's coaching?" she snickered, and glanced over her shoulder for her mother's approval.

"Actually," Waverly spoke out, "she coached me. We're in the same age bracket, right? Fourteen to seventeen for the Atlanta pageant?"

To Lexi's delight, Vera and Rose both blanched. "Well, good luck to you guys in Atlanta."

Lexi had learned over the years to cut off awkward situations. She nudged Stephen in the chest with her shoulder to indicate it was their time to depart.

Ernest's dark eyes flashed between Stephen and Lexi. He extended his gold, Rolex-clad hand out for Stephen to shake. Like a gentleman, Stephen released his arm from around Lexi's shoulder to accept the handshake. "Ernest Laing, Laing Diamonds."

Inwardly Lexi groaned. The man still used the same line from ten years ago. When she was young and naive, the line had worked on her. Ernest knew exactly how to smooth talk Lexi into almost anything. Prior to working for him, she'd became acquainted with him on the set of a local modeling shoot. Ernest's company loaned out jewelry. He'd helped cover her body in diamonds with her even more infamous dress. After she graduated from fashion school, Lexi ran into Ernest again and he'd made an offer she couldn't refuse. She'd believed everything he said about his life and his young daughter's desire to become a beauty queen, and even the claim his marriage was over.

While shaking Stephen's hand with one of his, Ernest reached into the breast pocket of his jacket and produced a business card. "Give me a call whenever you and the lil' lady decide to settle down. I know exactly what she likes." To make matters worse, Ernest gave Lexi a wink.

Skin crawling, she tried not to roll her eyes. Oblivious to the barb, the kids giggled at the idea. She waited for Stephen to correct him, but instead he released Ernest's hand and draped his arm lovingly over Lexi's shoulder.

"I'll keep this in mind." He pulled Lexi up to his side again; this time he planted a kiss on her forehead. "I've been trying to get the lil' lady—" he mocked Ernest's twang "—to settle down for quite some time."

The mental score card dinged past one hundred.

No comparison between the men. Stephen was taller, stronger, more chivalrous and way more handsome out of the two. Lexi knew it. Rose knew it, hence the sneer across her face as she looked between them. The woman lived to embarrass Lexi. Lexi still believed the gossip leaked to the press was set up by Rose, who decided one day she wanted her husband back—a title Lexi had no idea Ernest owned.

"Yes, well be careful with this one. She has a nasty habit of—"

"We need to get going," Stephen cut Ernest off. He kept his arm still secured around Lexi's shoulder, but nodded his head toward the exit sign for the kids.

Lexi's heart soared; her feet barely touched the ground. No one had ever come to her defense before. She'd had men fight over her, women be catty with her for her appearance, but no one had ever blatantly stood up for her as Stephen did.

Once they got outside, he didn't drop his arm from her shoulders. She wanted to thank him properly, but the kids were in tow. Mr. Keenan had already pulled the Hummer up to the doors, with the caravan of mothers not far behind. With the sun already setting, they needed to get the kids home and in bed and ready for school tomorrow.

"Real cool of you back at the hotel," Kimber said.

Lexi pretended to be asleep in the back of the stretch Hummer limousine. Philly rested her head in her lap. The keyboard of Kimber's phone went off as she sent texts to her friends while she spoke to her uncle.

"What's that?" she heard Stephen ask.

"The jerk back at the pageant," said Kimber. "I wanted to hit him."

Stephen chuckled softly. "Violence is never the best way to solve a problem."

"Yeah, but I didn't like the way any of those people spoke to Lexi."

A silent pause. She guessed Stephen had nodded his head in agreement. A part of her wondered if the Laing incident reminded him of their first meeting. Lexi knew she'd prove his opinion of her wrong. After this evening, however, she worried again. If he ever learned the truth of her relationship with Ernest, he might never let it go.

"So you like Lexi?" Stephen asked his oldest niece.

"She's pretty cool. Nate liked coming to the shop to see her, but she never looked at Nate the way she looks at you."

Another silent pause before he spoke again, "What do you think that means?"

"She likes you, but I don't think I want you to date her."

Instead of another pause, Stephen began to cough to stifle a laugh. "What?"

"C'mon, Uncle Stephen, you like Lexi. But you are not the boyfriend-girlfriend kind of guy."

"I'm not?" Stephen's voice rose with curiosity.

"Lexi is the best thing ever."

"You're sixteen, little girl. What do you know?"

For the rest of the drive, Lexi kept her grin to herself and focused on keeping her eyes closed to stay out of the rest of their conversation. Sleep and dreams of Stephen's lips on hers took over. She dreamed they were on River Street with the Savannah River as their backdrop, and his lips were caressing hers—his soft, sensual lips. The back of his fingers brushed against her cheeks; the warmth fueled her soul. His touch felt so real. Stirring, Lexi's eyes opened slowly and she realized she hadn't been dreaming. Stephen's face hovered over hers.

"Did you enjoy your nap?"

Still disorientated, Lexi struggled to sit up with Stephen's help. At some point on the ride back, she had laid her head in his lap. Her hands went to her disheveled hair and she tried to maintain some calmness. "How long have I been asleep?"

"About an hour."

"Where are all the kids?"

"Everyone made it home." Stephen moved to his side of the seat. "This is our last stop before we head back."

Lexi glanced around the space, empty except for Philly and Kimber curled up next to each other across from them. The leather seats were covered with plastic tiaras, gum and candy wrappers, soda bottles and a massive amount of glitter.

"We've been driving around town for the last hour while you slept and called out my name."

"I did not!" Her hands flew to her mouth in embarrassment. Any trace of the lip gloss she had applied earlier had disappeared. "Oh, my God, what did I say?"

"You asked me to kiss you, but other than that you behaved."

The shadow of the driver blocked the streetlight. Lexi peered across Stephen's chest. "I did not," she said back to Stephen.

Stephen tapped on the window and miraculously the back door opened. He stepped out to thank his driver, then reached his hand back inside to help her out. Together they walked back to the double doors of her building. Stephen entwined his fingers with hers.

"I'd invite you in, but well, you know." Lexi nibbled on her bottom lip, not sure if she needed to be completely honest with Stephen at this point. She inhaled deeply when he leaned forward and tugged her hands close to his body. Lexi shifted her weight to her tiptoes and he leaned down to meet her lips. They shared a kiss—a deep and knee-buckling, but brief, kiss.

"No, it is late, and I've got to get my nieces home before Nate starts yelling at me." Stephen nodded.

They found themselves facing each other underneath the light. Lexi's heart slammed against her rib cage. "Yes."

"Plus," he nodded and cocked his head to the side. "I don't want everyone to get the wrong impression of us."

The word *us* rolling off his lips set a quiver in the pit of her stomach. Lexi began to giggle. Stephen's brows went up in question. "Yes, I am not sure how to explain to anyone we're dating after I've turned down a lot of single fathers."

"So we're dating now?" he asked.

Lexi's mouth gaped in a moment of horror; then it was Stephen's turn to grin.

"I'm messing with you." His onyx eyes bore down on her. "Damn straight we are."

He braced her shoulders and dipped his head for a kiss. Somewhere in the distance there had to be birds chirping or some sort of Disney moment when the prince and the princess kissed and fell in love. *In love?*

Lexi broke the kiss. She gulped for some air.

"You okay?" he asked caringly, stroking her cheeks.

"I'm fine. I—I need to—" She struggled for the words.

"Go inside?" Stephen let his arms linger over her shoulders, locking his fingers at the nape of her neck. "I've got quite the drive home."

"You know you don't have to go the long way…"

"Go inside," Stephen ordered gently.

Hesitating, Lexi sighed. She needed to clear the air between them and took a chance with a partial truth. "Look, I need you to understand something about my history with Ernest."

The smile he offered disappeared into his black beard. "I don't care about you and him."

"But I need you to know why I don't date parents."

Stephen pulled her close to his frame. His beard brushed against her chin when he dipped close to capture her lips. "I don't give a damn about Ernest. I don't expect you to have a blank history. Got it?" To prove his point, Stephen cupped her face and planted another mind-blowing kiss.

Chapter 11

"Didn't you attend a prestigious boarding school?" asked Stephen, rising to his feet when Lexi approached the picnic table. He slipped his hands into the pockets of his khaki pants and tried to still the beating of his heart as she neared. Lexi shook her head and flashed a smile. Behind her, children frolicked on the giant sheet of slippery plastic near the lake. Some of the older kids, his nieces included, zoomed down the makeshift slide directly into the blue lake. If she'd stayed down there a little longer, Stephen figured the kids would conspire to get her in the water, as they had to a few of their teachers who came out to attend the South-wood Summer Kickoff Picnic the Saturday after Memorial Day weekend. Wisely, most of the adults kept their distance. Stephen had made friends after being introduced by Nate, but when Nate went off to flirt with one of the single mothers, Stephen found himself longing for Lexi's return. Her long, black-and-white maxi dress flowed behind her, silhouetting her curvy frame and long legs.

She'd chosen comfortable shoes—a pair of black plastic flip-flops. Stephen always cringed at the sight of them. In San Juan, his *abuela* was quick at slipping her *chancleta* off her foot and throwing it across the room in a heartbeat whenever the boys acted up. Subconsciously he smoothed the back of his head.

Lexi flopped down on the wooden bench, resting her elbows on the red-and-white-checkered tablecloth secured by a plastic-covered ceramic bowl full of some casserole. The potluck picnic lunch brought out every casserole in the world. Not wanting to be left out, Stephen and Nate had hunkered down in Ken's modest kitchen and put together their mother's *pastelón* dish. They had to promise a Fourth of July visit with the grandchildren in order to get Elizabeth Torres Reyes to share her family's sweet lasagna recipe.

"I did," Lexi said, finally getting back to the question as she waved a mosquito from her face before reaching for the green bug spray from her oversize bag filled with all sorts of needed gadgets, including the boots she'd wear for a line dance on stage with the rest of Southwood's participants. She got the spray out first. "Come over here." She rose and took Stephen by his forefinger.

Stephen glanced down at her ringless fingers wrapped around his. A woman as beautiful as Lexi needed jewelry. "Hey." He flinched and coughed when she started spraying him from head to toe. "What are you doing?"

"Your head, in this weather—" she made a tsking sound "—not a good match. Now what is this nonsense about me and my boarding school?"

"You're a natural in the outdoors."

"I believe we've had this conversation before, Mr. Reyes." Lexi stood stock-still in front of him, both hands clasped now. Her lashes fluttered against her cheeks as she blinked, and Stephen inhaled the sweet, chocolatey scent he'd grown accustomed to. "What did I tell you I am?"

"Something about grits?" he teased, enjoying the arousing way her dress blew in the wind.

"Correct. I am a Girl Raised in the South. I clean up real good, but I love country music, my tea sweet, chicken fried and I will trade my stilettos for flip-flops any day."

"Flip-flops." His mouth curved upward.

"They're a Southern girl's glass slipper." She winked.

"Well, Cinderella, how about diamonds? I thought those were a girl's best friend?" Mentally, he created the perfect diamond in his head, something only royalty would wear. She was, after all, a queen.

A frown marred her beautiful features. The sun kissed her skin, browning her shoulders and reddening her cheeks. "I'm not one who needs diamonds to make me happy."

"Bad experience?"

"Yes, I'll tell you someday. Right now, tell me why you're standing over here all by yourself. Are you being antisocial?"

Stephen contained his frown and glanced around. The only person he wanted to be around stood right in front of him, and she had yet to share her deepest secrets and fears with him. His ex-girlfriend Natalia had opened up to him right away. Years later, now he realized she fed him enough about herself in hopes to gain favor when her aunt dropped the bombshell about using his ties to the Torres family to elevate her publicity.

"Have you made any friends yet?"

"I'm not antisocial. I made a few friends. Everyone wants to know what I'm going to do with the bakery. They're so friendly. A lot of them have said 'bless your heart' to me."

A set of birds flew out of the hanging moss when Lexi began to laugh. "Aww, 'bless your heart' is a nice way to say, 'Go…'" Her words trailed off when a man with a white collar over his black T-shirt asked for everyone's attention to bless the food. Townspeople gathered around and bowed their heads.

Like a stampede, wet children flocked the dozen picnic tables and began ripping off the plastic wrap and plastic container tops for the food. A man in a pair of overalls who'd been handling a large oblong grill hinged to the back of a rusty red pickup truck opened the lid and the scent of charcoal filtered through the air. Stephen's stomach growled. His mouth watered for one of the hot dogs or burgers, maybe both.

"What are you in the mood for?" asked Lexi when the line began to thin. "I can make a plate for you if you'll find us a spot under one of the trees."

You, he thought, but instead said, "How about a little of everything?" Off in the distance he found a spot free of red-ant colonies, underneath an oak tree shaded by the oversize branches and Spanish moss. The wide trunk supported his back as he pulled his legs up. Kimber and Marvin sat at a table with a bunch of other boys and girls, far away from both uncles. Philly ate on a blanket, teaching her new beauty walk to her friends. Nate leaned against a tree, cornered by a mystery woman while Keenan mingled with Lexi's assistant, Chantal.

"Don't get me wrong, but nothing but scandal has followed the Pendergrass family," a woman's voice said from the other side of the tree.

Hard to believe that a few weeks ago Stephen would have paid to gain any information on Lexi and her family. Well aware things were not rosy with her parents, he'd dropped the subject with her and waited until Lexi wanted to share what happened. And coming from a small town, Stephen did not like to eavesdrop on gossip, but the mention of Lexi's family's name piqued his interest.

"Mr. Pendergrass still won't show his face at any public function. I bet he still believes the youngest one isn't his."

"Mmm," said another voice, "after all these years? You know they're good for trying to keep secrets. Those two ain't foolin' nobody. Did you see the way they kept making googly eyes at each other all day?"

What? Stephen wanted to laugh.

"She wouldn't dare. Didn't she learn her lesson from the last time she got involved with a parent?"

"Girl, don't get me started. At least this one won't be here long. Hopefully, when Lexi's done with this one, it won't bring the trash TV people around here like the last time."

Stephen's teeth gnashed together when he heard a clap. Did they high-five each other?

"What about the oldest Pendergrass girl, running off with that man? See, that's why they're in trouble now. I refuse to believe Lisbeth Pendergrass was brought up to marry some swindler."

Lisbeth, Stephen recalled Lexi mentioning her older sister.

"—leaving her daughter behind like that. What a shame. You know what Lisbeth's husband did to those people, and it's a wonder something bad hasn't fallen on the entire family. God don't like ugly."

"Speaking of not liking ugly," the first woman said, lowering her tone. "You heard the man who brought Divinity's Bakery is planning on tearing down the block and building a high-rise apartment? All these big-city folks keep moving down here and taking over."

An apartment? Stephen thought. He had no idea what to do with the place. See, this was why he hated small towns. False gossip.

"Well I would not string the word *ugly* and that man together."

"Amen," the other woman said before another apparent high five.

"Did you say an apartment complex? Aren't things bad enough with the condominiums downtown? I swear I hate havin' to carry myself up to the City Hall to pay my bills. They got too much going on."

Stephen, so engrossed in eavesdropping, didn't hear Lexi's flip-flops flapping against the back of her heels. "Hey, getting you a little bit of everything required a couple of plates," she said, kicking the bottom of his leather boat shoes.

Immediately he rose to relieve her of the four plates she balanced on both hands and forearms. They carried a spoonful or two of every casserole, baked beans, coleslaw, potato salad and macaroni salad, mini sandwiches, a few hot dogs, sausage dogs, and a burger with a slice of tomato and lettuce spilling out.

"Oh, thank you! I can work a catwalk in six-inch heels,

wearing an eight-pound tiara balanced on my head like
it's nobody's business, but my waitressing skills are not
up to par."

"Lexi!" One of the gossiping ladies stepped out from
around the tree. Both women wore a set of velour jogging
outfits, jackets unzipped, one purple, one brown. "What
a pleasure to have you out here on this glorious day." The
woman in brown, probably in her sixties, had the decency
to avoid eye contact with Stephen. Her porcelain skin had
reddened and not from the sun.

"Hi, Mrs. Fields," Lexi said to the first lady, leaning over
to air-kiss her cheeks, then she reached over and hugged the
other gossiping woman. "Hi, First Lady Huggins. Allow me
to introduce to you one of Southwood's new residents, Stephen Reyes. Stephen, this is Mrs. Fields. She and her husband own the pharmacy down the street from our shops."

Stephen made a mental note to never step foot in their
establishment as he balanced the four plates in one hand.
Her small, fragile hands shook with his. The woman next
to her offered Stephen her boney hand to shake.

"And this is Mrs. Huggins. Her husband is the pastor
who blessed our food today. Would you ladies be so kind
and keep an eye on Stephen while I run and get us some
tea?"

Flustered, First Lady Huggins opened her Martin Luther
King Jr. fan and began cooling the beads of sweat around
her neck and forehead. "Mr. Reyes, we did not realize you
were sitting here."

Jaw clenched, Stephen nodded. "Aw, bless your heart."

The afternoon of fun in the sun for Southwood families
wound down to an evening of serenity. The sun set in the
distance over a row of pine trees, casting a golden glow
over the calm lake. Homemade ice cream in all kinds of
flavors—chocolate, vanilla, and the local favorite, butter pecan—were churned at the cleaned-off picnic tables.

Old folks with their hand cranks faced off against the new generation's electric ice-cream machines hooked up to a generator off the back of someone's truck.

Belly filled with chilled triangular slices of watermelon, Lexi set the rind down to save for the horses from the hayride later and stretched out on the docks beside Stephen. Finally, he rolled up the hem of his pants and stuck his feet in the water. Hoofbeats caused the water to vibrate.

"They're fine," she said, covering her eyes with the crook of her elbow. Stephen kicked the water.

"What?" He chuckled nervously. "I'm not worried."

Lexi readjusted herself on her elbows, admiring the way he fretted over the girls. Stephen had taken over more responsibility. With school officially over, Stephen had planned out all the activities he was doing with the girls, including a trip to his parents'. He'd invited Lexi, but she told him she'd have to think about it. Meeting the parents? So soon? It had only been two weeks since he burst through her front doors.

"Kimber is on a hayride with a bunch of kids." Lexi bumped her shoulder against his. "What can happen?"

Stephen raised a brow. "Seriously?"

"What?" she asked innocently, and studied his face.

"You have been sneaking kisses from me all afternoon right under their noses." Stephen kept his gaze straight ahead. The right side of his cheeks rose and he broke out into a grin.

Heart fluttering, Lexi rolled her eyes and sat upright, dipping her feet into the water beside his. "I did not sneak anything."

"So," he began slowly, "are you saying you did not wait until the kids went into the water to kiss me?"

"I cannot help if no one is paying attention to us." Lexi kicked a bit of water toward him.

"No one is paying attention now," he said with a challenge in his voice, "except for the folks living in the house across the lake."

Lexi didn't need to follow his direction to know what house. Instead she cocked her head to the side, "You're the one who said I've been stealing kisses." Okay, so she had stolen one or two here and there. She liked the excitement of asking him to help get things out of the trunk of her Cadillac, then stepping up on her tiptoes for a quick peck. "Maybe you need to steal some of your own."

Without hesitation, Stephen leaned to the right and brought his face to hers. He smelled of coconut sunscreen and bug spray. And he completely turned her on. His almond-shaped eyes stared down at her lips. The pulsating of her heart was erratic. She licked her lips in preparation and closed her eyes. Gently, his tongue grazed her lips and touched hers. She parted her lips wider, and her left hand supported her weight as she turned to him, her other hand pressed against his heart; the beat of his matched hers.

Fireflies danced around them and a cool breeze whipped between them. This day had been the closest thing to perfection she'd experienced in a long time.

A couple of teenagers in a paddleboat out in the center of the water were playing around, screaming. Stephen pulled away. "Say, who lives in the house over there?"

"Why? Are you interested in buying it?" For a few days last week, Stephen's driver had taken them around town to scout homes. Keenan took the long way around each time. Lexi assumed because it gave them more opportunity to make out in the backseat. Stephen gave her every experience she'd missed out on while away at an all-girls boarding school, including making out on the couch, worrying every time they heard the kids coming down the steps.

"Scouting." Stephen faced her. "I still have to make a living and I'm not sure I made enough friends today who want to entrust me to sell their homes. I got a text from one of the station producers while you were at the waterslides."

"It's a Sunday, Stephen."

"I'm sorry, but I had to take it. Doesn't the home remind you of Tara?"

"I know the house very well." Lexi cocked her head to the side and studied the manicured lawn from the distance. Typically her viewpoint came from the docks by the forty-foot yacht. A couple of yards away from the docks, the trees parted to offer a peek at the back of the plantation home. "My parents live there, so whatever plans you're thinking for them, forget it."

Water lapped against the docks, emphasizing the silence between them. Stephen came from a huge family, whether he wanted to be a part of it or not. His mother still wanted to see him. Hell, his mother wanted to meet her. What would Mrs. Reyes think of Lexi and her past?

"I'm sorry if I snapped." Lexi rubbed her shoulder against his. "I told you we're not close."

"Do you want to be?"

She half shrugged. "I did. I've tried, but I've brought so much embarrassment. It's too late."

"It's never too late, Lexi." Stephen wrapped his arm around her shoulders, absorbing the pain. She tried not to cry.

"I did try. My folks don't even bother returning my cards. At least then I knew they got them. My mother's handwriting would be delicately written on the front, *Return to Sender.* I have no family."

"Don't worry, you've got me."

Lexi walked on cloud nine for the next few months. She literally had an energy in her step, one she never realized she was missing until now. Her calf muscles absorbed the weight of her stride and the red shoulder bag dangling from her arm bounced against her hip. Her red-and-white polka-dot mules skipped her past the Foxx's café. This morning, Chantal had faxed over blueprints for an idea she had to build the store deeper instead of wider. She suggested Lexi build upward. The upstairs apartment would be turned into a private area for bridal consultations, and the expansion downstairs could hold pageant dresses and other formal gowns. They also went to a nearby hardware store and put in an offer in case Mr. Wheeler wanted to retire early.

As summer rolled on, her schedule remained busier than ever. Toddlers and teens flocked to her workshops every Saturday afternoon, and private sessions with Philly progressed so well, she had Philly help with the girls her age on Saturdays. The nights Lexi did not work with Philly, Stephen would pick her up for their dates after work—movies at the park, market days in the downtown square. The days Philly came to the shop, Stephen busied himself with some secretive project next door. Some days, their weekend excursions included the children.

Stephen let Keenan go as a driver and bought himself a family-friendly white sports utility vehicle. He still drove the long way around town, mysteriously avoiding short-cuts, but Lexi enjoyed the extra time they spent together.

They fell into a comfortable routine and Lexi loved every minute of it. For the Fourth of July, Stephen gathered everyone up and brought them to Villa San Juan to his family's hotel, Torres Towers. Everyone sat on the beach facing the Gulf and watched the fireworks.

Occasionally Stephen took solo trips to help with the process of transferring his office in Atlanta. Those nights, he and Lexi talked on the phone till all hours, talking through their binge marathons of old Cary Grant movies on Netflix.

Life with Stephen was perfect. Too perfect. Somewhere across the street, she heard a bird call out so loudly she stopped in her tracks to look around. Lexi shielded her eyes with her hand from the sunny, cloudless sky. Set in a permanent state of happiness, she continued on toward the store. After eating out every night, the walk wouldn't kill her. Hiking her purse back on her shoulder, she tore her gaze from the clouds and her eyes fell across the street. Kimber's familiar pink-and-lavender backpack slung across her shoulders caught her eye. Suspicion rose in Lexi's veins. Why did a kid need her backpack in the summertime? Kimber stood in front of a boy—not Marvin. Lexi's eyes narrowed. This summer, she'd gotten to be friends with Marvin since he picked Kimber up to take her to a lot of the town's social events for the teenagers of Southwood. This boy was a foot taller than Marvin and had a good fifty pounds on him. Nearby at a picnic table, Lexi spied the real Marvin seated in front of a pile of books.

Prepared to shout across the street at Kimber, Lexi raised her hands to cup her mouth to yell. Stephen was going to have a fit when he learned Kimber had broken his trust. Lexi still kept the secret about the dress because she thought Kimber had truly learned her lesson. But to Lexi now everything became clear as day.

She'd been using poor Marvin as a decoy while she secretly dated this man-child. Judging from the way the boy grabbed at Kimber's behind and slobbered all over her face, the two were well acquainted with each other. What was she thinking, kissing this boy across the street from her shop? What if Stephen had been in town?

Lexi was so focused on the couple across the street and trying to reach for the cell phone inside her purse she didn't hear the door to the bakery behind her open. A cold hand snaked around her mouth, preventing her from screaming, and dragged her inside. Panic struck every nerve in her body. Nothing bad ever happened in Southwood, so of course the first broad-daylight kidnapping would happen to her. Regrets flogged her mind. She wished she'd worked things out with her parents. She wished she had the chance to say goodbye to the Reyeses. She wished she'd shown Stephen how she really felt. If only she had the chance.

Chapter 12

Wildly, her eyes looked left and right, hoping, praying someone had witnessed this abduction. Jammed against this man's frame, she walked awkwardly backward into the bakery, where Lexi imagined being chopped into tiny pieces. Why did Stephen believe the myth of never having to lock doors in a small town?

Fear took over again once the doors to the bakery closed, trapping her inside… Her dark eyes glanced at the vaulted ceilings. On the occasions Lexi had indulged in the desserts at the bakery, she'd never studied the shop closely, but she realized things had changed. The lowered ceiling had been removed to reveal golden paint. The rafters were polished and sparkling. Thick plastic covered the marble flooring. She wondered if her dead body would be wrapped up in the plastic. The smell of fresh French bread returned, though, as well as the sweet and spicy scent of Stephen's cologne. Quickly she jerked away and spun around.

"You scared the hell out of me!"

Stephen stood in the center of the room in a pair of black chinos, a white oxford shirt and black shoes, scratching the back of his head. "I thought you saw me through the window."

"You're supposed to be in Atlanta! I was——" Though she was still reeling from her initial fright and anger, she remembered Kimber. Now was not the time to tell him. She planned to talk with Kimber first and encourage her to come clean with her uncles. They trusted her. "What are you doing here?" She waved her arms around the new office area. The walls were covered with framed photographs of Stephen handing over the keys of dream homes to several families. Photographs above the secretary's desk were shots of classic homes from famous movies alongside families standing in front of their own versions. Her heels clicked on the hardwood floors as Stephen led her to the back office space.

"When did all this happen? This work takes months!"

Before opening his office door, Stephen gave her a sneaky smile. Her stomach did a flip. "This is the power of Hollywood, *querida*." Stephen snapped his fingers and the lights flickered, a white screen lowered against the walls darkening. The ceiling turned the room into an orangey-yellow foggy haze. "While you've been busy with Philly, I've been doing some work on my own."

A familiar tune she currently could not put her finger on poured from the surround-sound speakers. "But what is all this?"

"I wanted to take you someplace you've never been before, and since you're so worldly and insisted on forcing me to watch all those movies with you, I came up with my own idea." Stephen extended his hand for her to take. "You don't like to dance, but here's something," He swept her into his arms. A panorama screen of the dance scene put them in the center of *An American in Paris*. She gasped when Stephen mirrored Gene Kelly swinging Leslie Caron into his arms. Lexi clung to Stephen's broad shoulders. Her hair floated through the air. Before she got dizzy, the walls flickered, changing from black to blue. They were surrounded by a body of water. Cool air whipped across her face from a perfectly placed and timed vent. Stephen stood behind her and held her arms out to either side like Jack and Rose in *Titanic*. His lips nibbled her neck. A chill of desire ran down her spine.

"I thought about all the locations I want to kiss you," he said against her earlobe.

"Oh, Stephen, I think this is so sweet and all, but I can't, I've got to go to..."

"Work?" His coy dimpled smile returned. "You mean

the thing you have to do next door?" He led her around in a bit of a circle. The room changed and they stood on a bridge, cars flying before them; he'd recreated the scene between Kate Hudson and Matthew McConaughey in *How to Lose a Guy in 10 Days*, leaning her against a bar as the actors did against a yellow cab. He cupped her face and his tongue traced the shape of her mouth. Lexi's knees buckled.

The sky around them reddened, a field surrounded them, and they were in *Gone with the Wind*, another movie they'd watched together on the couch of his brother's home. Lost in remembering the evening, she hadn't noticed the temperature drop or the next change of scenery, but he recreated the last kiss scene in *Love Jones*.

"Work has been taken care of," he whispered, "I am going to take care of you this afternoon. Want to tell me what made you so jumpy?"

Lexi stared at the hairs of his beard on his square chin. "I haven't been completely honest with you, Stephen."

"Sounds like we need to sit down." He led her toward a long black velvet chaise longue against the wall where the French doors of the kitchen separated the counter space. She braced her back against the arm and he sat beside her, pulling her legs into his lap. "You were shaking like a leaf."

"I don't want to ruin this moment." She bit her lip.

Stephen tugged at her ankle. "Talk. We've got all night."

"You scared me to death when you grabbed me."

"Is there something else going on with you?"

How did she begin to explain what she witnessed across the street? Kimber's blatant audacity to flaunt her lie in front of the shop was a slap in the face. Lexi had vouched for her with the dress, had taken the heat from Stephen's anger. And now here she was lying again.

"Oh." Lexi bit her bottom lip. "My mind is preoccupied with my sister and her family." In all honesty, Lexi's concern for her sister had been on her mind. While they weren't the closest, Lisbeth often dropped an email or a text to her every couple of weeks. Lexi hadn't heard from her or her niece in a while now.

In concern, Stephen cupped her face. "Anything I can help with? You can talk to me about anything."

Lexi smiled and pushed her sister and Kimber out of her mind. "I know."

"I have a cousin who works with the US Marshals. One phone call and we can locate your sister."

"You don't have to bring your family into this," Lexi said quietly. "If I don't hear from her by the end of the summer, maybe I'll take you up on your offer." She hated lying to Stephen. He'd shown her he wasn't the terrible monster she'd met first. But Lexi struggled with her place in this family matter. She'd already kept the secret about the dress. The last time she got involved in a family matter was with Ernest and look where that got her, a scandal to everyone in the pageantry world who knew about his nondivorce. Making her feel worse, his kind offer to help and ploy to get her to open up to him continued.

"You need to learn to trust me, not keep things from me. Okay?"

"Okay." She blinked.

"Are you hungry?"

"For food?" she asked wantonly.

Stephen straightened her upright again. "I've got dinner planned for us upstairs."

"I've got to get to work."

"Work is taken care of." He smiled and winked. "Andrew insisted on making me aware how he could handle the shop *and* work with Philly."

Slowly she shook her head, fighting with the angel and devil on her shoulders. She had work to do. Her services were needed next door, but her body wanted service in here. "I promise to take full responsibility if anything goes wrong."

"What did you have planned in here?"

Stephen cleared his throat and snapped his finger. Suddenly they were on a Greek balcony staring down at a village. He reached to the side of the sofa for a dish of Brie and red grapes, and fed her one piece of fruit. She nibbled on the tip of his finger.

"Are we alone?" she asked.

To answer her, he set the plate on the floor beside them and reached for her hips, yanking her down on her back. His hand slid under the hem of her skirt and up her thigh. "Something you wanted to do with me alone?"

Lexi bit the corner of her lip and batted her long lashes. "Well, I had one particular revelation when fighting for my life after being snatched off the street." She tried to hide her giggle when Stephen rolled his eyes at her dramatic antics. "Never mind."

Though she had no intention to leave, nor did she want him to let her go, she still had to pretend to make the effort to get away. Stephen caressed the curve of her waist, the pad of his thumb circling the buds beneath her bra. With kids at his home, they never got the chance to be alone. Their late-night movies were often marred with someone waking up and needing water. And they both just respected not having sex in the house. They made out a lot on the couch. Stephen would always get frisky, but they always broke apart like teenagers caught by their parents. It seemed too adolescent, but now faced with going the distance, Lexi shuddered. He was too fine to try and continue resisting.

"I'm sorry—go ahead and tell me what your last thoughts were before you nearly died."

A cord of desire pulled at her center the minute his mouth covered her neck. She opened her mouth to speak but she could only moan. Her only way to respond was to slip her hands under his shirt again and stroke his rock-hard abs. Her thumbs dipped down to the waistband of his slacks.

Stephen pulled back. "Hey now, I didn't set up this

date for that." He took her fingers and brought them to his mouth.

"Stephen, what my near-death experience taught me is I don't want to waste another second we have together, starting now."

He'd be lying if he said every inch of his body didn't ache to make love to her, but he wanted to respect her wishes and go slow. Lying on the couch making out with her left him in need of several cold showers. So if she continued to kiss him, lying so close, he worried he would not be able to stop.

"Don't tease me, woman," he growled playfully as she nibbled on his bottom lip.

Whatever he wanted to say got lost in his throat when she maneuvered out from under him, only to stand before him. A quick yank and the polka-dot strapless dress fell to the ground in a pool of red. She stood before him, a goddess of golden honey covered in a pair of tiny red lace panties and a red strapless bra. Hands on her hips, she tilted her head slightly up toward him for a kiss. Her blond hair spilled on one side of her shoulder, covering her left breast. Stephen stood to fit his body against hers. His hands stroked the curve of her waist; his fingers itched to pull off the material. Their mouths met and kissed deeply— passionately. Never before had he gotten lost in a kiss. As crazy as it seemed, he'd been content not making love. He did not need it—he wanted it, but kissing and a bit of touching here and there made him content, or so he thought.

"Do I look like I am teasing?"

A nerve in the back of his jaw twitched. *"¡Dios mío!"* His erection stiffened and strained against his pants.

Lexi's wide eyes blinked innocently as she stepped forward, pushing him onto the couch while she straddled his legs. Her breasts, so delectable, pushed against his face. Stephen kissed the valley between them and she ground her lower half against him. Her long lashes fanned against her cheeks each time. "Is something wrong?"

Innocent, his ass. This woman made seduction a profession. She had played the sweet Southern girl act for a while and he'd fallen for it. Grinning devilishly, Stephen shook his head. He was done with playing the good boy if she was finished playing the good girl.

"Not at all," he breathed.

"Why are you leaving me the only one undressed, then?"

Her fingertips unbuttoned his shirt. Stephen helped, trying to control his eagerness. With her still in his lap, he lifted his hips, slid his pants down his legs and kicking out of his pants, stripped down to his black boxers. Lexi reached for his waistband. "Let me."

Lexi slipped off his legs and cradled her body between his thighs. Her warm breath against his belly button made him aware he'd been shivering with nervousness. Stephen slouched into the cushions of the couch. A pink tongue darted out of her mouth, tracing the area between the fabric of his briefs and his skin. Her fingers moved to his hips and slowly peeled down the material, freeing his throbbing cock. Lexi took her thumb and rolled the precum and spread it around and down the shaft. Maneuvering to her knees, she braced her hands on his thighs and slid her red lips over him, taking him deeply to the back of her throat. Stephen reached for the cushions, trying to maintain his cool, but as she bobbed her head up and down, suctioning each time her mouth closed around the tip, he couldn't take it. His hands sank into her hair, guiding her to his oblivion. When he thought he might burst, Stephen jackknifed upward and swooped Lexi into his arms and laid her down on the couch. He needed her. Now.

Stephen hovered over her body. She slid her bra off and he kissed her on the collarbone. When Lexi pressed her hands against his bare chest, her breasts jutted forward in offering. He obliged, making love to one nipple at a time until her legs fell to the side. Stephen sent another trail of kisses down her smooth belly. The thin fabric of her panties didn't hide the moisture she'd exuded from their touching. He was ready to stroke her but not yet. His mouth craved another kiss. Providing one, Lexi's soft hands milked him softly and firmly. Stephen pulled his hips out of her way, returning to his trail of kisses. His thumbs parted the center of her legs and he blew a hot kiss through the red fabric of her panties. Lexi whimpered.

His tongue slipped the fabric to the side and stroked the length of the runway strip of hair. Liquid heat gushed onto his tongue as he went deeper into her slick folds. Above him, Lexi's breath went ragged. Stephen kissed, lipped and devoured her while her hips wiggled beneath him. He used his hands to raise her butt so he could feast on her.

"Stephen!" She cried out his name. Stephen pulled himself to his arms and balanced himself to hover over her. He made love to one nipple with his mouth, pulled back and made love to the other. He sat back a moment to look at his work. The twin peaks stood at full attention. Lexi's body squirmed beneath his. She gyrated her hips against his strained erection.

Stephen struggled with the idea of how to make love to her body properly, fast and hard or slow and easy. Eager, he did not want to wait another minute; he wanted to take her right here. Another part of him wanted to savor every inch of her delectable body. They only had a limited time together and he wanted to showcase all of his skills.

Lexi's hands ran all over the place. They traced circles at the back of his freshly shaven head, cupping his jaw by his beard, and on his neck and biceps; before he rose to his haunches they were all over his back. Stephen had been skilled in the way of pleasing a woman. He'd practiced self-control over the years and always found the right time to release himself but at a mere touch of her hands he was going to explode. This couldn't be normal, but then again Lexi was a world-class seductress. Even the way she breathed turned him on—short, shallow breaths as if she were impatient. He looked down at her in the flickering light of the setting sun on the background he'd set for them.

Out of habit, Stephen reached down between her legs to test her readiness. He slipped a long finger under the silky fabric and into the warm depth of her body. He prayed she didn't catch his eyes fluttering or the way he inhaled deeply. Her insides took him into her velvety embrace—decadent, moist and rich. Touching her so deeply almost ended him.

He tried to play it as cool as possible again as he stood up and reached down for a condom from his wallet. Lexi rolled to one side, faced him and wrapped her warm hands around his thighs and brought him to her face. The bend of his knees almost made him buckle when she took him in her mouth again. He braced himself just to keep from falling. Her talented tongue licked, sucked and even nibbled. He couldn't breathe. Like a child on Christmas morning, he couldn't wait.

In one swift move, he went from one end of the couch to the other. He yanked those panties off, rolled the condom on and dived into her wet crevice. For half a second, a flash of panic quickened in Lexi's eyes, and at the same moment a slight barrier held him back for a moment as he entered her tight body. Her walls hugged his erection; he moved his hips deeper and met the same resistance. She was wet but not ready. He dipped his head down and took a nipple into his mouth. Stephen tried to stand up but Lexi locked her legs around his waist.

"Make love to me, Stephen, please," she mewed, "please."

Stephen had not planned for this. Desire clouded his common sense. She seduced him and made him lose every hold on reality. Hips moving again, he pushed onward, deeper and slower. Lexi's hips rose to meet his with each thrust. Like a jockey urging its mount on, she pressed her hands against his rear end and urged him faster. Soft moans echoed in his ear. The light flickered across her face, exposing her pleasure. Lexi arched her back, bringing her body closer. Her Cupid's-bow mouth parted in a gasp when he hooked her knees around his arms and drove into her, trying hard as hell to not lose control.

Their bodies moved in perfect rhythm. He couldn't control himself any further. She moaned with each pump, hands still on him, knuckles clenched until they spun out and her entire body jolted and fell back into the couch. Her lower half trembled in orgasm. He was so taken that he suddenly lost control, spilling himself.

Sweat poured down his body. He quickly got to his knees and knelt before her naked body. Her dewy skin glistened. Lexi turned her head to his; in the light he could see her blush.

"My God, woman," Stephen breathed.

"What?" Lexi blinked innocently.

The floor chilled his knees. Emotions trudged through his body. Hating the way she casually threw his question back, Stephen stared at the spot on her shoulder he'd kissed. "I didn't plan for our first time to be on my office couch."

She reached over and pulled him by the neck. He liked the way she knew how to take charge. Her soft lips pressed against his. "Well, now every time you have a meeting in here, you can be reminded of me. What other room can we christen?"

Stephen tickled the soft inside curve of her waist. "You're not going to let me catch my breath?"

"Not a chance, old man," Lexi teased. "We have a lot of making up for lost time to do."

A shrill ring came from her phone in her purse by the door. Lexi struggled to get up while trying to maintain modesty. She grabbed his white pullover and slipped her arms through the sleeves and tugged the hem over her ample behind as she crossed the new hardwood flooring.

Stephen enjoyed the sight of her in his clothes, her long legs tiptoeing out of his office. Stephen followed her to the doorway, watching as she bent over and he got a peek at her sunshine below. Unabashed by his own nakedness, Stephen got his second wind.

Like Lexi's place next door, Stephen's too had an apartment upstairs. That entrance was sealed off with a closed door between his office and Nate's. The wooden staircase was littered with rose petals. He'd planned on surprising Lexi with a tour of the studio and an early dinner. The kitchen upstairs still had their dinner warming in the oven. A round table held a vase of her favorite orchids and a string quartet played through the air from one of the many music devices left over by the sound-machine guys who had helped set up this afternoon for him.

Okay, so maybe he went into a little overkill on the romance. Hell, what good were his Hollywood connections if he did not call in a favor or two? To top off the evening, he'd had the folks from Owen's drive over family-style spaghetti and meatballs. He broke off a piece of the crispy garlic bread and popped it into his mouth, hoping the crunch would drown out her conversation as he made his way back downstairs, two steps at a time. Is this what people did when they were in love?

Stephen stopped in his tracks. Love? When the hell did that happen? Earlier this summer he'd stormed into her office and blamed her for almost ruining their lives. Now his mind floated the word *love* around? This was not supposed to happen. In like, yes. Lust, definitely. But love?

"Yes," Lexi went on to whomever was on the other line. Stephen tried not to eavesdrop. "No, I'm not worried about the space…Girl, I am working a new angle…Please, my name is Lexington Pendergrass. I always get what I want, no matter the price…Grits and Glam Gowns is going to double when you return."

Double? Working an angle? Lexi twirled a strand of

hair around her index finger and turned around. Their eyes met. Stephen's narrowed on hers. Had he wasted a summer with Lexi? Was history repeating itself? She wouldn't be the first woman alive to seduce him for one reason or another, whether it be the use of his wealth, his family name, or now to get a piece of property. His cell phone rang. Stephen trotted over to the couch to retrieve his pants.

Andrew's shriek on the phone snapped Stephen's attention. "Oh, my God, Stephen, I'm so sorry to interrupt! I had no idea it was going to happen. There's blood everywhere! Philly's in the ER."

Chapter 13

A candy apple! Who knew a candy apple could cause so much damage?

Lexi adjusted her purse higher up on her shoulder and shook her head at the smiling darling with alligator tears in her hazel eyes. She would never have guessed from the horror on Stephen's face when he hung up his cell phone that this would be the result of an innocent bite out of a delicious treat. Her two front teeth got stuck in the sticky sweet and when she had tried to pry her mouth off, the apple ripped them out.

The silence between them on the way over unnerved her, especially with the way his jaw twitched. Moments before he received Andrew's call, Stephen had glared at her angrily. She probably should not have taken the phone call after they made love, but the cell phone ring excited her. She hadn't talked to her best friend in ages.

Nate was already waiting for them at the hospital and he explained what had happened while walking back to Philly's room.

"I'm sorry! She asked if she could have one of the apples in the fridge," Andrew wailed again from his corner of the doctor's office. Blood covered his lime-green button-down shirt. "I didn't know those candy apples from the fair were still in there!"

"It's okay," Nate said, holding Philly in his arms. "Philly has been told about taking things that don't belong to her, especially sneaking sweets."

"I asked if I could have an apple." Philly smiled a toothless grin and beamed at everyone in the room. Everyone had dropped what they were doing to be here for her. "Can I still do the pageant?"

All eyes turned on Lexi. This time she did not mistake the chilling glare coming from Stephen. Maybe his nerves were rattled. "We have our ways around this."

"So I can still do the show this weekend if I promise not to eat any more sweets?"

In order for Philly to perform in a high-glitz pageant, she'd need a flipper, false teeth for a pageant, and they needed to work quickly in order to get it to arrive in time. If Lexi recalled correctly, one of the judges at the fair was a dentist. Maybe she could get him to work some magic. "I think so."

"Of course," Stephen said, tight-lipped. "You're Lexi Pendergrass. You always get what you want, right?"

The condescending tone confused her. Nate raised his brow, too.

"So," Nate drawled, looking at the doctor dressed in light blue scrubs, "are we allowed to bring our patient home?"

As the doctor gave the directions on how to care for Philly over the next few days, Lexi tried making eye contact with Kimber. The real Marvin stood dutifully by Kimber's side. Now things became clearer; Marvin tried to put his hand over her shoulder, but she kept knocking him off.

One by one the Reyeses exited the small waiting room. Lexi reached out to catch Stephen's elbow before the automatic doors closed. The reopening of the doors made enough noise to interrupt everyone in the waiting room and draw their attention from their books, magazines and iPods. She gave an apologetic smile all around before turning back to Stephen.

"Hey." She smiled when he turned around. "Is everything okay?"

His cold eyes bored through her. "Yes."

"The evening is still early. Do you want to finish our date?"

With her needing to lean her body to make eye contact

with him, she already realized things were wrong—way wrong.

"I think, given what's happened tonight, it's best I stay home with the family. You understand, right?"

No, she wanted to say, but she plastered a smile on her face, she squared her shoulders and inhaled deeply. Shaking her hair off her shoulders, she nodded. "Sure."

Awkwardly Stephen leaned down and kissed her cheek. When he pulled away, he gave her a tight smile and turned back around to leave.

"Are you and my boo having difficulties?"

Lexi gave Andrew a sideways glance as she watched Stephen leave. He didn't even so much as look back at her or ask her how she was going to get home. "I'm not sure."

For comfort, Andrew draped his arm around her shoulders. He smelled like candy apples and hospital. The antiseptic scent reminded her this was a place for the sick. "Well, I'm really sorry to cut off your evening like this. I had no idea we were training a candy-apple junkie. This is all my fault."

Lexi patted Andrew's arm and laid her head on his shoulder. "Nate told me to make sure you did not blame yourself. Philly has a major sweet tooth." Hell, she'd witnessed it herself in Savannah.

"What are we going to do? Her smile alone brought her twenty-five points."

"We will buy her one."

"What the hell, Stephen?"

Living in Ken's home had its perks. Stephen was able to monitor the girls better and make sure things stayed on track. He enjoyed bonding with them, as well. Living with Nate had a list of drawbacks. Lack of privacy topped the list of things Stephen disliked about moving in.

Stephen stood in Ken's office, staring at the wedding photograph of his brother and Betty. Driving down Country

Road Seventeen brought back memories he'd suppressed for over six months. In trying to gain custody of the girls and making the transition with his business and living situation, he'd never grieved for Ken. He understood and accepted he had died. Or so he thought. Traveling down Seventeen, passing the spot where the wreckage was found hit him hard. The yellow do-not-cross tape was gone. Blood splatters had been washed away by rain and residue, but Stephen still knew. He knew his brother was dead. And he'd had to confront that fact with Lexi driving his car to go see his niece, whom he should have been with.

"What?" Stephen played dumb.

Without asking permission to stay, Nate took a seat in the maroon rolling chair at the computer. "Lexi."

The mere mention of her name made him want to drink. From a half bar next to the brown pullout couch, he helped himself to a scotch, no ice, and welcomed the burning liquid. The purpose of moving down to Southwood was to take care of his nieces, not fall in love. Stephen wasn't sure he could forgive himself for losing focus because of Lexi. "What about her?"

"We care a lot about her. She's been good for us."

"And I haven't?"

Nate's eyes widened. "Seriously, Stephen you need to chill out with that."

"I'm putting in my dues." Stephen tossed back another drink. He softened his tone, knowing Nate did not deserve his wrath. "Sorry, I did not mean to sound selfish. I need to clear my head."

"So this means you won't be on the house phone at all hours of the night?"

Stephen tried to lighten the mood with a fake laugh. He shook his head and sighed. "I don't understand the problem. Everyone has a cell phone in this house but Philly. Why is it important if Lexi and I talked on the phone? Never mind. I doubt you'll have to worry about it much."

"You're pitiful. You need to snap out of this funk. No one asked you to fall in love with her."

The blood in his veins ran cold with irritation. "What? You don't know what you're talking about."

"I'm not stupid or blind, Stephen. You're so predictable, and you're angry because you've fallen for her."

"Why do you think I am in love with Lexi?"

"Clearly, you've never been in love, but one of the main signs is she's the only person you want to be with. Everyone else comes in second place."

Instead of his brother's words helping, they made Stephen feel guiltier. He'd moved his life down here to be with the girls, not meet a woman to fall in love with. Crossing the room to the window, Stephen clasped his hands behind his back and focused on the neighbors across the street putting out their trash. He'd already taken care of theirs. In Atlanta he paid someone else to take out his trash. He'd become domesticated. "You came off like a cold ass to Lexi."

Cold did not begin to describe how he'd treated Lexi at the hospital. For a split second, he admittedly had compared her to his ex Natalia. But deep down inside he was flat-out scared. Did she really care for him or what he could offer? To top everything off, Lexi had forced him to face his fear of driving down the road where his brother had died. No man wanted his woman to think he was weak. Nate might have been the one person to talk to about this, but he jumped to the wrong conclusion. "Stay out of my business, Nate."

"You brought Lexi into the fold of the family."

"Who signed Philly up for this pageant?" Stephen retorted.

"The fold of the family, *hermano*," Nate repeated.

People could say whatever they wanted about Lexi Pendergrass as long as they remembered one thing—she was a professional, a professional model, professional pageant coach and professional businesswoman. She plastered a smile like no one's business. She hadn't seen Stephen since he gave her the cold shoulder at the hospital. She'd be lying if she said she didn't care, but as the cliché went, the show must go on.

Somehow, the venue of the Southern Style Glitz Pageant in Atlanta bustled to life. Families arrived in limousines, carriages, on the shoulders of a coordinated entourage— anything to attract attention. Lexi checked in to her hotel room right next door to Philly and Kimber. Everyone's rooms adjoined at some point, except for Stephen's. Nate mentioned he'd already headed over to his home in Berkeley Lake. Did he plan on attending today? She refused to believe he'd gotten what he wanted and left. She'd never been so humiliated.

A soft knock at her hotel door brought her out of her pity party. Lexi turned from her somber stare out onto Peachtree Boulevard. "C'mon in."

Kimber spilled into the room, shutting the door secretively behind her. Her hazel eyes were wide. "Can you talk?"

"Of course, sweetie." Lexi had been meaning to talk to the girl since seeing her on the street. With everything going on in the past seventy-two hours, she hadn't made the time.

"I'm in some trouble."

Lexi's knees buckled. She pressed her backside against the window to steady herself. *Dear sweet Jesus, no.* Kimber's beauty belonged on television, but not *16 and Pregnant.* Nervously she smiled, pulled her hair into a side ponytail and waved Kimber to take a seat.

Instead of sitting at the table, Kimber sat with her back to Lexi on the royal-blue comforter of the queen-size bed. Kimber rocked back and forth a few times without saying a word.

Heart racing, Lexi chewed her bottom lip. "Kimber,

you're making me nervous," she finally said. "Whatever is going on, you can tell me."

"All summer long, I have been lying to everyone!" Kimber blurted out with a cry.

"Oh?" Lexi's voice rose in pitch and she asked, "What do you mean?"

"Marvin isn't my boyfriend. He's my cover."

Lexi waited for the other shoe to drop.

"Philip is a varsity football player at Southwood Central and he's the reason I stole the dress. He's the most popular boy ever and he is totally into me."

A slight pressure built up in the back of Lexi's head. "Kimber—" she tried to keep any sign of panic out of her voice "—what exactly did you do to get his attention?"

Kimber turned around, her hazel eyes wide. "Not *that*!" She covered the opening of her pink polo shirt. "The dress I took sealed the deal and elevated me from sophomore to sophomore *hottie*, and Philip noticed, too."

Relaxing, Lexi stretched out across the bed and patted Kimber's arm. "Why the cover boyfriend?"

"Marvin is Philip's cousin. Marvin goes to school with me and I don't want my uncles to freak out because Philip is from the wrong side of the tracks."

Lexi did not imagine Nate judging anyone. He dated women from all walks of life in Southwood. Stephen, on the other hand, she thought, might take issue with *any* boy who wanted to date Kimber. "Oh, Kimber." Lexi scooted around the bed so she was seated next to the upset girl and wrapped her arm around her shoulders. "You need to tell your uncles."

"How? They barely like Marvin."

"What if you invite Philip here to the pageant?" Somehow Lexi doubted Stephen would cause a scene in front of a room full of people, if he even came at all.

"You think?"

"Yeah, sure. I'll stand by your side to support you."

Kimber picked up her cell phone and began texting. Lexi tried to concentrate on being with Stephen again. He hadn't called. She missed their late-night chats. Nate told her an emergency had taken him away, which she still struggled to believe. A vibrating buzz came from Kimber's phone. She made a little squeal and looked up at Lexi, "He'll be here tonight for dinner! I can't wait! Thank you, Lexi!"

So, dinner it was, Lexi thought, steeling her nerves.

"What are you going to wear?" Kimber asked, taking Lexi out of her thoughts.

"Me?"

In a matter of seconds, Kimber made the conversation about Lexi. Quickly, she flipped onto her stomach and lay down on the bed, face resting in her hands with her elbows propped up. "I'm pretty good at keeping quiet about secret relationships. You and Uncle Stephen aren't."

Lexi tried not to grin. "We're friends."

"You guys haven't been friends since you danced the night Philly won at the Peach Blossom. My *abuela* said he's never brought anyone home to Villa San Juan, and yet you came."

"Philly and I work together, regardless of the location." Lexi rolled her eyes and shook her head at the same time. "You're a child," she said with a grin. "I'm not going to discuss this with you." She slid off the bed and slunk over to her closet.

"So do you deny having feelings for Uncle Stephen?" Kimber rose to her knees, folded her arms across her chest.

"I…I…I think he is a very nice man."

"So does Natalia Garcia Ruiz."

Ears perking, Lexi glanced over her shoulder. "Who?"

Kimber's mouth twitched with a smile. "Not according to the tea being spread around Southwood."

Lexi had been around enough of the young kids these days to understand "tea" was code for gossip. After years of being the center of a scandal, Lexi frowned at the unwanted attention. She shook her head from side to side. "People are going to talk." Lexi shrugged.

"So you don't care if Uncle Stephen has been up here being caught on camera with one of the biggest reality stars around?"

The corners of Lexi's eyes twitched. "Of course not. What do I care if he meets up with what's her face?"

"Her name is Natalia Garcia Ruiz, and she's only the biggest internet sensation. Her family's only got the biggest perfume line, Azúcar. I can't believe you don't use her products."

"Sorry." Lexi shrugged her shoulders and went back to flipping through her clothes. Their conversations never revolved around exes. Her heart plummeted into her stomach.

"She's also the woman Uncle Stephen took out the other night to Owen's."

A pang stabbed at the center of her heart. Lexi's mouth formed an O, and she tried to smile and shrug the hurt off. Owen's? "Your uncle meets lots of people in his business."

"Not like I know a lot about the place, but it has these curtained booths and they were photographed exiting." Kimber started pressing the buttons on her phone. "Here, let me pull it up."

"You don't need to." Lexi's voice squeaked. How foolish of her. He'd pulled the same routine with her.

"According to what I overheard from Uncle Nate talking, they dated."

"Well, good for them." She put out her chin.

"Yes, but you and Uncle Stephen belong together." Kimber's eyebrows rose in amusement.

"Let's not talk about this." Lexi quickly changed the subject. "How about we call Chantal and get her to bring something spectacular for you to wear to dinner tonight, and in the meantime, we'll get a little pampered?"

In a matter of a half second, Kimber scrambled off the

bed and was right by Lexi's side. "You don't need to ask me twice!"

Lexi remembered those days where a mani-pedi healed all wounds. Her mother taught her a long time ago about the importance of therapeutic shopping. Days like today, Lexi wished she were in a better place with her parents. Trying not to think about the past, she draped her arm around Kimber's shoulder.

"Lexi, check out who arrived." Kimber stopped walking once the elevators dropped them off at the lobby and nodded in the direction of the commotion going on at the front desk.

As expected, Rose Laing screeched at the front desk clerk. Somehow the pageant had lost their registration. Somehow it was always someone else's fault. *Poor Vera*, Lexi thought. She stood off to the side, completely humiliated by her mother's antics. Ernest Laing strolled around the lobby, casual as could be with his cell phone and dark sunglasses, while he stared at the behinds of the women on their way to the pool. Lexi shook her head. Nothing much had changed.

Unfortunately, the lobby lacked the different options to make a quiet exit. To the left of them sat the pageant registration team ready to take on-the-spot late registrations. To the right of them a group of two- to three-year-old girls from a pageant troupe worked on their cupcake walks, which meant their outstretched arms made it harder to walk by.

Taking a deep breath, Lexi grabbed Kimber's hand and dragged her forward. "Lexi, I'm not sure I can keep quiet if she starts talking to you all crazy again."

"We'll take the high road," Lexi said, "We'll see who's so smug when Waverly wins in Vera's category."

Of course Rose noticed Lexi coming. She stepped in front of their path and gushed out a fake hello. "Well, I didn't think we would run into you here!"

With a tight smile, Lexi tried not to look directly into Rose's bright peach pantsuit. The flash of a smile from Vera disappeared quickly. "Why wouldn't we be here, Rose?"

"Oh, you didn't read the newsletter?" Rose reached into her giant matching purse and pulled out the weekly *Pageant Press* paper.

On the cover Waverly stood in front of a wrecked motorcycle. Bottles of beer lay everywhere. Waverly held a helmet and was covered in grime from head to toe. Lexi didn't need to read the article. Each pageant contestant was supposed to keep a clean nose and stay out of trouble.

"I figured, with your little beauty queen headed off to jail, you wouldn't even show up. Funny how you tarnish ever pageant you're near."

Kimber lurched forward but Lexi held her back. "I'm not here for Waverly. I have another client."

"Who?" Rose and Vera chorused.

With her hand on her hip, Kimber stepped forward. "Actually, she's been training me in the teen category."

Chapter 14

Awkward—the understatement of the year.

Stephen drew a blank for words when Lexi entered the formal dining room on the rooftop of the Brutti Towers. Philly chatted aimlessly about everything she'd seen today. Chantal and Andrew drove up with the team to help out and helped fill the void of silence. Kimber and Lexi arrived at the same time. Kimber wore a new frock, pink, of course.

Stephen couldn't take his eyes off Lexi and her simple strapless black dress. Her hair, knotted in the back, directed his eyes to the silver-and-onyx necklace wrapped around her neck. Even though they sat right next to each other at the head of their table, she barely made eye contact with him.

Before everyone arrived for dinner, Nate had pulled Stephen aside to inform him he'd taken the liberty of explaining his absence, telling Lexi business called Stephen away to handle damage control. His dinner with Natalia had gone well. Natalia had needed a place to film a commercial in Atlanta and none of his assistants were good enough for her. She'd finally gotten the attention she wanted without having to use him or his family connections. Stephen was glad to call her a friend now. All the reality star wanted to do was go back home to Puerto Rico and hide from the world; she hated having all her secrets aired on national television. He hated to admit it, that traveling down Country Road Seventeen where the orange spray paint still stained the pavement, memorializing where his brother died, was another skeleton in his closet. He'd managed to avoid the road this long. For a moment, he had been paralyzed with what to do but Lexi took control of the situation, dragging him to her car and racing down the road. Whether or not she knew it at the time, she'd reached for his hand and given it a squeeze of assurance as they drove by the marked spot. Despite how things were left at the hospital, seeing this place again brought back the rush of feelings and desire for her. He wanted to hold her. Kiss her.

"Can we dance?" Stephen leaned over and whispered into Lexi's ears.

Lexi pretended to dab her white napkin over her lips. "Not on your life."

He leaned an inch from her bare, gardenia-scented shoulder. "Lexi."

"Stephen," she countered quickly.

"Don't be like this." He turned his head so only she could see his face. He might as well sit in her salad plate. "I want to talk to you."

Finally she gave him a smile—one baring her teeth, but still a smile. "We're here for Philly, Stephen. We are going to focus on Philly."

"Don't forget we're here for me, too, now." Kimber, seated on the other side of Lexi, leaned over; obviously she'd been listening to their conversation.

Stephen sat up a bit so he could see his niece. "What are you talking about?"

"I entered the pageant today."

"Yay!" Philly clapped her hands, "We can do the cupcake walk together!"

"Thanks, kiddo," Kimber said, smiling, "but I'm entering the big-girl pageant."

Something clicked in Stephen's mind and sparked anger. No one consulted with him on anything. "Over my dead body," Stephen growled, recalling the teenagers flirting with the male judges earlier this summer in Savannah.

"She can do the pageant," Nate, the Judas, stepped in. "We'll find a dress shop up here."

"One is en route as we speak," said Lexi. "Did you know, I had no idea you were interested in pageantry but the first time you came upstairs to the apartment above the store, I had a vision for a dress for you."

Kimber beamed and Philly sat, cheering.

"I am well acquainted with the dresses you sell in Kimber's size," Stephen sneered at Lexi.

"Excuse me?" Lexi jerked her head at him.

Anger blinded him. How had he forgotten so quickly? Stephen imagined his sixteen-year-old niece wiggling her hips on the stage in a dress from Grits and Glam Gowns. He didn't want her suffering from the problems Natalia said she'd received from people objectifying her at the young age of eighteen. Stephen did not appreciate Lexi and Nate making decisions for the girls without including him.

"I'm going to go get a drink at the bar." Stephen glared at his brother and at Lexi. "When I come back, I want to pretend like this didn't happen."

Crudely he pushed his wrought-iron chair away from the table. People looked, but he didn't care. He found a spot at the bar closest to the edge of the rooftop filled with other miserable men who didn't want to be at this event, either. He asked the bartender for a whiskey and sat and drank with his back to his family.

"Long weekend ahead?" asked the man seated next to him.

Stephen barely lifted his head from his tumbler and nodded. "Didn't we meet?"

The man slowly nodded, recognizing Stephen from his drunken fog. "Yeah, you're with Lexi Pendergrass. Ernest," he said, extending his hand, "Ernest Laing."

"Yeah," Stephen said.

Ernest took in a deep breath of the cooling air and shook his head. "Man, you don't gotta tell me nothin'. I recognize that look in your eyes. Biggest mistake of my life was not picking her. Lexi is some hellcat in bed. Am I right or am I right?"

"What in the hell did you just say to me?"

Drunkenly, Ernest shook his head. "Don't get me wrong, my wife is smoking hot, but damn, what a bitch. Lexi, she sure did know how to heat up a man's bed."

Stephen took several deep breaths of air. "Man, if you do not shut your mouth right now, you're going over the side of the building." Stephen pushed away from the bar. He and Lexi needed to talk—*now.*

At the door, a security guard held his arms out, keeping someone who looked exactly like Marvin from entering the rooftop. Stephen did a double take.

"Mr. Reyes!" Marvin's voice cracked when called out to Stephen.

"What's going on?" Stephen asked the maître d.

"Mr. Reyes—" the maître d's face reddened "—I am sorry to interrupt your dinner, but these gentlemen say they're here with you and your family."

Stephen nodded his head and the guard let Marvin in but held his hands up again. He recognized the little Marvin fellow, but he had no idea who the grown man-child was standing next to him. The boy was close to Stephen's height and had the nerve to sport a trimmed goatee like a grown man. His white shirt was a size too small to cover his overdeveloped chest and with his sleeves rolled up, Stephen figured the dark sky prohibited him seeing the boy's tattoos. "I don't know who this guy is."

"Uncle Stephen!" Kimber skidded to a stop at his side. "This is what I wanted to talk to you about. I want you to meet my boyfriend."

"I met your boyfriend, Kimber. Marvin. This is who has been coming to see you and pick you up to go study." Stephen poked his finger against Marvin's bird chest. The push was hard, not enough to crack the boy's rib cage but enough to knock him into the man-child standing behind him.

Kimber wedged herself between the boys and her uncle.

"No, Marvin's not my boyfriend. This is Philip." Kimber reached for the giant. "Lexi said…"

"Lexi?" Stephen snarled and blinked in disbelief. He turned his angry glare at her. She'd come to stand by Kimber's side. "You knew about this."

Wide-eyed and in shock, Lexi slowly nodded. "Yes, but…"

"Gonna throw this into the bucket of secrets you keep from me?"

"It's not what you think," Lexi tried to say.

What else was he supposed to think? She'd hidden everything about herself. Stephen brought his nose to hers and gritted his teeth. "How many different ways are you planning on trying to ruin my family?"

"Uncle Stephen!" Kimber cried.

"Stephen!" Nate barked, snatching him by the arm and pulling him away. In the instant it took Stephen to glare at the spot on his arm where his brother touched him, Lexi had stormed off.

Out of the corner of his eye, he saw Marvin and his friend back out of the door.

Kimber dramatically sobbed and took off out the door, crying, "Philip is my boyfriend. And I love him!"

When Stephen had made the phone call to arrange for the Southern Style Glitz Pageant to take place at this hotel back in the beginning of the summer, he had no idea it would triple the number of entries. Stephen had received a text from Gianni Brutti this morning, thanking him and cursing him—a running theme for him in the past twenty-four hours.

Stephen knew the funk he was in had spoiled everything today. Any other time, he would have cracked up at the outrageous dance routines mothers would do behind the judges' table while their daughters performed. Maybe the little two-foot-tall zombie girls would have made him laugh if he had someone next to him. It took Stephen a few minutes to decide if he wanted to come to the pageant show at all. He'd been too afraid to see what Kimber and Philly planned to wear. No amount of Torres rum could keep the horrific images out of his mind, but he tried. Now he paid the price.

Thank God it wasn't the talent part. He didn't think he'd be able to sit through the noise. Maybe in an hour or two the medicine he took would kick in. Stephen sat in his seat, arms folded; everyone had lost their damn minds. A snarl on his upper lip only reminded him of his hangover. Why, for God's sake, was everyone so perky at eight in the morning?

To make matters worse, they were only in the beauty portion of the show. The pageant world needed to call this the world's longest and slowest walk. Stephen stifled a triggered yawn, not meaning to mock the boy resting his head on his mother's shoulder in the seat in front of him.

I'm with you, kid, he thought to himself.

Stephen learned judges frowned on parents who had to coach their kids behind the judges' backs. Well, Philly had this contest on lock. Now he understood why Lexi made her practice over and over. Even on vacation, she made her practice. The one person who didn't practice was Kimber. She wouldn't even speak to him on the phone when he tried to wish her good luck this morning. As much as it pained him, coparenting did not work, not with Nate undermining him at every turn. Last night, he had not appreciated being outnumbered. Kimber had lied to them, and they rewarded her by letting her compete in a pageant she hadn't prepared for in order to satisfy Lexi's revenge against the Laings.

A woman in front of him turned around when he snorted. She curled her lip in disgust and turned back to the event on stage. Why should it matter if one more person hated him? Stephen spotted an empty seat closest to the front of the stage with better access to cheer on Philly.

She was in the next age group, four- to six-year-olds. Nate buzzed around somewhere. Stephen cut his eyes to the left and right and found Kimber's fake boyfriend, Marvin, and her real boyfriend, Philip. His lip curled like the woman in front of him. This new boyfriend was exactly what he had feared—tall, a jock, tattoos and facial hair. Kimber tried explaining all about Philip—all the things he should have been told when they started to date. A round of applause shook him out of his funk. At least now Philly would be up. The emcee told everyone they would take a five-minute break and would resume with the next age group. There was no point for Stephen to get up. He stretched his legs a little farther, this time adding his arm. His back popped against the back of the chair. Out of the corner of his eye, he caught a glimpse of her. *Lexi.* The glittering pink-and-black T-shirt with Team Philly across the front caught his eye in the sea of waiting mothers and children. Her long, slender hands rested on Philly's shoulders. When Lexi turned to talk to the ladies near her, he easily read the back of her T-shirt: Team Kimber. He wondered how she found the time to make a shirt.

Three ailments afflicted him at once. *Anger* for her being so intrusive with his family; *anger* at her for still making his body stiffen like Pavlov's dog at the mere sight of her; and of course *anger* for her betrayal and secrets.

"Mami always told us if you frown like that your face might freeze," teased Nate as he started coming down Stephen's aisle.

Why Nate needed to come here baffled him. "Go away," Stephen groaned.

Still coming, Nate shook his head. "Last night you had this same sourpuss mug on your face, and see here, you still got the same."

The emcee tapped on the metal microphone. Waverly had done a more entertaining job in Savannah. "Ladies and gentlemen, if you'll return to your seats, we'll get started on the four- to six-year-olds. If you have a child in the seven to twelve, please get them ready."

Stephen pinched the bridge of his nose. Pressure relieved it a little. "Where have you been all morning?"

Nate shook his head. "Philly's flipper arrived. I had to make sure she got it."

Stephen shook his head. "I am mad you know what a flipper is."

Nate stretched out his legs and inhaled. "Keep in mind that it's the little things that get me all these numbers." He waved to an Indian woman with a dolled-up baby on her lap.

"I've said it before, man—you're sick." Stephen shook his head.

"Sick, but at least one of us has been with a woman in the last twenty-four hours. Can you say the same thing?" Nate teased.

"What number is Philly?"

"She's next, I think."

Stephen tried to judge if Philly was next or not by the order of the mothers behind the judges. The last girl exited the stage and the mother walked behind the judges table to meet her on the other side of the stage. A wave of anger washed over Stephen when his eyes darted to the empty space behind the judges. Lexi had abandoned her? His thoughts were drowned out by the applause erupting from the room.

At the center of the stage stood his poised Philly, in a custom-designed peach-colored dress. Her little legs walked slowly in her white Mary Jane shoes. White ruffles fluffed the bottom of the dress. Strategically placed sparkles caught every aspect of the light. She glittered on the stage. Philly walked with her head held high and smile wide. Her front teeth now were perfectly white and even.

"The flipper," Nate whispered and tapped his two front teeth.

Unlike all the other girls who needed help, Philly stopped at the *X* on the stage without having to look down. She cradled her cute little baby cheeks at the judges and showed off her perfect cupcake hands as she turned around to walk back behind stage. Not once did she turn her head for guidance from Lexi. After she blew the judges an air-kiss from her glossed lips, she exited the stage, where Lexi waited. The crowd rose to their feet in applause. Lexi swung Philly in her arms and visibly mouthed how wonderful she was.

"That's our girl!" Nate whooped, pumping his fist in the air.

"Where was Lexi before?" Stephen frowned.

Nate rolled his eyes. "Didn't you pay attention to when Lexi trained her?"

He paid attention to Lexi, not necessarily her words.

"Even though those mothers are behind the judges—" Nate pointed his long finger up ahead to where one overly plump mother imitated the cupcake walk with her hands down as if fluffing an imaginary tutu "—the judges are aware. They take off points on their scoring cards if the parents are too obnoxious. Lexi is off to the side. Check out how irritating those mothers are. They're ridiculous."

"Speaking of obnoxious." Stephen cleared his throat.

Nate nodded and winked, "Yeah, you've been obnoxious."

He ignored his brother's comment. "What's with this Philip guy?"

Slinking in his seat, Nate groaned and rested his head on the back of the chair to view the high ceiling. "He's a good guy, Stephen. Do I like the way Kimber went about it? No. If you're going to live here with us, you need to understand and accept the fact that Kimber is sixteen and not the angel on the pedestal you've placed her on."

"You need to be quiet talking about Kimber."

"Accept it," Nate said with a carefree shrug. "We're not the holiday uncles who come in town and shower the girls with gifts. We're parents now and we need to realize our kids are going to mess up. Are you up for the job, or do you want to go back to your big old mansion in Berkeley Lake and visit us on vacation?"

Stephen did not like the idea of not being with his nieces. He hated Nate's veiled threat. "Well, big brother, you've got some thinking to do." Nate gave Stephen's knee a hard pat. "I'm going to go upstairs, give Lexi this pager." He extracted a square black buzzer with a red center which reminded him of something a commercial restaurant would hand out when a table was ready. "I want to watch Philly get ready for talent."

The other girls weren't done on stage, but Stephen got up, not caring about seeing about the rest. He wanted to spy on Kimber. What kind of outfit had Lexi designed? Lexi had worked day and night for Philly's dress. When did she have time to complete one for Kimber?

"Stephen, right?"

One of the last people Stephen wanted to run into was the woman he held responsible for Kimber entering the pageant. Rose Laing, Lexi's former boss. She exited the doorway of the hotel's bar and tugged at the hem of her low-cut leopard-print tank top—her steps a bit wobbly. "Hello." Stephen gave a short nod with his bald head.

"You out here all by yourself?"

Stephen wanted to button up his shirt with the way the woman leered at him. Something about the way she spoke to him creeped him out. "I'm about to find my family."

"Lexi?" The corners of her eyes where he expected to see crow's feet trembled. A sly smile tried to appear but obviously Botox worked for her. "She should know better than to leave a handsome man like yourself down here all alone."

"Well, I'm a big boy," Stephen said, backing up as she closed the gap between them. Someone ought to teach her about personal space. Her breath smelled like gin.

"Yes, you are." A weird growl came from the back of her throat. "You know I am a firm believer in returning favors. Lexi slept with my husband. I think turnabout's fair play. You and I should get together."

"Whoa!" Stephen jumped when Rose reached out between his legs.

Pulling her head back in amusement, Rose gave a bit of a cackle. "You seem shocked. You didn't know?"

"Lexi's past is none of my business."

Now realizing he would not sleep with her, Rose stepped back and chose her next weapon. "Haven't you ever wondered why she stopped being a pageant coach?"

"No."

"Ever wonder why her little dress shop is so little? Why she tucked her tail between her legs and took off or why her parents want nothing to do with her?" Rose went on, "She has such a bad reputation. No one wants to buy from her." Rose sniffed the air and exhaled loudly, "And I'm not saying this because I caught her and Ernest."

Stephen's jaw twitched as he ground his back molars together. "Ma'am, what happened in the past is not any of my concern."

"Of course not," Rose said with a throaty laugh. She dug her phone out of the lace lining of her bra and flipped her screen on. "You're not concerned anymore. This is you in the photograph with Natalia Ruiz, no?"

For some reason Stephen took the bait and craned his neck to view her screen. He shook his head, trying to figure out why his picture would be in Rose's phone. "You've moved on to better things."

"You'll have to excuse me," Stephen grumbled. He needed to find Lexi and find her fast. The last thing he wanted her to think was he'd gone to Natalia last night while angry. Dinner was strictly business. He might be mad as hell with Lexi, but not crazy.

"Don't say I didn't warn you. Good luck to your niece today," Rose called out. "Remind her second place is nothing to sneeze at."

In order to get a better assessment of Kimber's walk, Lexi thought it would be a good idea to watch her go from room to room. Lexi propped open Kimber and Philly's door and Nate's to judge. After a summer of monitoring pageant walking with cupcake hands, Kimber managed the art well. Nervously, Kimber chewed on her bottom lip, waiting for Lexi's opinion, while the boyfriends stood off to the side, tossing a football to each other.

Lips curving into a slow smile, Lexi couldn't keep the girl in suspense any longer. "You are awesome!"

Kimber's sister and fake boyfriend cheered for her. Her new boyfriend picked her up and swung her around in the air. "Oh, thank God!" Kimber cried. "Miss Chantal and Andrew ran those old tapes of you in the store. I've been studying your walk all summer!"

"You've mastered it, Kimber." Lexi beamed. "I want you to remember, I will always be off to the side watching you, in case you need reassurance," Lexi said, patting Philip's large arm to set Kimber down. He let her down easy but still kept his arm protectively over her shoulder while he one-handedly caught a football toss from Marvin.

Nodding, Kimber blushed, "I've got this!"

"I still don't want you to feel like you have to go through with this."

"Are you kidding me?" Kimber gasped. "I'm sorry, but that brat's mother needs to be shut down."

"She wasn't always mean," Lexi mumbled to herself. Her heart ached for Vera and the pressure her mother must be putting on her now to win. "I'm a big girl. You don't have to worry about me."

Kimber reached out to pat Lexi's arm. "Please. After

how Uncle Stephen acted last night, it's the least I can do."
She gave Lexi an apologetic smile.

Bottom line, Stephen still held her responsible for the
dress and still thought less of her for wearing the garment.
Funny how the dress Kimber stole was what brought Stephen and her together.

Someone knocked rapidly at Lexi's door. Nate went to
answer and Chantal came flying inside with a garment bag
in her arms. "Geez, you would think the presidential cam-
paign was being held here," Chantal breathed. "None of
the guards would let me through. I had to give all my IDs
to them. Thankfully Andrew spotted me and vouched."

Lexi crossed the room to half hug her and take the garment bag from her. "Thank you for doing this."

"Yes, thank you," Kimber said.

"Tell me you love the dress and we'll be even," said
Chantal, stepping backward. Lexi handed Nate the hanger
to hold up while she unzipped the black garment bag. A
collective gasp filled the room. The dress blinded them
with sunset-orange beauty—perfect to kick off the fall season right around the corner. With Kimber's hazel eyes and
amber coloring, the floor-length gown with a sweetheart
neckline was a sure winner.

"Lexi," Andrew said, waltzing through the adjoining
doors. He lowered his voice when he peeked into the other
room and he realized Philly had fallen asleep on the bed.
"You won't believe this, but from wearing this shirt around
I've already gotten orders for six new clients for your October workshop." He ducked out of the way of the hurtling
football.

"I don't have any October workshops."

The ball whirled his way again, and this time Andrew
caught the pigskin and tossed it back with force. "You better tell her, Chantal."

"Chantal?" Lexi said her name low and slow.

"Sorry, too many people were asking me about your services, so I started a sign-up sheet."

"You're busy until next summer," said Andrew.

Lexi wanted to grab Andrew's hands and twirl around the room out of sheer excitement, but she contained her joy with a close-lipped squeal. Kimber needed to change into the dress, so Nate kicked the boys out and closed the door for the women. While Kimber went into the bathroom to change, Lexi glanced over at Philly and grinned. A plate of apple slices remained untouched. Lexi preferred Philly continue the talent portion well rested. She hated when parents offered their children candy and Go-Go Juice—a mixture of high caffeine and sugar drinks.

"How are you doing?" asked Chantal.

"I'm fine. Didn't you hear Andrew? Business is booming." Lexi plastered on a toothy smile.

Chantal sat down on the bed and patted the space next to her. "I *heard* him. I also *saw* the picture of Stephen and Natalia Ruiz on *Reala-tea*."

Did everyone follow the blogs but her? "Whatever." Lexi shrugged.

Not believing her, Chantal rolled her eyes. "Don't try and be tough."

"I'm not trying." Lexi attempted to sound cheerful and hoped she came off the same. "I've got too many things going on in my life, thanks to you."

Nate knocked on the adjoining doors before poking his head in. "Everybody decent?"

"We are," Lexi answered. Kimber mumbled from the bathroom and Chantal went in to help. A few minutes later, Kimber twirled into the bedroom in a ray of autumn sunshine. The boys rushed in to see all the fuss. Philip, clearly smitten, stood speechless. After a while, Chantal ushered the boys out on the promise of getting some food from downstairs. Everyone left through the boys' room, leaving Nate and Lexi alone.

"Mind if I hang out in here? I can't take another argument between Andrew and your cousin, Henri, over decorations for a pretend wedding."

"Is your masculinity threatened?" Lexi teased.

Nate chuckled. "No." He leaned against the doorjamb and sighed, shoving his hands in his pocket and training his penetrating deep green eyes on her. "How are you doing?"

"Why does everyone keep asking me if I'm okay?"

"Because last night was pretty crazy and my brother is a jerk."

Lexi relaxed and smiled. "I'm fine, I promise."

"Listen," he began, "I didn't get a chance to apologize to you."

"I didn't stick around—" she shook her head "—but you don't need to apologize. Stephen is a grown man, Nate," said Lexi. "What he says and does isn't your responsibility."

"I know you saw the picture in the gossip blogs."

A heavy sigh escaped from Lexi's lungs. "I promise you, I don't pay attention to those things. If Stephen was on a date, he was free to do so."

From the other room, Kimber's shrill scream rang through the air. The two of them rushed into the room next door. The floor was a mess, door wide-open, and Philip sat on a bed clutching his jaw, Kimber in front of him, staring her uncle down.

"You had no right!" Kimber yelled at Stephen.

"I had every right. This *man* had his hands all over you."

Nate came between Kimber and Stephen. "Relax, Stephen. They're a couple of kids making out."

"Where in the hell were you with this going on?"

"I was right here." Nate folded his arms across his chest.

Stephen pushed his chest against his brother's. Lexi feared they were going to come to blows. After all, Stephen had just hit a teenage boy. "No, you weren't here because you would have seen this punk groping our niece. What had you so distracted?"

Nate didn't say her name; his eyes flickered in Lexi's direction. Stephen spun around. His cold eyes narrowed on her, chilling her to the bone. Her heart seized against her chest. She'd never seen such a wild look in his eyes. The man had gone mad. She had no idea what she'd done so wrong, and as high-and-mighty as she wanted to claim Stephen was, it didn't lessen the pain. Lexi was positive if they all stood still, everyone would hear her heart breaking.

"You!" he growled. She was sure she made a squeaking noise. "I swear to God, haven't you done enough? I already know what lengths you'll go through just to get my property, but I'll be damned before I let you teach Kimber your little tricks. First, you sell Kimber your dress, then talk her into this and now you're moving on to my brother?"

Lexi's hands flew to her mouth, covering her face. Nate jerked Stephen's arm and slugged him one good time across the face. Stephen's head turned slightly at the blow but stopped when Kimber screamed.

"Stop!" Kimber cried, tears running down her face. Lexi wanted to comfort her but hesitated. Fortunately Nate reached around and supported her. "She didn't sell me the dress!" Kimber blurted out. "I stole it." Stephen gasped and Nate nodded his head. "I stole it one day when Uncle Nate came into the shop. I took it because I wanted to impress Philip."

"Kimber! You didn't have to do that," Philip said behind her.

"Boy—" Nate shot a glare over his shoulder "—shut up."

"Lexi took the rap for me," Kimber continued, "and never said anything, but she did talk to me about it. She's talked to me about so many other things, even about being truthful to you guys about Philip."

The room grew quiet for a second too long, Lexi staring at the ground, her arms folded across her chest awkwardly. She felt Stephen's eyes on her, but she refused to give him the satisfaction of eye contact.

"How is she trying to get your property if I'm helping her expand the apartment above her shop?" Nate chimed in.

Another silence fell across the room. Embarrassed to the hilt, Lexi wanted to bury her head in the sand. A haughty laugh filled the open door.

"This is classic." Rose snickered. She turned her head to exaggerate her laugh with the other two pageant mothers. The door had been left open and they were in the hallway. "I tell you, ladies, drama follows her wherever she goes."

Lexi had to stop wondering if this day could get any worse. The buzzer in her back pocket went off. The show had to go on.

Chapter 15

A hangover would have been something survivable. Stephen didn't think he could handle much of anything else today. Humiliation, loss, shame, jealousy. He'd been an ass. His family hated him. Hell, he hated himself. His fist still ached from where he had punched Kimber's new boyfriend but it was nowhere near as painful as his jaw, where Nate had punched him. He deserved it. No amount of physical pain hurt as bad as his heart did at the idea of losing Lexi.

Ever the professional, Lexi held her composure during the talent portion for the toddlers. She kept her dark eyes focused on the stage. Before anyone else occupied the prime location, Stephen sat in the front of the ballroom and angled himself off to the side to get a view of the contestants backstage. He watched with guilt as she smiled brightly after Philly finished her rendition of the "Star-Spangled Banner" in her patriotic red, white and blue skirt and top. Lexi had been correct to add a tap-dance routine with patent leather shoes and white lacy socks. It differed from all the cloggers in cowboy boots he'd seen already.

Lexi. His heart ached at the thought of her name. She knew everything—she really did. She knew Kimber better than he; she had gained Kimber's and Philly's trust before he did. She knew what to say and what not to say and why. Stephen had to admit, he may have gone even more ballistic if he had learned Kimber stole. Lexi could have pressed charges against her, but that wasn't her style. At any point, she could have told Kimber's secret. But she didn't. Because she was Lexi, and she knew what was right.

During Kimber's beauty walk, Lexi's smile filled with pride, wide and toothy, and she laid her hand over her heart as if she was legitimately touched. Stephen tried shifting in his seat in hopes of catching her attention but while her smile for Kimber never faltered, she always managed to never look quite at him.

Despite the family ignoring him, the pageant continued. The snarky view he'd taken on changed. He was the crazy one. Guilt crippled his insides each time Lexi glanced over him and into the crowd. Stephen focused on the dress Kimber wore and remembered being with Lexi when she picked up the fabric. Everything she touched seemed to blossom, the dress, his family. Him. Given Lexi's magical touch, it began to made sense why the Laings held on to their bitterness. They understood the loss of having Lexi out of their lives.

The idea of Lexi exiting his life scared him. He needed her. He needed her in his life. Nausea swept through him. He slid his hand down the length of his sweating face and shifted in his seat. He sat and listened to the emcee announce Kimber's age group without a sour thought on the length of the competition.

"You look as miserable as I feel."

Stephen's eyes turned upward to the hooded stranger standing over him. "Waverly?"

Dressed in a red sweatshirt with the hood up and a pair of oversize glasses on her face, Waverly nodded nervously and took a seat next to him. "Hi!" she said quickly.

"Aren't you banned from here?" His eyes narrowed on the girl.

Waverly slipped her glasses down the slope of her nose. "Aren't you?" she asked sarcastically.

"Bad news travels fast, huh?" He slouched back down in his seat. The room had thinned out for everyone to get ready for the next part. The judges were deliberating over their scorecards.

"More like fast texts and blogs."

"What?"

The lights on Waverly's phone came to life when her

finger swiped across the screen. "Natalia Ruiz, Stephen? Seriously?" said Waverly, holding the photograph of him exiting the booth with Natalia the other evening. "I hope you know you lost all your points on the scorecard and you're a douche for the way you treated Lexi. She's a good person."

Stephen nodded and accepted the teenager berating him. In this world of technology, of course someone had shown her. The question was when. He only found out about it today, but his meeting with Natalia was the night before. If she'd seen it yesterday, it easily explained her attitude toward him at dinner. The teenager took a break from giving him an earful. Waverly sat back into her seat and sighed.

"So you came this way to tell me about myself?"

"Actually, I came looking for Lexi, but I got here right after the beauty segment ended. I can't run into anyone." She nodded her head toward the judges' table, where Rose Laing had strolled over with a tray of cookies.

The two of them snorted in disgust at the desperate woman. "I hate her. She will do anything to win."

"So it seems." Stephen sighed.

"I blame her for my accident." Waverly folded her arms across the front of her sweatshirt.

"The motorcycle accident?"

"Yeah."

Stephen sat up in his seat. "Did she run you off the road?"

Waverly shook her head. Her hood came off but she quickly put it back on. "Not the actual accident but the pictures after." People began wandering around the room. Waverly stretched her legs against the chair in front of her. "Ohmigod, I forgot how boring this part is when I'm not working a pageant. They seriously need to learn how to entertain while we wait."

"Let me ask you something." Stephen cleared his throat and turned toward Waverly. "This scorecard I keep hearing about. Do you and your friends keep one on your boy-friends?"

Waverly gave him a side-eye glance. "Why?"

"Lexi mentioned one before. I was curious what my score would be."

"I wasn't kidding when I said you're at a total zero right now." She blew a bubble from a piece of gum he didn't re-alize she had.

"What do I need to do to bump my score up in her eyes?"

He listened intently to Waverly's ideas about making things right. The beauty queen came up with a bevy of ideas, the majority of which he shot down. They'd been so engrossed in their conversation he hadn't noticed the room filling back up or when Nate reentered the room. No one from his family or from Grits and Glam Gowns acknowl-edged Stephen.

"Ladies and gentlemen, are you ready for the final event of this evening?" The emcee's voice brought a round of ap-plause from the packed room.

"She sounds tired," Waverly commented as she leaned over. "I don't think I've been to a bigger pageant. At this point, we'll never get through it until tomorrow evening."

Stephen was eager to watch Kimber in the next event. Like their mother, the girls' talents lay in their singing. He also feared, after tomorrow, Lexi might walk out of his life for good. Could he imagine living in the same town as Lexi and not being able to be with her?

The music began and one by one the teenage girls worked their talents. Stephen closed his eyes during most of the routines. Anyone who dared to clap should have been shot. A few girls showcased clogging, baton twirl-ing, juggling and even some gymnastics. The buildup of excitement for Kimber mounted. She had this in the bag. The red curtains moved and he caught a glimpse of Kimber in a simple solid white dress and a white gardenia tucked behind her ear—a scene right out of *Lady Sings the Blues*, another movie they'd stayed on the phone and watched.

"Kudos for Lexi's choice in costume," Waverly whispered behind her hand. "The judges will enjoy the break from the stripper outfits some of the other girls wore."

With hope, Stephen craned his neck to try and find Lexi in her usual spot off to the side. She wasn't there. His eyes averted to the spot behind the judges' table. No way would she stand behind them to coach Kimber from the front. Kimber didn't need help.

Waverly stated the obvious "Lexi's not here. Where'd she go?"

"I'd like to know."

"This isn't like her. She's always backstage. Something's wrong." A vise-like grip clamped down on Stephen's hand.

Stephen shot to his feet before she finished her statement. Yanking her hand, he dragged her down to where Nate was. Kimber was on stage, singing a Billie Holiday medley with a set of powerful lungs .

"What's going on?" Nate hissed in a whisper and with a frown. "Waverly?"

"I need you to keep a close eye on her," said Stephen.

He ducked out of view from the onlookers and made his way to the lobby. Nate, not following his orders, was hot on his heels. Any sign of tension between the brothers dissipated. Once the ballroom doors closed behind them, Stephen filled Nate in on what happened to Waverly.

"And you're afraid something's happened to Lexi?" Nate asked stroking his chin.

"You're the one who said she is always off to the side." Stephen stretched his neck all around toward the other entrance to the backstage of the ballroom. He found a few late stragglers making their way down the hallway. He took off with fast strides, not wanting to alarm anyone with a full run. Nate was behind him, spouting off the *excuse me, pardon me, sorry* to all the people they shoved out the way.

"Stephen—" Nate nodded his head in the direction of a stout woman wearing a headset on top of her bouffant hairstyle "—the coordinator. Excuse me, ma'am?"

The woman licked her chops at the sight of Nate. "Well, hello, Mr. Nate. I hoped to get a chance to meet you this evening. Two nieces in the competition—are you excited? They're certainly the crowd favorites." She scrunched up the tip of her nose as she batted these come-hither glances at him.

"Thanks, we wish them the best of—"

Stephen did not have time for pleasantries; he stepped forward, glanced at her name tag and asked gruffly, "Peggy, have you seen Lexi Pendergrass?"

Taken aback by his rough tone, the woman cocked her head to the side at him, and then saw the resemblance. "Oh, you're brothers?" She purred and slipped her cat's-eye glasses down the slope of her long nose. "I hope you guys are going to enter the Mr. Southern Style Glitz Pageant in the morning."

"Have you seen her?"

"Yes," Peggy went on, oblivious to their impatient sighs, "and may I say what a joy to have her in the circuit again. Such a shame the way she got caught up in drama with the Laings. *I* for one rooted for Lexi and Ernest. She was the best thing to ever happen to Vera."

"What?" Nate asked, doing a double take.

"Everyone knows how desperate Rose was to get her husband back. He'd seen how good he was with Lexi and Vera. Oh, look at me, gossiping. I don't care what the cameras caught. I don't care how many diamonds he's donated to the circuit."

Stephen's height allowed him to glimpse above everyone's head. Kimber was exiting the stage to a standing ovation and he didn't want to upset her with his presence. He tapped Nate's shoulder. "I don't think I should be here when she walks off the stage." He turned his attention to the gossiping woman, "Ma'am, do you know where Lexi went?"

"Oh, yeah, sure, she went looking for your other niece."

"What?" Nate and Stephen chorused.

"Yes, she walked off the stage on the wrong side."

And Stephen didn't notice this? Damn it!

Peggy barely finished before Stephen took off toward the back of the stage behind the curtains. Maybe he could meet her halfway. Philly got off the stage a while ago. Why hadn't anyone noticed? Stephen took a few deep breaths and tried to remain calm. He tried to remember to take long, slow breaths again when he made it to the other side of the curtain and still saw no sign of Philly or Lexi. He craned his neck and made eye contact with Nate, who threw his hands in the air, indicating he hadn't found them.

Before he ran upstairs to check the rooms, Stephen figured he needed to check outside to be safe. The door slammed shut behind him. Access to the streets was blocked on either side with a satellite truck and a catering van. Stephen tested the closed door but the slam already told him he was locked out of the back entrance. He began squeezing by the satellite van and walking down the alley and back through to the front of the building.

The smudged brass bar of the revolving door's entrance warmed his hand. "Do you have ID, sir?" The gray-and-maroon-uniformed guard stepped in Stephen's way.

"ID?"

"It's okay, Barry." Lexi appeared at the guard's side, her manicured hands on Barry's forearm. "He's with me."

From the way Barry gave Stephen a once-over, Stephen could only imagine what he was thinking. "Thanks," Stephen mumbled, passing by Barry. With no idea of how Lexi would treat him, he stiffened when she neared.

Lexi placed her hands on her hips. "Now is not the time to be mad at me."

"I'm not mad." Stephen reached for Lexi's arm. Her

warm skin electrified him. "We need to talk after we find Philly. What happened?"

Folding her arms across her chest, Lexi's eyes watered and she looked around the lobby. "One minute she was doing just fine on stage, the next she exited the complete opposite. I ran back behind the curtains, figuring Nate caught the mistake and met her in my spot."

"No—" Stephen shook his head "—he didn't. He's backstage looking for her."

"I've posted guards at the exits."

A part of him was amazed she thought so quickly and the other part of him wasn't. The lobby swarmed with contestants and their families, and with all the chaos, Lexi had been able to pull guards from their duties.

"Follow me." He laced his fingers with Lexi's. They fit perfectly, as they should.

"Stephen." Lexi pulled her hand away a bit, but he tugged her back gently.

"We're going to find Philly." He took a chance and tipped her chin with his free hand. "Together."

A line began to form into the hallway leading to the outside pool. Stephen elbowed his way through the parents with Lexi in tow. There, outside, sprawled out on a white beach chair sat Philly, still in her tap-dance outfit, licking away on a candy apple. So much relief flooded Stephen's senses, he almost cried. Lexi did. Blood began to pulsate in his fingertips and his temples throbbed.

"Philly!" Lexi dashed to the five-year-old's side and knelt on the ground. "You had me worried."

"Philly, what were you thinking?" Stephen sat down at the bottom edge of the little diva's seat. Every visible inch of her seemed okay. "You bought a candy apple after what happened?"

"I don't want to do the pageant anymore," Philly announced.

"Okay," Lexi said softly and pressed the back of her

hand against Philly's red-stained cheek. "Do you feel forced?"

"No," Stephen interrupted with more force, "you're not quitting this pageant. Lexi's worked hard. Uncle Nate, Kimber… Hell, Philly," he cursed and winced at the same time when both ladies looked up at him, "you're not a quitter. You made a promise and you're seeing this thing through to the end."

"But I don't want to do it if you're going to be unhappy." Philly's bottom lip quivered, her brown puppy-dog eyes watering as she looked at him.

"What? I've never been prouder."

"But you've done nothing but yell at everyone. And I don't want Miss Lexi to leave us, so I'll just stop."

"Philly," Lexi cooed, wrapping her arms around her. "What gave you the impression I'd leave?"

"You left Vera Laing. She told me not to count on you for pageants. So if I leave pageants, will you stay?"

Lexi glanced over at Stephen. He shrugged his shoulders, not sure what to say but sure the two of them both wanted to throttle the Laings. "Sweetie, when the pageants are over, you can always come and see me anytime."

Taking another chance, Stephen reached over and pulled Lexi against him. "Lexi isn't going anywhere, Philly. I promise."

Long false lashes blinked back the giant tears. Stephen's heart ached for Philly. "But you're mad at Miss Lexi."

"I'm not mad at Miss Lexi, I'm mad at myself."

"Philly!" Nate's voice boomed across the Olympic-sized pool.

"Is everyone mad at me?" asked Philly.

Lexi began to leave. Maybe she thought this was a private moment. Stephen held on to her hand to prevent her from walking away. "Philly, walking off and not telling anyone is so dangerous. You could have fallen in the water.

Someone could have snatched you up and we'd never know how to find you. I can't have you doing that ever again."

"Am I in trouble?"

"You're certainly not finishing this candy apple." Stephen reached for the wooden Popsicle stick holding the half-eaten apple. "You will finish the pageant, and then we will discuss your punishment later."

Nate stormed over and took Philly away after Stephen filled him in, all the while still holding Lexi's hand. It dawned on him she may have wanted to leave with Philly, but not before they talked. Stephen stood to face her.

"We need to talk, as well," he said, glancing into her eyes.

This time Lexi pulled harder on her hand and pulled herself loose. "No—" she shook her blond head "—we don't."

"Lexi, I'm sorry." Stephen stepped forward, his hand already feeling empty. "Let me explain. I lost my mind." The fact she didn't breeze by him gave him hope. He took a step closer; the bottom of the lounge chair scraped against his calf. "What can I say?"

Lexi sidestepped his attempt to reach for her hand. "There's nothing to say. One day you're telling me how I can count on you, the next you make insinuations about me like you have from day one." Her dark eyes glanced around the pool before she leaned forward and gritted between her teeth, "Day one, Stephen."

"Everything okay, Miss Lexi?" asked the security guard, Barry.

A plastered smile pressed on Lexi's face indicated to anyone paying attention that all things were okay. The plastic smile did not reach her eyes, and in the last rays of summer light, Stephen shivered. "We're good," she called out to Barry. To Stephen, her smile ceased. "We're not good. In fact, we're done."

"Lexi, please listen to me."

"I can't, Stephen." Lexi sighed and folded her arms underneath her breast. "Philly means the world to me, and I can't stand the idea of her hating me the way Vera hates me. She thinks I left her when it didn't work out between me and her dad. Oh, and yes—" she slapped her hand against her denim-clad thigh "—I dated a married man, but in my defense, I didn't know they were married until Rose decided she wanted to be a wife and mother again. Ernest told me he was single and I foolishly believed him. That's why they hate me."

As much as he wanted to know, Stephen no longer cared about her past. "Lexi."

"I'm serious, Stephen. Let's just call it—"

Never before had Stephen been more grateful for the pageant parents to live up to their reputation when a mother, not happy her child's teeth were stained black with the free candy, tossed over the food table into the pool. Pandemonium broke out, and out of instinct, Stephen grabbed Lexi by the arm and guided her through the drama into the lobby.

"Now that I'm done parenting," he said, proudly admitting what he was, "go back to the pageant and wait for me. I promise I'll be right back," said Stephen over the noise of screams, alarms and police whistles. "I love you, Lexi."

So much for promises, Lexi thought miserably to herself as she sat in her seat in the ballroom of the Brutti Hotel. She tried to keep a happy face as she sat next to Nate and Andrew. At the end of the row, Philly sat in Philip's lap based on the notion they shared the same name. Kimber and Marvin were at the end. Last night, she'd stayed up in her room, waiting to hear back from Stephen. Around midnight she realized what a fool she'd been for giving him a second chance. Who wanted a man who was so quick to humiliate her? Did it matter if he apologized? Well, she was done waiting—even if she'd literally just walked through the doors twenty minutes ago, not wanting to miss a call.

"All right, ladies and gentlemen. We're back at it," the

emcee said. "Crowning time!" Applause drowned out the emcee. Everyone was ready for the weekend to end. "Well, before we conclude, we have a little surprise for everyone."

"I am so tired." Lexi yawned and laid her head on Nate's shoulder. "Wake me when they're done."

"This year we've decided to have one more treat to liven everyone's spirits with a little fun and send everyone off on a good note. We want to thank all the parents and participants for coming. Moms, we thank you for all your devotion and hard work."

Music began to play, a violin twanged. Lexi made out the Charlie Daniels Band's infamous "Devil Went Down to Georgia." She stifled a giggle and shook her head.

"Moms, grandparents, god-mamas, coaches, we thank you for getting your girls here on time. Dads, brothers, uncles, we thank you for your patience. So without further ado, we would like to introduce the men of the Southern Style Glitz Pageant." The room broke out in catcalls and whistles. "Ladies and gentlemen, coming to you from right here in the Peach City, uncle of two of our contestants, Philly and Kimber Reyes—please put your hands together for Stephen Reyes."

Lexi sat straight up. Her ears barely caught the names of the rest of the surprise contestants. A dozen men lined the back row of the stage and waited for their turn. Some men dressed in suits, a few in Speedo bathing suits and others casual in jeans.

She blinked in disbelief but sure enough, walking slowly to the center of the stage right on the masking-taped *X*, was Stephen Reyes, head shaved, beard trimmed, in a pair of snug jeans and a pink personalized Grits and Glam Team-Kimber Team-Philly T-shirt. He took it in good stride as he slowly spun around for everyone to see, and all the mothers, with no shame, hollered out for him.

Without moving her head, she cut her eyes to Nate. He was laughing and filming the whole event. Down front, in the middle of the aisle but directly behind the judges, Andrew spun in the same slow motion with his hand on his hip for Stephen to copy. Stephen didn't seem to have any trouble keeping his composure. He kept his hands in perfect cupcake hold and kept his almond-shaped eyes glued to Lexi. Her heart stopped and jump-started ten times over as he was on the stage. As he exited, another father came out and then another and another. No one generated the same excitement as Stephen.

"Thank you, gentlemen." The emcee fanned herself. "Did the temperature get hotter or am I going through a spell?"

Unless Lexi had hit menopause, it was the temperature. Heat crept down her face, across her neck and down her spine. She pushed away from the row of chairs to run over and meet Stephen as he exited the stage.

"You're nuts!" Lexi cried, wrapping her arms around his neck. "Is this why didn't call me? Did Andrew have you working all night?"

"For you, Lexi, only for you," he said.

"Ah-hem," the emcee interrupted, "Will all contestants please remain on the stage while we tally the scorecards?"

Stephen planted one more kiss against her lips before jumping back onstage. The crowd cheered for him. Lexi shook her head and covered her mouth while she laughed all the way to her seat. Her personal scorecard went off the charts for him.

"This just might be a tough one to call," the emcee chuckled, not believing the lie. "We'll go by the judges' score…" She paused for a moment, pushing her glasses back up on her face. "Oh, I stand corrected, a unanimous vote. Ladies and gentlemen, your first and new Mr. Southern Style Glitz is none other than Mr. Stephen Reyes."

Stephen stepped forward from the back; he blew ridiculous kisses at the audience members like Philly. At least he had been paying attention during her rehearsal! Once

Stephen was fitted with a king-size crown, the other men all took a bow before disappearing back behind the curtain.

"You're not going to show anyone that tape, are you, Uncle Nate?" Kimber asked from the end of the row.

Still laughing to the point of tears, Nate nodded his head. "I've already uploaded this directly to the web."

When the men came back into the audience, Stephen was given a standing ovation. Everyone cleared the way for Lexi to come out into the aisle and for them to meet halfway. Her mouth twitched with a smile and desire to kiss him. He didn't need to be asked. Stephen took her in his arms and wrapped her up in a hug.

"Lexi, I'm so sorry for what I put you through. I was fighting a ghost—my brother. Thanks to you, I finally understood what he tried to tell me about finding the right woman and wanting to settle down. I'm just sorry in order for me to understand, I hurt you in the process. I embarrassed you and to prove that it'll never happen again, I will go to any length to top what I've done to you. You must have thought I was such an ass."

"Well, if the shoe fits…" She grinned.

"It did," he whispered, "but I promise, if you'll allow me, I will do whatever is necessary to make things up to you. Nothing happened between me and Natalia. We had dinner to talk, for closure. You're the only one I want. You're the only one I…you're the only one I love."

"Stephen, it's okay." She kissed his jaw. The crown tilted off his head so she straightened it.

"I love you, Lexi."

Her heart melted. She bit her lip as he set her down. She'd found her prince, crown and all. "I love you, too, Stephen."

Through the microphone, the emcee cleared her throat. "Are we ready to announce the winners of this weekend?"

Stephen took Lexi's hand in his and led her to the

Reyeses' row. She didn't have to sit through the rest of the event. She already knew who the real winner was tonight. The Reyes family.

Epilogue

Seated on a king-size bed strewn with golden, orange, yellow and red rose petals, Lexi shook her head to the upbeat song's tempo as Stephen strutted his stuff in the privacy of her bedroom in the condominium they shared. At the end of summer, they had moved to the top floor in a bigger place with more rooms for the kids when they came over.

"I'm beginning to think you're making fun of me," Stephen said, slowly spinning around to reveal his ripped torso in a pair of white boxer briefs. "How many nights are you going to make me do this?"

As far as Lexi was concerned, she'd never get tired of Stephen working the faux runway of carpet before the bed. It had been a few months since they'd returned home as the winners of the Southern Style Glitz Pageant. Kimber insisted on keeping her Miss Ultimate Grand Supreme Queen trophy at Grits and Glam Gowns in the new storefront window on the corner of Sunshine Boulevard and Sunshine Street. Philly slept with her Mini Grand Supreme trophy every night. Every morning and evening Lexi walked by her desk she pressed a kissed finger to the framed photograph of her and Stephen in his first and only beauty pageant sash. Right next to the photograph sat a simple congratulations card signed "Mom and Dad."

"Forever," Lexi hummed to herself. Her parents had yet to make an appearance at Grits and Glam Gowns but the card was a definite start in the right direction and there was always hope. Maybe they realized their daughter was a pillar of the community. She'd taken out the photograph her parents sent her in her congratulations card and set it on her nightstand.

This weekend Stephen and Lexi had celebrated their six-month anniversary by hanging inside and decorating for the Halloween party they had planned for everyone later at Grits and Glam Gowns. Their *Saturday Night Fever* costumes hung over the door of their walk-in closet. With the renovations upstairs and down the street, their businesses boomed. The former upstairs apartment had been converted into a bridal salon with a special Realtor right next door.

"Happy six-month anniversary," Stephen said when the song ended. He stood at the end of the bed and stroked her red-painted toenail.

Lexi curled her toes and grinned. "I cannot believe it has been six months since you stormed into my life."

Stephen cocked his head to the side and gave a lazy smile. "*Storm* is such a strong word."

"*Barged, intruded, disrupted?*" She offered a range of words, but anything else she wanted to say got lost in her yelp when he grabbed her by the ankles and yanked her body down to the edge of the bed. She rested her heels on his shoulders while he stroked the length of her calf. "You can't be serious about going another round?"

"Didn't I say I'd make love to you every hour on the hour?" He dipped his head to kiss her ankle. "We're already behind schedule."

This morning Stephen had woken her up with breakfast in bed, catered by Henri's restaurant. And every night since returning, he had been at Lexi's side. He showered her with gifts. She refused to take the space next door but had stood back and admired him as he donned a pair of workman's boots and helped remodel Grits and Glam Gowns.

"New picture?" asked Stephen, when he stopped fiddling around. "Let me see."

Lexi reached over and handed him the photograph in the frame by her nightstand. "You want to see a picture of my parents before you're about to make love to me?"

"Scandalous woman." Stephen winked. "Why have I never noticed this picture?"

"My mother sent it to me yesterday." Lexi felt her cheeks rise as she beamed. "It's a start, right?"

"Your dad runs a bank, right?"

"Yes, David and Mary Pendergrass in the flesh." Her smile dropped. "Well, sort of."

"I've met this man before. He's the one who suggested I give you the Dancing Lady orchids."

A shaky hand touched her mouth. "What?" she gasped.

"Yeah, crazy—" Stephen set the picture down on the nightstand "—almost like I got his permission to pursue you."

"Sure." She sighed with a playful smile. Her hands rolled through the soft petals, lifting them and letting them fall back onto her bed. "Are we getting back to your talent portion?"

With that, Stephen began to crawl onto the bed, stalking the length of her body with each move. Lexi used her elbows and scooted back to fit Stephen between her legs. She went to wrap her arms around his neck but he pulled back. "Wait, I have something for you."

"Stephen, really." Lexi shook her head, rubbing her neck against the soft, pink fluffy robe from the spa day he'd surprised her with in her living room this morning. "You've done too much already."

"I don't think I can ever stop doing too much, Lexi."

Blushing, she rolled her eyes. "You've already fed me grapes by hand, helped build my little castle in the store, barely let me step foot anywhere without you carrying me. You're treating me like some sort of princess."

"Well, you know, if the tiara fits…"

As he reached for the drawer of the nightstand, he stumbled to the ground. Lexi stifled a giggle until he righted himself, on one knee with a black velvet box in his hands. Lexi's hands flew to her mouth. The one-and-a-half-carat princess crown diamond blinded her. "Stephen! It's big enough for a queen!"

"Well, Reyes does mean 'kings.'" Stephen shortened the distance between them, greeting her with a kiss. "So what do you say? Will you put me out of my bachelor misery and be my queen?"

"I do."

* * * * *

1809

COMING NEXT MONTH
Available March 22, 2016

TONIGHT
by Nana Malone and Sienna Mynx
This collection features two stories from fan-favorite authors. Prepare to be swept away as two couples embark on an odyssey of secret longings and scorching desires set against the backdrop of glamorous Las Vegas and a private Caribbean island.

FALLING FOR AUTUMN
Bare Sophistication
by Sherelle Green
Lingerie boutique owner Autumn Dupree is a realist when it comes to relationships, until Ajay Reed arouses a passion she never knew existed. Can Ajay convince Autumn that they both need to take a leap of faith?

TENDER KISSES

ned

han

nce

iven

their love finally ready for the spotlight?

Spotlight on temptation

The tall, sexy stranger who just barged into Lexi Pendergrass's shop looks like a perfect ten to her. But not only does Stephen Reyes accuse the former beauty queen of selling his young niece a scandalous dress, he then prevents Lexi from buying her dream property next door. Not exactly Mr. Congeniality. Even still, beneath their bickering simmers an inconvenient chemistry that's shaking Lexi's legendary poise to the core.

Real estate mogul Stephen has had his world rocked twice in recent months. First, he became guardian to his late brother's children. Now he's falling for a feisty Southern beauty who, when she isn't coaching his pageant-crazy niece, is schooling him in desire. He misjudged her once. Now he's using all his seductive talents to win Lexi for now and forever...

Once Upon a Tiara

$6.50 U.S./$7.25 CAN.

ISBN-13: 978-0-373-86444-7

50650

CATEGORY
AFRICAN-AMERICAN

9 780373 864447

EAN

Ⓢ

HARLEQUIN®
™KIMANI™
ROMANCE
harlequin.com